好記口訣 + 圖解文法 + 回顧筆記

用對方法，

學好**英文文法**就是這麼簡單！

捷徑文化
Royal Road Publishing Group

1.

" 文法口訣輕鬆記 "

1. 動詞只能有一個
2. be 動詞、一般動詞選一種
3. 兩種一起做進行，一般加上 i

文法口訣輕鬆記

針對較複雜的文法觀念，會在每個核心文法的開頭附上一段韋婕老師親自錄音的好記口訣，讓你用最容易記憶的句子學會原本枯燥無味的文法觀念！

2.

" 文法觀念說給你聽 "

動詞（V.）分成兩大類：

一、be V.：am / is / are

二、一般 V.：am / is / are 以外的動詞，

文法觀念說給你聽

針對每個文法都有最精確的觀念剖析，一個一個跟著學，就能學會文法的重要觀念。

3.

" 圖解文法一看就懂 "

be V. 和 一般 V. 的結合用法

be V.
am、is、are

一般V.
eat（吃）、drink（喝）、
play（玩）、walk（走）……

be V. + V–ing
正在……

圖解文法一看就懂

除了文字上的文法觀念剖析，《暢銷增訂版》更以真正的圖解搭配圖表來呈現文法概念，透過具有邏輯性的圖像來學習文法，讓記憶與理解都能長長久久！

Part 1—基本詞性篇

Unit 01　什麼是動詞？

1.

文法口訣輕鬆記　◀ : Track 001

1. 動詞只能有一個
2. be 動詞、一般動詞選一種
3. 兩種一起做進行，一般加上 ing！

1. 動詞只能有一個
　一個句子只有一個動詞（除非有連接詞連結 2 個以上的動詞，詳 Chapter 06 Unit 02 對等子句的用法。）

2. be 動詞、一般動詞選一種
　動詞有兩大類：「be V.」與「一般 V.」，不可同時使用，須擇一選用。

3. 兩種一起做進行，一般加上 ing！
　一般 V. 須加上 ing 才可與 be V. 形成進行式
　➔ be 動詞+ V-ing（正在……）。

2.

文法觀念說給你聽

動詞（V.）分成兩大類：

一、be V.：am / is / are

二、一般 V.：am / is / are 以外的動詞，統稱為一般動詞，又叫作普通動詞。

★ 這兩種動詞不能一起使用，例如下面這兩個句子：
　1. I am go to the supermarket. (X)
　2. She is write a letter to Tom. (X)

016

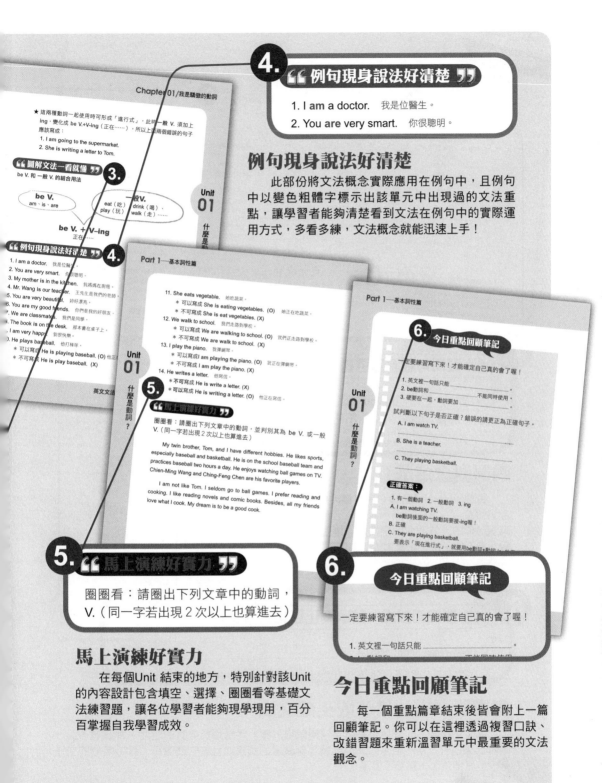

4.

例句現身說法好清楚

1. I **am** a doctor.　我是位醫生。
2. You **are** very smart.　你很聰明。

例句現身說法好清楚

　　此部份將文法概念實際應用在例句中，且例句中以變色粗體字標示出該單元中出現過的文法重點，讓學習者能夠清楚看到文法在例句中的實際運用方式，多看多練，文法概念就能迅速上手！

Chapter 01/我是驕傲的動詞

★ 這兩種動詞一起使用時可形成「進行式」，此時一般 V. 須加上 ing，變化成 be V.+V-ing (正在⋯⋯)，所以上面兩個錯誤的句子應該寫成：
1. I am going to the supermarket.
2. She is writing a letter to Tom.

3.　圖解文法一看就懂

be V. 和一般 V. 的結合用法

be V.
am、is、are

一般 V.
eat (吃)、
play (玩)、
drink (喝)、
walk (走)⋯⋯

be V. + V-ing

Unit 01 什麼是動詞？

4.　例句現身說法好清楚

1. I am a doctor.　我是位醫生。
2. You are very smart.　你很聰明。
3. My mother is in the kitchen.　我媽媽在廚房。
4. Mr. Wang is our teacher.　王先生是我們的老師。
5. You are very beautiful.　妳好漂亮。
6. You are my good friends.　你們是我的好朋友。
7. We are classmates.　我們是同學。
8. The book is on the desk.　那本書在桌子上。
9. I am very happy.　我很快樂。
10. He plays baseball.　他打棒球。
　　* 可以寫成 He is playing baseball. (O)
　　* 不可寫成 He is play baseball. (X)

英文文法⋯⋯

Part 1─基本詞性篇

11. She eats vegetable.　她吃蔬菜。
　* 可以寫成 She is eating vegetables. (O)　她正在吃蔬菜。
　* 不可寫成 She is eat vegetables. (X)
12. We walk to school.　我們走路到學校。
　* 可以寫成 We are walking to school. (O)　我們正在走路到學校。
　* 不可寫成 We are walk to school. (X)
13. I play the piano.　我彈鋼琴。
　* 可以寫成 I am playing the piano. (O)　我正在彈鋼琴。
　* 不可寫成 I am play the piano. (X)
14. He writes a letter.　他寫信。
　* 不可寫成 He is write a letter. (X)
　* 可以寫成 He is writing a letter. (O)　他正在寫信。

Unit 01 什麼是動詞？

5.　馬上演練好實力

圈圈看：請圈出下列文章中的動詞，並判別其為 be V. 或一般 V.（同一字若出現 2 次以上也算進去）

My twin brother, Tom, and I have different hobbies. He likes sports, especially baseball and basketball. He is on the school baseball team and practices baseball two hours a day. He enjoys watching ball games on TV. Chien-Ming Wang and Ching-Feng Chen are his favorite players.

I am not like Tom. I seldom go to ball games. I prefer reading and cooking. I like reading novels and comic books. Besides, all my friends love what I cook. My dream is to be a good cook.

Part 1─基本詞性篇

6.　今日重點回顧筆記

一定要練習寫下來！才能確定自己真的會了喔！

1. 英文裡一句話只能 ＿＿＿＿＿＿＿＿＿＿＿。
2. be動詞和 ＿＿＿＿＿＿＿＿＿＿ 不能同時使用。
3. 硬要在一起，動詞要加 ＿＿＿＿＿＿＿。

試判斷以下句子是否正確？錯誤的請更正為正確句子。
A. I am watch TV.
B. She is a teacher.
C. They playing basketball.

正確答案：

1. 有一個動詞　2. 一般動詞　3. ing
A. I am watching TV.
be動詞後面的一般動詞要接-ing喔！
B. 正確
C. They are playing basketball.
要表示「現在進行式」，就要用be動詞+動詞+-ing⋯⋯

Unit 01 什麼是動詞？

5.

馬上演練好實力

圈圈看：請圈出下列文章中的動詞，V.（同一字若出現 2 次以上也算進去）

馬上演練好實力

　　在每個 Unit 結束的地方，特別針對該 Unit 的內容設計包含填空、選擇、圈圈看等基礎文法練習題，讓各位學習者能夠現學現用，百分百掌握自我學習成效。

6.

今日重點回顧筆記

一定要練習寫下來！才能確定自己真的會了喔！

1. 英文裡一句話只能 ＿＿＿＿＿＿＿＿＿＿＿。

今日重點回顧筆記

　　每一個重點篇章結束後皆會附上一篇回顧筆記。你可以在這裡透過複習口訣、改錯習題來重新溫習單元中最重要的文法觀念。

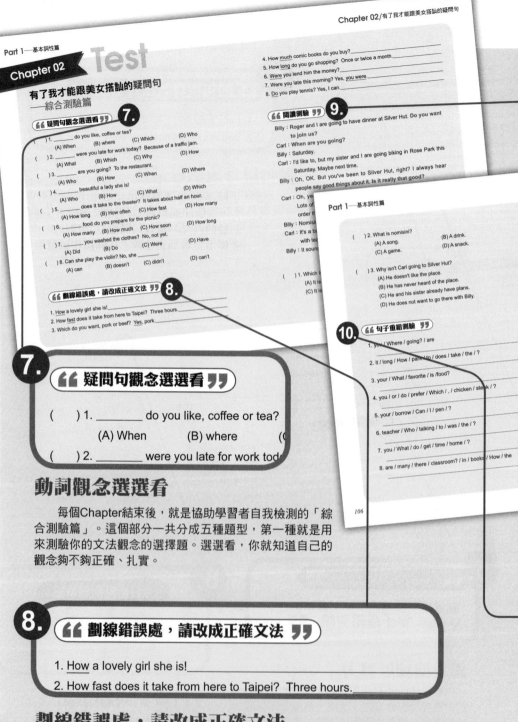

Chapter 02

Test

有了我才能跟美女搭訕的疑問句
—綜合測驗篇

疑問句觀念選選看 7.

( ) 1. _____ do you like, coffee or tea?
    (A) When   (B) where   (C) Which   (D) Who

( ) 2. _____ were you late for work today? Because of a traffic jam.
    (A) What   (B) Which   (C) Why   (D) How

( ) 3. _____ are you going? To the restaurant.
    (A) Who   (B) How   (C) When   (D) Where

( ) 4. _____ beautiful a lady she is!
    (A) Who   (B) How   (C) What   (D) Which

( ) 5. _____ does it take to the theater? It takes about half an hour.
    (A) How long   (B) How often   (C) How fast   (D) How many

( ) 6. _____ food do you prepare for the picnic?
    (A) How many   (B) How much   (C) How soon   (D) How long

( ) 7. _____ you washed the clothes? No, not yet.
    (A) Did   (B) Do   (C) Were   (D) Have

( ) 8. Can she play the violin? No, she _____.
    (A) can   (B) doesn't   (C) didn't   (D) can't

劃線錯誤處，請改成正確文法 8.

1. How a lovely girl she is!_____
2. How fast does it take from here to Taipei? Three hours._____
3. Which do you want, pork or beef? Yes, pork._____

4. How <u>much</u> comic books do you buy?_____
5. How long do you go shopping? Once or twice a month._____
6. Were you lend him the money?_____
7. Were you late this morning? Yes, you were._____
8. <u>Do</u> you play tennis? Yes, I can._____

閱讀測驗 9.

Billy : Roger and I are going to have dinner at Silver Hut. Do you want to join us?
Carl : When are you going?
Billy : Saturday.
Carl : I'd like to, but my sister and I are going biking in Rose Park this Saturday. Maybe next time.
Billy : Oh, OK. But you've been to Silver Hut, right? I always hear people say good things about it. Is it really that good?
Carl : Oh, ye... Lots of ... order t...
Billy : Nomisi...
Carl : It's a b... with tea...
Billy : It soun...

( ) 1. Which i...
    (A) It is ...
    (C) It is ...

Part 1—基本詞性篇

( ) 2. What is nomisini?
    (A) A song.   (B) A drink.
    (C) A game.   (D) A snack.

( ) 3. Why isn't Carl going to Silver Hut?
    (A) He doesn't like the place.
    (B) He has never heard of the place.
    (C) He and his sister already have plans.
    (D) He does not want to go there with Billy.

句子重組測驗 10.

1. you / Where / going? / are
2. it / long / How / park / to / does / take / the / ?
3. your / What / favorite / is /food?
4. you / or / do / prefer / Which / , / chicken / steak / ?
5. your / borrow / Can / I / pen / ?
6. teacher / Who / talking / to / was / the / ?
7. you / What / do / get / time / home / ?
8. are / many / there / classroom? / in / books / How / the

106

7.

疑問句觀念選選看

( ) 1. _____ do you like, coffee or tea?
    (A) When   (B) where   (

( ) 2. _____ were you late for work tod

動詞觀念選選看

每個Chapter結束後，就是協助學習者自我檢測的「綜合測驗篇」。這個部分一共分成五種題型，第一種就是用來測驗你的文法觀念的選擇題。選選看，你就知道自己的觀念夠不夠正確、扎實。

8.

劃線錯誤處，請改成正確文法

1. How a lovely girl she is!_____
2. How fast does it take from here to Taipei? Three hours._____

劃線錯誤處，請改成正確文法

除了選擇題，改錯題也是這次《暢銷增訂版》特別增新收錄的題型。每個句子第一眼看起來都很正常，但是如果你能發現劃線處的錯誤並且將它們改正，就證明你的文法觀念非常清楚、一點都不混淆！

❝ 閱讀測驗 ❞

Billy：Roger and I are going to have dinner a
　　　to join us?

Carl：When are you going?

閱讀測驗

收錄歷屆國中基測閱讀測驗試題，帶你了解基測閱讀測驗的考試重點和模式，此外，在Chapter 中學習過的文法概念，於閱讀測驗的內文中皆以粗體變色字標示出，學習者能清楚看到文法觀念在閱讀中的應用，更能意識到閱讀時該注意哪些文法重點。

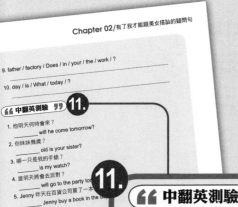

Chapter 02/有了我才能跟美女搭訕的疑問句

9. father / factory / Does / in / your / the / work / ?

10. day / is / What / today / ?

❝ 中翻英測驗 ❞ 11.

1. 他明天何時會來？
_____ will he come tomorrow?

2. 你妹妹幾歲？
_____ old is your sister?

3. 哪一只是我的手錶？
_____ is my watch?

4. 誰明天將會去派對？
_____ will go to the party to

5. Jenny 昨天在百貨公司買了一本
_____ Jenny buy a book in the de

6. 你會騎腳踏車嗎？

7. 你為何上學遲到？

8. 他是做什麼工作的？

9. Bill 喜歡哪一種水果？

10. 那個高個子的男孩是誰？

英文文法簡單到不行──暢銷增訂版 *107*

11.

❝ 中翻英測驗 ❞

1. 他明天何時會來？
_____ will he come tomorrow?

2. 你妹妹幾歲？

中翻英測驗

將中文句子翻譯成英文，同樣需要紮實的文法基礎，因此也能夠有效檢測出學習者的文法能力，同時還可以訓練百分百的寫作能力！韋婕老師這次更貼心為讀者分別難度，前面五題採填空式翻譯，後五題再完全自我發揮。不管你的程度如何，都可以試試看！

10.

❝ 句子重組測驗 ❞

1. you / Where / going? / are

_____

句子重組測驗

十題的英文句子重組測驗，能夠有效檢測出學習者的文法觀念是否正確，一起來挑戰看看吧！

親愛的老師、同學們，
我把英文文法變簡單了！

首先，感謝王總編、讀者和學生們的熱情支持，才有這本暢銷增訂版，讓我能和更多人分享學習**英文文法的圖像口訣密技**。「文法」一直是學生的學習困擾，也是許多英文老師教學上的難處，如何把像法條般硬梆梆的文法，學得輕鬆有趣、教得清楚有效，依我多年的教學經驗與師訓分享，發現**透過文法口訣**與**圖像概念**，著實能建立起學習者的清晰架構，不再混淆；也分享給許多教學者這種自創的教學法，相信多年來已看見成效。

這本「暢銷增訂版」，除了將口訣修編得更琅琅上口，讓學習者可運用簡短的口訣帶出關鍵的文法觀念，接著再配合文法圖像及詳細的解說，更容易理解，也更能夠透過圖像加強記憶的長久性。為能和大家分享口訣的原創，感謝出版社讓我有機會親自進錄音室錄製了MP3，透過聲音讀者可和我更貼近。平常上課我就會自然而然輕鬆地帶入口訣並配合文法圖像，發現不喜歡英文的孩子也開始感興趣了，「**原來這麼簡單喔！**」，一位學生突然這麼說。

另外師訓時許多老師告訴我，這些都是我多年教學經驗累積下來的法寶，竟願意將寶物和大家分享，這在補教界是很難得的。但認識我的都知道我的座右銘是：**成長、分享、交流**。怎能獨享呢？口訣流傳出、隨口能唸出，學習有樂趣、教學有幫助，這才是我要的教學舞台！

既然是增訂版，那還有哪些新增的內容呢？

文法變得輕鬆易學，但練習是不可少的，畢竟懂是一回事，運用又是另

一回事。因此每單元增加了**回顧筆記**，讓學習者將概念快速的複習一次，加深印象！而每章節主題複習單元除原有閱讀測驗、句子重組、中翻英，特別新增**選擇題**、**改錯題**，讓題型變得豐富多樣，觀念清楚正確，怎麼考都不會倒！

　　還是最感謝**捷徑文化總編輯** Jessica 對我的信賴與支持、給予的機會與鼓勵，每一本書都可看見她的用心與巧思規劃，她的認真與堅毅，也讓我看到女性的美。相知相惜幾年來成了無話不談的好友，我很感念這份書上無法獲得的情誼。也感恩細心體貼的**主編侑音**以及捷徑文化編輯超優團隊，你們創造出了每一本優質暢銷書！

　　誠如李國修老師的名言，我追隨著：「人，一輩子能做好一件事就功德圓滿了！」我希望我一直在教學的舞台不斷創作分享，讓台灣的英語教學與學習有了微變化，有了微進步！

Part2
進階運用篇

Part1
基本詞性篇

針對英語初學者（英檢初級、多益 550 分以下程度）特別規劃英文文法觀念概述及運用說明，學習者們可以透過此篇徹底了解英文的文法邏輯與架構，打下完美的基礎。

Chapter01 / Verb
我是驕傲的動詞

本篇動詞的學習重點如下：

Unit 01 什麼是動詞？

Track 001

文法口訣輕鬆記

1. 動詞只能有一個
2. be 動詞、一般動詞選一種
3. 兩種一起做進行，一般加上 ing！

1. 動詞只能有一個

一個句子只有一個動詞（除非有連接詞連結 2 個以上的動詞，詳 Chapter 06 Unit 02 對等子句的用法。）

2. be 動詞、一般動詞選一種

動詞有兩大類：「be V.」與「一般 V.」，不可同時使用，須擇一選用。

3. 兩種一起做進行，一般加上 ing！

一般 V. 須加上 ing 才可與 be V. 形成進行式
➔ be 動詞＋ V-ing（正在……）。

文法觀念說給你聽

動詞（V.）分成兩大類：

一、**be V.**：am / is / are

二、**一般 V.**：am / is / are 以外的動詞，統稱為一般動詞，又叫作**普通動詞**。

★ 這兩種動詞不能一起使用，例如下面這兩個句子：

1. I **am go** to the supermarket. (**X**)
2. She **is write** a letter to Tom. (**X**)

★ 這兩種動詞一起使用時可形成「進行式」，此時**一般 V.** 須加上 **ing**，變化成 **be V.+V-ing**（正在……），所以上面兩個錯誤的句子應該寫成：

1. **I am going to** the supermarket.
2. She **is writing** a letter to Tom.

圖解文法一看就懂

be V. 和 一般 V. 的結合用法

be V.
am、is、are

一般V.
eat（吃）、drink（喝）、play（玩）、walk（走）……

be V. + V–ing
正在……

例句現身說法好清楚

1. I **am** a doctor.　我是位醫生。
2. You **are** very smart.　你很聰明。
3. My mother **is** in the kitchen.　我媽媽在廚房。
4. Mr. Wang **is** our teacher.　王先生是我們的老師。
5. You **are** very beautiful.　妳好漂亮。
6. You **are** my good friends.　你們是我的好朋友。
7. We **are** classmates.　我們是同學。
8. The book **is** on the desk.　那本書在桌子上。
9. I **am** very happy.　我很快樂。
10. He **plays** baseball.　他打棒球。

　　＊ 可以寫成 He **is playing** baseball. (O) 他正在打棒球。

　　＊ 不可寫成 He **is play** baseball. (X)

11. She **eats** vegetable.　她吃蔬菜。

　　＊ 可以寫成 She **is eating** vegetables. (**O**)　她正在吃蔬菜。

　　＊ 不可寫成 She **is eat** vegetables. (**X**)

12. We **walk** to school.　我們走路到學校。

　　＊ 可以寫成 We **are walking** to school. (**O**)　我們正走路到學校。

　　＊ 不可寫成 We **are walk** to school. (**X**)

13. I **play** the piano.　我彈鋼琴。

　　＊ 可以寫成I **am playing** the piano. (**O**)　我正在彈鋼琴。

　　＊ 不可寫成 I **am play** the piano. (**X**)

14. He **writes** a letter.　他寫信。

　　＊**不可**寫成 He **is write** a letter. (**X**)

　　＊**可以**寫成 He **is writing** a letter. (**O**)　他正在寫信。

Unit
01

什麼是動詞？

馬上演練好實力

圈圈看：請圈出下列文章中的動詞，並判別其為 be V. 或一般 V.（同一字若出現 2 次以上也算進去）

　　My twin brother, Tom, and I have different hobbies. He likes sports, especially baseball and basketball. He is on the school baseball team and practices baseball two hours a day. He enjoys watching ball games on TV. Chien-Ming Wang and Ching-Feng Chen are his favorite players.

　　I am not like Tom. I seldom go to ball games. I prefer reading and cooking. I like reading novels and comic books. Besides, all my friends love what I cook. My dream is to be a good cook.

Solution 公佈答案

中譯：

　　我的雙胞胎兄弟，湯姆，和我有不同的嗜好。他喜歡運動，特別是棒球和籃球。他是棒球校隊並且每天練習棒球兩小時。他喜愛在電視上看棒球比賽。王建民和陳金鋒是他最喜愛的球員。

　　我不像湯姆一樣。我很少去看球賽。我比較喜歡閱讀和烹飪。我喜歡看小說和連環漫畫。此外，我的朋友全都喜愛我煮的東西。我的夢想是成為一名好廚師。

My twin brother, Tom, and I have different hobbies. He likes sports, especially baseball and basketball. He is on the school baseball team and practices baseball two hours a day. He enjoys watching ball games on TV. Chien-Ming Wang and Ching-Feng Chen are his favorite players.

I am not like Tom. I seldom go to ball games. I prefer reading and cooking. I like reading novels and comic books. Besides, all my friends love what I cook. My dream is to be a good cook.

be V. 依序有：is / are / am / is / be，共 5 個
一般 V. 依序有：have / likes / practices / enjoys / watching / go / prefer / reading / cooking / like / reading / love / cook 共十三個

Unit
01

什麼是動詞？

Unit 01

什麼是動詞？

今日重點回顧筆記

一定要練習寫下來！才能確定自己真的會了喔！

1. 英文裡一句話只能 .... 。
2. be動詞和 .... 不能同時使用。
3. 硬要在一起，動詞要加 .... 。

試判斷以下句子是否正確？錯誤的請更正為正確句子。

A. I am watch TV.

....

B. She is a teacher.

....

C. They playing basketball.

....

正確答案：

1. 有一個動詞　2. 一般動詞　3. ing
A. I am watching TV.
　　be動詞後面的一般動詞要接-ing喔！
B. 正確
C. They are playing basketball.
　　要表示「現在進行式」，就要用be動詞+動詞-ing的用法。

動詞時態──現在式

Unit 02

一、現在式總論

文法觀念說給你聽

「現在式」的使用時機：

一、表示習慣，常常跟 every day、always 等頻率副詞搭配使用。

二、表示目前的動作、狀態。

三、表示存在及事實。

四、表示不變的真理。

五、格言。

圖解文法一看就懂

例句現身說法好清楚

1. This **is** my mother.　這是我媽媽。→ **事實**
2. I **go** to school early every day.　我每天很早去上學。→ **習慣**
3. We **love** fruit.　我們喜愛水果。→ **目前狀態**
4. The earth **moves** around the sun.　地球繞著太陽運行。→ **真理**
5. No news **is** good news.　沒有消息就是好消息。→ **格言**

Unit

02

動詞時態——現在式

二、be 動詞現在式

文法口訣輕鬆記　🔊 *Track 002*

> **1. am、are、is 怎麼配？**
> **2. I am 我最大，you 配 are**
> **3. 其餘單數用is，複數一律共用are**

1. am、are、is 怎麼配？

　　be 動詞現在式有 am、are、is三種，需跟著主詞作變化。

2. I am 我最大，you 配 are

　　主詞若為I（我）配用am；主詞若為you（你／你們）則配用are。

3. 其餘單數用is，複數一律共用are

　　主詞若為第三人稱單數配用is；若為複數則
一律配用are。

文法觀念說給你聽

我們先從英文的be「是」的現在式變化介紹起。be動詞的變化形式很多，光是現在式就有am /are / is 三種方法可以說。到底怎麼配用呢？

· 先記得**I am**（「我」用am）和 **you are**（「你」配are）。

· 其他分為兩大類：

一、單數：he（他）/ she（她）/ your sister（你妹妹）就配**is** ➜ he is / she is / your sister is

二、複數：we（我們）/ they（他們）/ the boys（男孩們）就配**are** ➜ we are / they are / the boys are...

圖解文法一看就懂

be動詞─am/are/is的用法

I
am
（我）

第三人稱單數
（he, she, it）
+ is

複數、you（你／你們）
+ are

例句現身說法好清楚

1. I **am** a teacher; you **are** a student.　我是老師；你是學生。
2. He **is** a dancer, and I **am**, too.　他是舞蹈家，我也是。
3. Your sister **is** very lovely.　你妹妹很可愛。
4. Her grandfather **is** very kind.　他的祖父很慈祥。

5. They **are** my friends.　他們是我的朋友。

6. Tom and Peter **are** classmates.　湯姆和彼得是同學。

❝ 馬上演練好實力 ❞

A. 選選看

(　　) 1. You _____ my classmate.

　　　　(A) am　　　(B) are　　　　(C) is　　　　　(D) be

(　　) 2. I _____ a doctor, not a teacher.

　　　　(A) am　　　(B) are　　　　(C) is　　　　　(D) be

(　　) 3. Sally _____ somtimes late for school.

　　　　(A) am　　　(B) are　　　　(C) is　　　　　(D) be

(　　) 4. They _____ usually busy on Monday.

　　　　(A) am　　　(B) are　　　　(C) is　　　　　(D) be

(　　) 5. Jacky and Linda _____ good friends.

　　　　(A) am　　　(B) are　　　　(C) is　　　　　(D) be

B. 填填看

6. I _____ from Taipei.　我是從台北來的。

7. You _____ my best friend.　你是我最好的朋友。

8. The man _____ Tony's father.　那個人是東尼的爸爸。

9. _____ your father at home?　你爸爸在家嗎？

10. We _____ in the same class.　我們在同一班。

Solution 公佈答案

解答：1. (B)　2. (A)　3. (C)　4. (B)　5. (B)

　　　　6. am　7. are　8. is　9. Is　10. are

Unit
02

動詞時態──現在式

今日重點回顧筆記

一定要練習寫下來！才能確定自己真的會了喔！

1. be動詞現在式有 _____ 、 _____ 、 _____ 三種，需
跟著_____作變化。
2. 主詞I 配用_____；you則配用_____。
3. 第三人稱單數用_____；複數一律用_____。

試判斷以下句子是否正確？錯誤的請更正為正確句子。

A. Your teacher are great.

....

B. She and I am good friends.

....

C. The boys are from America.

....

正確答案：

1. am/are/is，主詞　　2. am/are　　3. is/are
A. Your teacher is great.
主詞「your teacher」是第三人稱單數，後面接is。
B. She and I are good friends.
She and I 有兩個人，是複數，後面接are。
C. 正確

三、be動詞─現在式否定句&疑問句

🔊 *Track 003*

Unit
02

動詞時態──現在式

📣 文法口訣輕鬆記 📣

1. be動詞easy
2. 否定後加not，疑問就搬be
3. 搬到主詞前，形成疑問句

1. be動詞 easy
　be動詞的否定／疑問句很簡單，不像一般動詞需用助動詞do/does。

2. 否定後加not，疑問就搬be
　否定句只要在be V.後面加上not；而疑問句則需搬動be V.。

3. 搬到主詞前，形成疑問句
　將be V.搬到主詞前即可輕鬆改成疑問句。

📣 文法觀念說給你聽 📣

一、beV.之否定句
中文「不是」，其否定字「不」是加在動詞前，而英文是在
be V. 之後 + not
例：am not➜通常不縮寫
　　are not➜縮寫成**aren't**
　　is not➜縮寫成**isn't**

二、beV.之疑問句
中文是句尾加上「**嗎?**」，而英文是將 be V. 搬到**句首大寫**，句尾加「**?**」
例：Am I～? / Are you～? / Is he～?

三、beV.之否定疑問句

搬BeV.至主詞前；主詞後加not

例：Am I not ~ ? / Are you not ~ ? = Aren't you ~ ?

Is he not ~ ? = Isn't he ~ ?

圖解文法一看就懂

Unit

02

動詞時態──現在式

否定句

主詞+be V. + not...

I am **not**...

You are **not**...

He is **not**...

疑問句

be V. + 主詞...?

Am I ~ ?

Are you ~ ?

Is he ~ ?

例句現身說法好清楚

1. She **is** a singer.　她是歌手。

➔She **is not** a singer.＝She **isn't** a singer.　➔ **否定句**　她不是歌手。

2. I **am** a student.　我是學生。

➔I **am not** a student.　➔ **否定句**　我不是學生。

3. You **are** my classmate.　你是我的同學。

➔You **are not** my classmate.　➔ **否定句**　你不是我的同學。

4. Thomas **is** a cook.　湯瑪士是廚師。

➔ **Is** Thomas a cook?　➔ **疑問句**　湯瑪士是廚師嗎？

5. **Is** she a businessman?　她是商人嗎？

➔ Yes, she **is**.　➔ **肯定簡答**　是，她是。

➔ No, she **is not**. ➔ **否定簡答** 不，她不是。

➔ Yes, she **is a businessman**. ➔ **肯定詳答** 是，她是商人。

➔ No, she **is not a businessman**. ➔ **否定詳答** 不，她不是商人。

6. **Are** you a teacher? 你是老師嗎？

➔ Yes, I **am**. ➔ **肯定簡答** 是的，我是。

➔ No, I **am not**. ➔ **否定簡答** 不，我不是。

➔ Yes, I **am a teacher**. ➔ **肯定詳答** 是的，我是老師。

➔ No, I **am not a teacher**. ➔ **否定詳答** 不，我不是老師。

7. **Isn't** Judy your new student? Judy不是你的新學生嗎？

Yes, she **is**. 是，她是。（肯定簡答）

No, she **is not**. 不，她不是。（否定簡答）注意：簡答需用代名詞

8. **Aren't** the students in the gym?

= **Are** the students **not** in the gym? 學生們不是在體育館嗎？

不可寫成: Are not the students in the gym? (**X**)

Unit 02

動詞時態──現在式

馬上演練好實力

A. 選選看

( ) 1. _____ your brother at home?

　　(A) Am 　　(B) Are 　　(C) Is 　　(D) Be

( ) 2. Is this your pen? No, it _____.

　　(A) are 　　(B) aren't 　　(C) is 　　(D) isn't

( ) 3. _____ Tony your classmate?

　　(A) Are 　　(B) Aren't 　　(C) Is not 　　(D) Is

( ) 4. Where _____ your sister?

　　(A) am 　　(B) are 　　(C) is 　　(D) be

( ) 5. Is this your watch? No, it _____.

　　(A) aren't 　　(B) is 　　(C) am 　　(D) isn't

B. 填填看：

6. She **is not** a doctor. = She _____ a doctor. （縮寫）

7. You **are not** late. = You _____ late. （縮寫）

8. Tom is in the park.

➜ _____ （改為否定句）

9. Your father is always busy.

➜ _____ （改為疑問句）

10. Are they your classmates?

➜ _____ （否定簡答）

Unit
02

動詞時態——現在式

Solution 公佈答案

解答：1. (C)　2. (D)　3. (D)　4. (C)　5. (D)　6. isn't　7. aren't
　　　8. Tom is not in the park.　9. Is your father always busy?
　　　10. No, they aren't.

Unit
02

動詞時態——現在式

今日重點回顧筆記

一定要練習寫下來！才能確定自己真的會了喔！

1. be動詞的否定句，在be動詞後面加上_____。
2. be動詞的疑問句，需將be動詞放在主詞_____。
3. is not可縮寫成_____；are not則縮寫成_____。

試判斷以下句子是否正確？錯誤的請更正為正確句子。

A. Tony is not at home.

B. Lily and Sally are your cousins?

C. Is not she your classmate?

正確答案：

1. not　2. 前面　3. is / are

A. 正確

B. Are Lily and Sally your cousins?
　　疑問句中，be動詞要放在主詞的前面。

C. Isn't she your classmate? 或 Is she not your classmate?
　　疑問否定句中，is和not如果要接在一起，一定要縮寫成isn't才行！

四、一般動詞現在式

文法口訣輕鬆記 🔊 *Track 004*

> **1. 一般動詞現在式,何時加s?**
> **2. I、you、複數用原形,其餘單數加s**

1. 一般動詞現在式,何時加s?

一般動詞現在式,什麼時候加「s」?就加在第三人稱單數(像是he, she, Mary, your friend...)這些主詞的動詞後面。

2. I、you、複數用原形,其餘單數加s

主詞是 I、you、複數如:we(我們)/ they (他們)/ the boys(男孩們)的時候就用原形動詞。

文法觀念說給你聽

　　英文的動詞現在式分成「原形 V.」及第三人稱專用的單數動詞「V.+s」,到底怎麼使用?注意!**除了 I / you 一定接原形 V.**,如 I eat / you eat,其他則分為兩大類:

一、單數:主詞是單數,如 he / she(他/她)/ your sister(你妹妹),就配用 **V.+s** ➔ he eats / she eats / your sister eats...

二、複數:主詞是複數,如 we(我們)/ they(他們)/ the boys(男孩們),就配用**原形V.** ➔ we eat / they eat / the boys eat...

總結:主詞只要不是 I、you 或複數就需V. + s

動詞現在式加s的用法

1. V.**＋s**（如：cooks / likes / eats...）

2. 字尾 x / o / s / z / sh / ch → **＋es**（如：do → does / watch → watches）

3. 子音＋y → **去y＋ies**（如：study → studies / hurry → hurries）

🔖 圖解文法一看就懂 🔖

一般動詞現在式規則：

主詞　　　　　　　　　　　　　動詞

```
┌─────────────────────┐         ┌──────────┐
│  I、You、複數         │         │  原形V.   │
│ （we, they, the students,     │          │
│   Tom and Tim...）   │         └──────────┘
└─────────────────────┘

┌─────────────────────┐         ┌──────────┐
│  第三人稱單數          │         │  V. ＋ s  │
│ （he, she, Mary, your │         │          │
│   friend...）        │         └──────────┘
└─────────────────────┘
```

🔖 例句現身說法好清楚 🔖

1. I **play** basketball everyday.　我每天打籃球。

2. Mr. Lin **goes** to work by car.　林先生開車去上班。

3. My brother **watches** TV every day.　我弟弟每天看電視。

4. Amanda **studies** English every morning.　亞曼達每天早上讀英文。

5. You have a cat; he **has** a dog.　你有一隻貓；他有一隻狗。

注意：have → has，不可寫成**haves**

6. Frank and I **play** basketball together after school.

= Frank **plays** basketball with me after school.

法蘭克放學後和我一起打籃球。

7. I **wash** the dishes after dinner every day. 我每天晚餐後洗碗。

→ She **washes** the dishes after dinner every day. 她每天晚餐後洗碗。

注意：動詞跟著主詞走，動詞記得作變化

❝ 馬上演練好實力 ❞

一、選選看：請從選項中選出符合題目的答案

( ) 1. Cathy _____ the piano every day.

　　(A) play 　　(B) is play 　　(C) plays 　　(D) are play

( ) 2. My brother _____ a car.

　　(A) is wash 　(B) wash 　　(C) washs 　　(D) washes

( ) 3. Joe _____ math very hard.

　　(A) study 　(B) studys 　　(C) studies 　　(D) is study

( ) 4. They _____ math very hard.

　　(A) study 　(B) studys 　　(C) studies 　　(D) is study

( ) 5. Your brother _____ math very hard.

　　(A) study 　(B) studys 　　(C) studies 　　(D) is study

二、寫寫看：請根據題目右方的提示，寫出空格中的正確答案

1. I like hamburgers.

➜ _____

（主詞改成 Tom）

2. You watch TV in the living room.

➜ _____

（主詞改成 Your brother）

Unit
02

動詞時態──現在式

3. She studies English every day.

→ _____

（主詞改成 We）

4. Tom gets up early every morning.

→ _____

（主詞改成 Tom and Mary）

5. We have a cat.

→ _____

（主詞改成 Jenny）

Unit

02

動詞時態——現在式

Solution 公佈答案

一、選選看：1. (C) 2. (D) 3. (C) 4. (A) 5. (C)

二、寫寫看：

1. Tom likes hamburgers.

2. Your brother watches TV in the living room.

3. We study English every day.

4. Tom and Mary get up early every morning.

5. Jenny has a cat.

今日重點回顧筆記

一定要練習寫下來！才能確定自己真的會了喔！

1. 一般動詞現在式，需跟著_____作變化。

2. 主詞I/you/複數，配用_____動詞。

3. 第三人稱單數動詞，字尾需加上____。

試判斷以下句子是否正確？錯誤的請更正為正確句子。

A. Your brother studys hard.

....

B. She plays tennis well.

....

C. The students goes to a movie together.

....

正確答案：

1. 主詞　2. 原形　3. s

A. Your brother studies hard.

　　study的結尾是y，所以第三人稱單數動詞變化要去y加上-ies才對。

B. 正確

C. The students go to a movie together.

　　The students是複數，go的後面不需加上-es。

Unit
02

動詞時態──現在式

五、一般動詞現在式否定句&疑問句

文法口訣輕鬆記

1. 一般動詞否定、疑問要人幫，助動詞來幫忙
2. 否定 don't / doesn't 擋在動詞前
3. 疑問要由 Do / Does 來引導

Unit
02

動
詞
時
態
|
現
在
式

1. **一般動詞否定、疑問要人幫，助動詞來幫忙**
   一般 V. 和 be V. 不一樣，需要助動詞 do / does 來幫忙形成否定和疑問句。

2. **否定 don't / doesn't 擋在動詞前**
   否定句在 V. 之前加上助動詞，變成「don't / doesn't＋原形 V.」。

3. **疑問要由 Do / Does 來引導**
   疑問句在句首加上助動詞，變成「Do / Does ～＋原形 V.」。

文法觀念說給你聽

一、一般 V. 之否定句：

在動詞前加上助動詞，變成「don't / doesn't ＋原形V.」，而且
do not →縮寫成 don't，例如：I don't know.
does not → 縮寫成 doesn't，例如：He doesn't know.

二、一般 V. 之疑問句：

在句首加上助動詞，變成「**Do / Does ＋原形V.**」，像是Do I ～？/ Do you ～？/ Does he ～？

例如：**Do you know her? / Does he know her?**

補充：

否定疑問句這樣寫，例如：

Do you not ～？＝ Don't you ～？

Does he not ～？＝ Doesn't he ～？

高分小撇步

> 主詞為第三人稱單數，一般 V. 之s 已轉給 does / doesn't，所以注意動詞要變回原形 V.！

圖解文法一看就懂

一般動詞現在式的否定句 & 疑問句：

否定句（～不～、～沒有～）				
主詞	＋	助動詞	＋	原形動詞～
I、you、複數	＋	don't	＋	原形動詞～
第三人稱單數	＋	doesn't	＋	原形動詞～
疑問句（～嗎？）				
助動詞	＋	主詞	＋	原形動詞～
Do	＋	I、you、複數	＋	原形動詞～
Does	＋	第三人稱單數	＋	原形動詞～

Unit
02

動詞時態——現在式

例句現身說法好清楚

1. **I don't** like swimming; she **doesn't** like jogging.
   我不喜歡游泳；她不喜歡慢跑。

2. **Do** you know the man over there?
   你認識在那裡的那個男人嗎？

3. Jenny **goes** to a movie with you.
   珍妮和你去看電影。

   → Jenny **doesn't go** to a movie with you. →否定
   珍妮不跟你去看電影。

4. **Does** Jenny **go** to a movie with you? → 疑問
   珍妮要跟你去看電影嗎？

   → Yes, she **does**. → 肯定簡答　是，她要。

   → No, she **doesn't**. → 否定簡答　不，她不要。

5. **Doesn't** Jenny **go** to a movie with you? → 否定疑問
   珍妮不跟你去看電影嗎？

   → Yes, she **goes** to a movie with me. → 肯定詳答
   是，她和我去看電影。

   → No, she **doesn't go** to a movie with me. → 否定詳答
   不，她不跟我去看電影。

6. They **eat** dinner at the fast food restaurant.
   他們在速食店吃晚餐。

   → They **don't eat** dinner at the fast food restaurant. → 否定
   他們不在速食店吃晚餐。

7. **Do** they **eat** dinner at the fast food restaurant? → 疑問
   他們在速食店吃晚餐嗎？

   → Yes, they **do**. → 肯定簡答　是，他們在。

   → No, they **don't**. → 否定簡答　不，他們不在。

8. **Don't** they **eat** dinner at the fast food restaurant? → **否定疑問**

他們不在速食店吃晚餐嗎？

→ Yes, they **eat** dinner at the fast food restaurant. → **肯定詳答**

是，他們在速食店吃晚餐。

→ No, they **don't eat** dinner at the fast food restaurant. → **否定詳答**

不，他們不在速食店吃晚餐。

馬上演練好實力

一、選選看：請從選項中選出符合題目的答案

(　　) 1. _____ you go to work late?

(A) Are　　　　(B) Is　　　　(C) Do　　　　(D) Does

(　　) 2. Ann _____ to school.

(A) aren't go　(B) don't go　(C) doesn't go　(D) don't goes

(　　) 3. We _____ dinner at the restaurant.

(A) aren't have　(B) don't have　(C) doesn't have　(D) don't has

(　　) 4. _____ your brother play the computer game every day?

(A) Is　　　　(B) Are　　　　(C) Do　　　　(D) Does

(　　) 5. Does she bake a cake? No, she _____.

(A) isn't　　　(B) aren't　　　(C) doesn't　　　(D) don't

二、寫寫看：請根據題目右方的提示，寫出空格中的正確答案

1. She **does not** play the piano. = She _____ play the piano.（縮寫）

2. You **do not** eat dinner. = You _____ eat dinner.（縮寫）

Unit
02

動詞時態──現在式

3. Jack studies hard.

➡ _____（改為否定句）

4. Tom walks in the park.

➡ _____（改為疑問句）

5. Does he live in Taipei?

➡ _____（否定簡答）

Unit
02

動詞時態──現在式

Solution 公佈答案

一、選選看：1. (C) 2. (C) 3. (B) 4. (D) 5. (C)

二、寫寫看：1. doesn't 2. don't

3. Jack doesn't study hard.

4. Does Tom walk in the park?

5. No, he doesn't.

今日重點回顧筆記

一定要練習寫下來！才能確定自己真的會了喔！

1. 一般動詞現在式，否定句／疑問句需用_____詞來形成。
2. 否定句：主詞I/you/複數，配用助動詞_____；第三人稱單數則用助動詞_____。
3. 疑問句：主詞I/you/複數，配用助動詞_____；第三人稱單數則用助動詞_____。

試判斷以下句子是否正確？錯誤的請更正為正確句子。

A. Do your grandfather get up early?

....

B. My sister don't give me a hand.

....

C. They don't like fast food at all.

....

正確答案：

1. 助動 2. don't / doesn't 3. Do / Does
A. Does your grandfather get up early?
　　your grandfather是第三人稱單數，需用助動詞does。
B. My sister doesn't give me a hand.
　　my sister是第三人稱單數，否定句的助動詞要用doesn't。
C. 正確

英文文法簡單到不行──暢銷增訂版　*041*

Unit
02

動詞時態──現在式

Unit 03 動詞時態──過去式

一、be 動詞過去式

文法口訣輕鬆記 ◀ Track 006

1. be 動詞過去式，只有 was、were
2. am、is 換 was
3. are 變作 were

---

1. be 動詞過去式，只有 was、were
　　be 動詞的過去式型態，只分成 was 和 were 兩種。

2. am、is 換 was
　　I am → I was；he is → he was

3. are 變作 were
　　you are → you were；they are → they were

文法觀念說給你聽

一、be 動詞的「現在式」和「過去式」比較：

1. 現在式：be V. 分成 **am / are / is**
2. 過去式：be V. 只分 **was / were**

I	＋	am	→	過去式用 was
第三人稱單數（He / She / It...）	＋	is		
You	＋	are	→	過去式用 were
複數主詞	＋	are		

二、一般動詞過去式的變化方式：

一般動詞的過去式變化方式，不分人稱，一律在字尾加上**(e)d**，但是另外有不規則變化的情況，在往後的章節會另作介紹。

三、過去式的使用時機：

1. 常見過去式的使用時機有下面這幾種：

   (1) **yesterday** (morning / afternoon / evening) 昨天（早上；下午；傍晚）

   (2) **this morning** 今天早上

   (3) **last** night 昨晚

   (4) **last** week 上星期

   (5) **last** Saturday 上週六

   (6) **last** year 去年

   (7) **last** September 去年九月

2. 以下這幾種時機也適用過去式，但經常被誤用，所以要特別注意

   (1) **before** 以前

   (2) ...(three days) **ago** ……（三天）以前

   ＊ ago 不可以單獨使用，一定要在前面加上一段時間。

   (3) the day before **yesterday** 前天

   (4) the other day 前幾天

   (5) in the past 在過去

   (6) **then** (＝ at that time) 那時候

   (7) in 2001 在 2001 年（過去）

Unit 03

動詞時態──過去式

圖解文法一看就懂

現在式 → 過去式的變化技巧：

一、be V.	am	→	was
	is		
	are	→	were

二、一般 V.	V＋(e)d
	不規則變化

Unit 03

動詞時態──過去式

例句現身說法好清楚

1. I **was** late for school this morning.　我今早上學遲到了。
2. We **were** at the party last night.　我們昨晚在宴會上。
3. Sherry **was** short **before**, but she **is** tall **now**.
   雪莉以前是矮的，但現在她是高的。
4. They **were** in the same class **last year**, but they **are** in different classes **now**.
   他們去年在同一班，但現在他們不同班。
5. Eric **was** heavy **before**, but he **is** thin **now**.
   艾瑞克以前是胖的，但現在他是瘦的。

二、be 動詞過去式否定句&疑問句

文法觀念說給你聽

以下是 be 動詞過去式的否定句與疑問句的寫法：

一、否定句：be V. ＋ not

was not = wasn't

were not = weren't

例如：He **was not** at home last night. 他昨天晚上不在家。

二、**疑問句**：be V. 在句首

Was ～ ? / Were ～ ?

例如：**Was** he at home last night**?** 他昨天晚上在家嗎？

三、**否定疑問句**：

Wasn't ～ ? / Weren't ～ ?

例如：**Wasn't** he at home last night**?** 他昨天晚上不在家嗎？

Unit
03

動詞時態──過去式

圖解文法一看就懂

be 動詞過去式的否定句和疑問句這樣變：

否定句	I	+	wasn't ～
	第三人稱單數		
	You	+	weren't ～
	複數		

疑問句	Was(n't)	+	I	～ ?
			第三人稱單數	
	Were(n't)	+	You	～ ?
			複數	

例句現身說法好清楚

1. You **were** in America **last month.**　你上個月在美國。

2. You **weren't** in America **last month**. ➜ **否定**　你上個月不在美國。

3. **Were** you in America last month? ➜ **疑問**　你上個月在美國嗎?

4. **Weren't** you in America last month? ➜ **否定疑問**

＝**Were** you **not** in America last month?　你上個月不在美國嗎?

5. **Was** he late yesterday?　他昨天遲到了嗎?

→ Yes, he **was**. ➜ **肯定簡答**　是的，他是。

→ No, he **wasn't**. ➜ **否定簡答**　不，他沒有。

→ Yes, he **was** late yesterday. ➜ **肯定詳答**　是的，他昨天遲到了。

→ No, he **wasn't** late yesterday. ➜ **否定詳答**　不，他昨天沒有遲到。

Unit
03

動詞時態——過去式

❝ 馬上演練好實力 ❞

選選看：請從選項中選出符合題目的答案

(　　) 1. Tom ＿＿＿＿ busy this morning.

     (A) is   (B) was   (C) are   (D) were

(　　) 2. I ＿＿＿＿ at my shop yesterday.

     (A) am not   (B) wasn't   (C) weren't   (D) aren't

(　　) 3. ＿＿＿＿ he at home last night?

     (A) Is   (B) Are   (C) Were   (D) Was

(　　) 4. Were you happy at the party last Saturday? Yes, ＿＿＿＿.

     (A) I were   (B) I was   (C) you were   (D) you was

(　　) 5. Jenny and John ＿＿＿＿ neighbors before.

     (A) was   (B) were   (C) is   (D) are

(　　) 6. Was your uncle busy last weekend? No, ＿＿＿＿.

     (A) he isn't (B) my uncle wasn't (C) he wasn't (D) he weren't

(　　) 7. He was late for work yesterday, but we ＿＿＿.

      (A) weren't　　(B) were　　　　(C) wasn't　　　(D) was

(　　) 8. The river ＿＿＿ clean before, but now it is dirty.

      (A) were　　　(B) are　　　　(C) is　　　　　(D) was

Solution 公佈答案

解答：1. (B)　2. (B)　3. (D)　4. (B)　5. (B)　6. (C)　7. (A)　8. (D)

Unit 03

動詞時態──過去式

Note 筆記手札

有沒有不太熟悉的文法觀念呢？有的話就把它們寫在這裡，之後多做幾次複習吧！加油！

Unit

03

動
詞
時
態
──
過
去
式

今日重點回顧筆記

一定要練習寫下來！才能確定自己真的會了喔！

1. be動詞過去式，可分成_____和_____。
2. 主詞I／第三人稱單數配用_____；主詞you／複數配用_____。
3. 否定句可將was not縮寫成_____；were not縮寫成_____。

試判斷以下句子是否正確？錯誤的請更正為正確句子。

A. Your classmate was late today.

....

B. I were sorry about that bad news.

....

C. He weren't at home yesterday.

....

正確答案：

1.was/were　　2. was/were　　3. wasn't/weren't

A. 正確

B. I was sorry about that bad news.
　　I的be動詞過去式要用was。

C. He wasn't at home yesterday.
　　he的be動詞過去式否定形式用wasn't。

三、一般動詞過去式的不規則變化

文法口訣輕鬆記　　　🔊 *Track 007*

> **1.** 一般動詞過去式，「ed」規則來變化
> **2.** 字尾加「ed」，有「e」就加「d」
> **3.** 「y」的前面是子音，去「y」加上「ied」
> **4.** 短母音要注意，重複字尾加「ed」

1. 一般動詞過去式，「ed」規則來變化

　　一般動詞過去式，在字尾加上「ed」作規則變化。

2. 字尾加「ed」，有「e」就加「d」

　　通常在一般動詞字尾加上「ed」就是過去式，例如「played」。
如果字尾已經有「e」則只需要加「d」，例如「closed」。

3. 「y」的前面是子音，去「y」加上「ied」

　　「y」的前面如果是子音就要去「y」加上「ied」，例如：
study→studied。

4. 短母音要注意，重複字尾加「ed」

　　子音結尾，而且其前面的母音為短母
音，就必須重複字尾加「ed」，例如：
jog→jogged。

文法觀念說給你聽

前面我們學過了 be 動詞的過去式，只分成was / were 兩個。而一般動詞
卻有較多的變化，須特別留意。一般動詞過去式的種類有：

Unit 03

動詞時態──過去式

一、規則變化：

1. 通常在字尾＋ed，即可代表過去式。

像是cooked（煮）/ played（玩），需注意 ed 的讀音。

2. 過去式不變。

像是cut（切）/ put（放），需注意與現在式的區別，尤其是主詞為第三人稱單數時。

例如：現在式：He **puts** his textbooks on the table by the window.

　　　過去式：He **put** his textbooks on the table by the window.

　　　　　　　他把課本放在窗邊的桌上。

注意： 第三人稱單數現在式，動詞需＋s

二、不規則變化：有口訣，用技巧，保證讓你快速學會！將詳述於後。

❝❝ 圖解文法一看就懂 ❞❞

這些都是過去式規則變化的動詞：

過去式 ➡ 動詞＋ed		過去式 ➡ 動詞（去y）＋ied	
現在式	過去式	現在式	過去式
call（打電話）	called	study（研讀）	studied
talk（講話）	talked	hurry（趕快）	hurried
watch（觀賞）	watched	fry（油炸）	fried
		cry（哭）	cried
過去式 ➡ 動詞（字尾e）＋d		過去式 ➡ 動詞重覆字尾＋ed	
現在式	過去式	現在式	過去式
like（喜歡）	liked	stop（停止）	stopped

love（愛）	loved	shop（購物）	shopped
hate（討厭）	hated		
save（節省）	saved		
close（關）	closed		

這些是「現在式／過去式同形」的特殊字：

現在式	過去式	現在式	過去式
cut（切）	cut	hurt（傷害）	hurt
put（放）	put	cost（價值）	cost
let（讓）	let	quit（停止）	quit
hit（撞擊）	hit	shut（關閉）	shut

現在式和過去式「同字不同音」的特殊字：

現在式	過去式
read [rid]（閱讀）	read [rɛd]

ed 發音唸唸看：

無聲			有聲		
字尾是無聲子音： [p]，[k]，[f]，[s]， [ʃ] (sh)，[tʃ] (ch)	＋ed	唸 [t]	字尾是母音或有聲子音： [b]，[g]，[l]，[m]， [n]，[r]，[v]，[z]	＋ed	唸 [d]
特殊：[t]＋ed ➜ 唸 [ɪd]			特殊：[d]＋ed ➜ 唸 [ɪd]		

〝 例句現身說法好清楚 〞

1. My brother watches TV every day.　我弟弟每天看電視。
→ My brother watched TV **last night**.　我弟弟昨晚看電視。
2. Amanda studies English every morning.　亞曼達每天早上讀英文。
→ Amanda studied English yesterday afternoon.　亞曼達昨天下午唸英文。

Unit 03

動詞時態——過去式

3. They **played** baseball after school **yesterday**.　他們昨天放學後打棒球。

4. He **hurried** home to tell us the news.　他匆匆回家告訴我們這個消息。

5. It **rained** a lot yesterday evening.　昨天晚上下很大的雨。

6. He **read** an English book last week.　他上週讀了一本英文書。

注意：read 在此為**過去式**，現在式應配用第三人稱單數動詞 → He reads...

7. John **quit** his job last month.　約翰上個月辭職了。

8. Mary **invited** me to the party.　瑪莉邀請我去派對。

Unit
03

動詞時態──過去式

四、一般動詞過去式的不規則變化

❝ 文法口訣輕鬆記 ❞　🔊 *Track 008*

1. 這群動詞很有趣，過去母音都是「a」
2. 游泳完，跑過來，坐下來，唱首歌，搖個鈴
3. 就給你喝水，預備開始，原諒我變得這麼厲害 a a a Ya ↗

1. **這群動詞很有趣 過去母音都是「a」**
   將下列11個動詞有劃線的母音字母改為「a」，就可以變成過去式。

2. **游泳完，跑過來，坐下來，唱首歌，搖個鈴。**
   swim變swam、run變ran、come變came、sit變sat、sing變sang、ring變rang。

3. **就給你喝水，預備開始，原諒我變得這麼厲害 a a a Ya ↗**
   give變gave、drink變drank、begin變began、forgive變forgave、become變became。會了吧！都是改 a a a a a Ya ↗。

「文法觀念說給你聽」

一、不規則變化的動詞：

可以歸納出常用的 11 個動詞，其動詞過去式只要將母音字母改成「a」，
即可輕鬆學會。例如：swim → swam / run→ ran

二、一般動詞過去式不規則變化的用法：

動詞的現在式需注意第三人稱單數＋ s，過去式則不需區分，一律都一
樣。

例1：He **swims** very well. → He **swam** very well. 他游得很好。

例2：You **swim** very well. → You **swam** very well. 你游得很好。

例3：He **runs** very fast. → He **ran** very fast. 他跑得很快。

例4：You **run** very fast. → You **ran** very fast. 你跑得很快。

「圖解文法一看就懂」

有些動詞的過去式變化是**將母音變成 a**，以下是幾個最常見的例子：

現在式	過去式	現在式	過去式	現在式	過去式
swim（游泳）	swam	run（跑）	ran	come（來）	came
sit（坐）	sat	sing（唱）	sang	ring（鈴響）	rang
give（給）	gave	drink（喝）	drank	begin（開始）	began

延伸字：

現在式	過去式	現在式	過去式
forgive（原諒）	forgave	become（變得）	became

Unit 03

動詞時態——過去式

例句現身說法好清楚

1. My brother swims every day.
   我弟弟每天游泳。

→ My brother swam very well yesterday.
   我弟弟昨天游泳游得很好。

2. She sang an English song for us.
   她為我們唱一首英文歌。

3. They came here on business last Monday.
   他們上週一來這裡出差。

4. She became a famous writer.
   她成了有名的作家。

5. I forgave him for his rudeness.
   我原諒了他的無禮。

6. My father drank a lot of beer.
   我爸爸喝了好多啤酒。

7. It began to rain cats and dogs outside.
   外面開始下起了傾盆大雨。

Unit 03

動詞時態──過去式

今日重點回顧筆記

一定要練習寫下來！才能確定自己真的會了喔！

1. swim/run/come...這些動詞過去式只要將母音改成＿＿＿＿。
2. 一般動詞過去式，否定句和疑問句需用助動詞＿＿＿＿。
3. 常見的過去式變化：1. 將字尾d→＿＿＿＿／ ow→＿＿＿＿／ ay→＿＿＿。

試判斷以下句子是否正確？錯誤的請更正為正確句子。

A. Did Terry grew rice before?

....

B. He sayed sorry to her.

....

C. The boy didn't did his homework.

....

Unit 03

動詞時態──過去式

正確答案：

1. a   2. did   3. t / ew / aid

A. Did Terry grow rice before?

　　有did搭配，grow就不需要是過去式的grew，用原形grow即可。

B. He said sorry to her.

　　say的過去式是said，不是sayed喔！

C. The boy didn't do his homework.

　　有了didn't 搭配，do就不需要用過去式的did，用原形do即可。

五、不規則變化技巧篇 1

📖 文法觀念說給你聽 📖

你累了嗎？你還在一個一個背動詞過去式的不規則變化嗎？其實，只要按照下列技巧，按其變化規則即可輕鬆記住動詞之過去式不規則變化：

一、保留字首子音＋ ought / aught，讀作 [ɔt]。
例如：buy → **bought**

二、母音 i–e → o–e。 例如：write → **wrote**

三、母音 ea → o–e。 例如：wear → **wore**

Unit

03

動詞時態──過去式

📖 圖解文法一看就懂 📖

ought		aught	
buy（買）	**bought**	catch（抓；接住；趕上）	**caught**
think（想）	**thought**	teach（教）	**taught**
bring（帶來）	**brought**		
i–e → o–e		ea → o–e	
ride（騎）	rode	bear（出生）	bore
rise（升起）	rose	tear（撕）	tore
write（寫）	wrote	wear（穿）	wore
drive（開車）	drove	speak（說）	spoke
		break（打破）	broke
like → liked 為規則變化		**hear → heard 為不規則變化，需熟記**	

📖 例句現身說法好清楚 📖

1. Mother **bought** me a new pair of shoes.　媽媽買給我一雙新鞋子。

2. The policeman **caught** the thief. 　警察抓住了小偷。

3. I **rode** home on my bicycle. 　我騎腳踏車回家。

4. I **wrote** Jack that his father was not well.

我寫信給傑克，告訴他他的父親身體欠佳。

5. Frank **fell** down and broke his leg. 　法蘭克跌斷了腳。

六、不規則變化技巧篇 2

文法觀念說給你聽

再教你幾個技巧，讓你以群組方式記住下列常見動詞的過去式不規則變化：

一、字尾子音 **d → t**。例如：lend → lent

二、字尾 **ay → aid**。例如：**say → said**

三、字尾 **ow → ew**。例如：grow → grew

四、母音 **ee → e–t**。例如：keep → kept

圖解文法一看就懂

只要按照下列技巧，按其變化規則即可輕鬆記住這些動詞之過去式

d ➡ t		ay ➡ aid	
lend（借出）	lent	say（說）	said
send（寄）	sent	lay（放置）	laid
spend（花費）	spent	pay（付帳）	paid
build（建造）	built	repay（償還）	repaid
		注意：play ➡ played 為規則變化。	
ow ➡ ew		ee ➡ e - t	
grow（成長；種）	grew	keep（保持）	kept

know（知道）	knew	feel（感覺）	felt
blow（吹）	blew	sleep（睡覺）	slept
throw（丟）	threw	meet（遇見）➡ met / feed（餵）➡ fed	
		要訣：字尾已有 t / d，去掉一個 e 即可。	
		注意：see ➡ saw 為不規則變化，需熟記。	

Unit 03

動詞時態──過去式

例句現身說法好清楚

1. I **spent** NT300 on the hat.　我花了三百元買這頂帽子。
2. Who **lent** you the dictionary?　誰借給你這本字典？
3. We **paid** a very high price for the house.
　我們出了很高的價錢買下了這間房子。
4. They **grew** some vegetables last year.　他們去年種了一些蔬菜。
5. I **slept** very well last night.　昨天夜裡我睡得很好。

七、不規則變化熟記篇

文法觀念說給你聽

　　雖然有些動詞的過去式變化，是沒有規則可循的，必需熟記，但如果利用顏色標示出其變化的地方，可以加強記憶的印象喔！例如：get → got / take → took / hear → heard

　　另外，還可利用發音來幫助記憶，常常唸的話自然就可以學會。下列就列舉出常用的 25 個不規則變化動詞。

🔊 圖解文法一看就懂 🔊

重複多唸幾次這些動詞的過去式變化，會有助於你記憶喔！

現在式	過去式	現在式	過去式
go（去）	went	do（做）	did
see（看見）	saw	get（得到）	got
eat（吃）	ate	win（贏）	won
have / has（有）	had	take（拿；搭）	took
shake（搖）	shook	hear（聽）	heard
find（發現）	found	make（做）	made
fall（掉落）	fell	sell（賣）	sold
tell（告訴）	told	leave（離開）	left
light（點燃）	lit	lead（引導）	led
stand（離開）	stood	understand（了解）	understood
fly（飛）	flew	hold（握／抱／舉行）	held
lose（失去／迷路）	lost	mean（意指）	meant
feed（餵）	fed		

Unit 03

動詞時態——過去式

🔊 例句現身說法好清楚 🔊

1. Mr. Lin **went** to work by car yesterday morning.
   昨天早上林先生開車去上班。

2. I **saw** an accident on my way home.
   我回家途中看到了一個意外事故。

3. Frank **ate** fish for dinner yesterday evening.
   法蘭克昨天晚上晚餐吃魚。

4. I **heard** that she was ill.
   我聽說她生病了。

5. When I **got** home, I **found** a gift on my desk.

   當我回到家的時候，發現書桌上有個禮物。

6. He **took** a piece of paper and **began** to write a letter.

   他拿了一張紙並開始寫信。

7. This baseball team **won** the champion.

   這支棒球隊贏得了冠軍。

Unit 03

動詞時態──過去式

八、一般動詞過去式否定句&疑問句

文法口訣輕鬆記 🔊 *Track 009*

> **1. 現在式很麻煩，do / does 選一個**
> **2. 過去式很簡單，一律都用 did**

1. 現在式很麻煩，do / does 選一個

現在式的助動詞分為 do 和第三人稱單數要用的 does。

2. 過去式很簡單，一律都用 did

過去式的助動詞，不需分人稱或單、複數，

一律都用did。

文法觀念說給你聽

一般 V. 的過去式否定句 / 疑問句，須用「助動詞」來幫忙形成：

一、否定句： 將現在式的 don't ～ / doesn't ～ → **didn't ～**

例如：I didn't ～ / You didn't ～ / He didn't ～

二、疑問句： 將現在式的 Do ～？/ Does ～？→ **Did ～？**

例如：Did I ～？/ Did you ～？/ Did he ～？

📖 圖解文法一看就懂 📖

現在式否定 / 疑問 VS. 過去式否定 / 疑問之比較：

否定句 （～不～、～沒有～）	現在式	～ doesn't	+	原形動詞～
		～ don't		
	過去式	～ didn't	+	原形動詞～
疑問句 （～嗎？）	現在式	Do ～	+	原形動詞～
		Does ～		
	過去式	Did ～	+	原形動詞～

📖 例句現身說法好清楚 📖

1. Peter doesn't study hard. ➞ 現在式

➞ Peter **didn't** study hard **last year**. ➞ 否定，過去式　彼得**去年不**用功。

2. Do you have fun at Tony's party? ➞ 現在式

➞ **Did** you **have** fun at Tony's party **last night**? ➞ 疑問，過去式
你**昨晚**在湯尼的派對上玩得愉快**嗎**？

3. **Didn't** Jane help her mother with the housework **last Sunday**?

= **Did** Jane **not** help her mother with the housework **last Sunday**?
珍**上星期日沒有**幫她媽媽做家事**嗎**？

4. **Did** Amy go to school late **this morning**?　艾咪**今天早上**上學遲到了**嗎**？

➞ Yes, she **did**. ➞ 肯定簡答　是的，她遲到了。

➞ No, she **didn't**. ➞ 否定簡答　不，她沒遲到。

➞ Yes, she went to school late this morning. ➞ 肯定詳答
是的，她今天早上遲到了。

➞ No, she **didn't** go to school late this morning. ➞ 否定詳答
不，她今天早上沒有遲到。

5. Who **came** to school first **this morning**? Tony **did**.
今天早上誰第一個來學校的呢？**是**湯尼。

Unit 03

動詞時態——過去式

注意：一般動詞之簡答、簡寫用助動詞 **did**，不可用 be 動詞 **was / were**。

6. John **rode** a bicycle to the library **yesterday morning**, but I **didn't**.

約翰**昨天早上**騎腳踏車到圖書館，但我**沒有**。

❝ 馬上演練好實力 ❞

選選看：請從選項中選出符合題目的答案

(　　) 1. The rain_____, and the students played outside.

　　　　(A) stoped　　(B) stopped　　(C) was stop　　(D) stops

(　　) 2. David _____ a comic book last night.

　　　　(A) reads　　(B) read　　(C) readed　　(D) was read

(　　) 3. Helen _____ to school by MRT yesterday morning.

　　　　(A) goes　　(B) goed　　(C) did　　(D) went

(　　) 4. They _____ a bus to the park yesterday.

　　　　(A) take　　(B) was take　　(C) took　　(D) did took

(　　) 5. I _____ a letter to my English teacher last week.

　　　　(A) writted　　(B) write　　(C) wrote　　(D) didn't wrote

(　　) 6. Dad _____ a watch for me last month.

　　　　(A) bought　　(B) buys　　(C) buyed　　(D) buied

(　　) 7. She _____ up early yesterday, but I _____.

　　　　(A) gets ; don't (B) got ; wasn't (C) got ; didn't (D) got ; did

(　　) 8. _____ she _____ the piano last night?

　　　　(A) Does ; play (B) Was ; play (C) Did ; played (D) Didn't ; play

Solution 公佈答案

1. (B)　2. (B)　3. (D)　4. (C)　5. (C)　6. (A)　7. (C)　8. (D)

動詞時態 —— 未來式

文法口訣輕鬆記

◀ *Track 010*

1. 未來式，動詞前面加 will，動詞記得現原形
2. will 可換 be going to

1. 未來式，動詞前面加 will，動詞記得現原形

   助動詞 will 表示將要／將會，用 will 加原形 V.，
   形成未來式。

2. will 可換 be going to

   be V.＋going to 也可表示未來。

文法觀念說給你聽

一、未來式需用助動詞 will／be V.＋going to＋原形 V. 來形成，will 不需分人稱單複數

例如：I will buy... / You will buy... / She will buy...，也可以寫成

　　　→I am going to buy... / You are going to buy... / She is going to buy...

二、未來式的否定句：will not／won't＋原形 V. ～＝ be V.＋not goning to＋原形 V. ～

例如：I will not（won't）buy the watch. ＝ I am not going to buy the watch.

三、未來式的疑問句：將 will 搬到句首，也就是Will ～＋原形 V. ～？／Be V.＋going to＋原形 V. ～？

例如： Will you buy the watch? ＝ Are you going to buy the watch?

四、未來式的使用時機：

1. 常見的使用時機有這些：

(1) 明天（早上；下午；晚上）tomorrow (morning; afternoon; evening)

(2) 今天下午（傍晚） this afternoon (evening)

(3) 今晚 tonight

(4) 下星期 next week

(5) 下週日 next Sunday

(6) 下個月 next month

(7) 明年 next year

2. 以下這些使用時機比較難一眼看出，須特別注意：

(1) 後天 the day after tomorrow

(2) 再過三天 in three days

(3) 十小時之後 in ten hours

(4) 在未來 in the future

(5) 某時候 some time

(6) 未來有一天 some day

✓(7) 從現在開始 from now on

❝ 圖解文法一看就懂 ❞

將要／將會的英文用法：

	will	going to
肯定	wil＋原形動詞	be V.＋going to＋原形 V.
否定	will not（＝won't）	be V.＋not going to＋原形 V.
疑問	Will～＋原形 V.?	be V.～＋going to 原形 V.～?

will 之縮寫為 'll，例如：I will ＝ I'll、You will ＝ You'll

66 例句現身說法好清楚 99

1. We **will** (We'll) play basketball tomorrow.

= We **are going to** play basketball tomorrow.

　　我們明天要去打籃球。

2. Mom **will not** (= **won't**) work next weekend.

= Mom **is not going to** work next weekend.

　　下週末媽媽不用上班。

3. He'll come to work here from now on.

　　從現在起他將在這裡工作。

4. **Will** you play baseball with me tomorrow morning?

　　明天早上你要和我一起打棒球嗎？

→ Yes, I will. → **肯定簡答**　要，我要。

→ No, I won't. → **否定簡答**　不，我不要。

= **Are** you going to play baseball with me tomorrow morning?

　　明天早上你要跟我一起打棒球嗎？

→ Yes, I am. → **肯定簡答**　要，我要。

→ No, I am not. → **否定簡答**　不，我不要。

注意：will 問 → will 答 / be V. 問 → be V. 答

5. There **will be** a good movie on TV tonight.

= There **is going to be** a good movie on TV tonight.

　　今天晚上電視上將有一部不錯的電影。

注意：will ＋原形動詞be；不可加is / are。will be ＝ is going to **be**；不要
　　　　忘了 be

補充：未來式的其他用法

一、往返動詞（來去動詞）：

通常用「現在進行式」代替「未來式」，come（來）、go（去）、start

Unit
04

動詞時態──未來式

（出發、開始）、leave（離開）、leave for（動身前往）都屬於往返動詞，用法如下：

1. Christmas **is coming!**　聖誕節快到了！

2. The train **is starting**.　火車即將要開了。

3. We **are leaving** Taipei tomorrow.　明天我們將離開台北。

二、表示年齡要用 will；不用 be going to：

I **will be** fifteen years old next year.　明年我就要15 歲了。

三、第一人稱（I / we）可用 shall：

Shall we go to the party tonight?　我們今晚將去派對嗎？

四、表示即將發生可用 be about to：

We **are about to** start.　我們正準備出發。

The plane **is about to** take off.　飛機就要起飛了。

He **is about to** begin his term as President. 他即將開始他的總統任期。

五、表示計劃或安排好的動作可用「be V. ＋ to ＋原形V.」：

We **are to** meet at the gate.　我們約定好將在大門口見。

❝ 馬上演練好實力 ❞

選選看：請從選項中選出符合題目的答案

(　　) 1. My brother _____ stay at home tomorrow, but I will.

(A) will　　(B) willn't　　(C) will be　　(D) won't

(　　) 2. The weather _____ cold next week.

(A) will　　(B) willn't　　(C) will be　　(D) won't

(　　) 3. Will you go to the party next weekend? No, I _____.

(A) am not　(B) willn't　　(C) will　　(D) won't

(　　) 4. Are you going to visit your uncle next Sunday ? Yes, I _____.

     (A) won't　　(B) am　　　(C) will　　　(D) will be

(　　) 5. _____ she be a singer in the future?

     (A) Does　　(B) Do　　　(C) Will　　　(D) Is going to

(　　) 6. Alan _____ his homework this evening.

     (A) will do　(B) will doing　(C) will does　(D) will did

(　　) 7. _____ you going to have a piano lesson tomorrow?

     (A) Will　　(B) Do　　　(C) Are　　　(D) Can

(　　) 8. There _____ a good movie tonight.

     (A) is going to have　(B) will have　(C) will be　(D) is going to

Unit
04

動詞時態──未來式

Solution 公佈答案

1. (D)　2. (C)　3. (D)　4. (B)　5. (C)　6. (A)　7. (C)　8. (C)

Unit
04

動詞時態——未來式

今日重點回顧筆記

一定要練習寫下來！才能確定自己真的會了喔！

1. 未來式是用will後面加上＿＿＿＿＿＿形成。
2. 否定句是用will+not，可縮寫成 ＿＿＿＿。
3. Will可換成：be ＿＿＿＿。

試判斷以下句子是否正確？錯誤的請更正為正確句子。

A. Will he going to the concert tomorrow evening?

....

B. They willn't buy the house.

....

C. There will be an important game tomorrow afternoon.

....

正確答案：

1. 原形動詞　　2. won't　　3. going to

A. Is he going to the concert tomorrow evening?
　　未來式是will加上原形動詞，而will也可以替換成be going to。所以這裡用Will he go...或Is he going...都可以喔！

B. They won't buy the house.
　　will的否定形式是won't，不是willn't。

C. 正確

動詞時態 ——進行式

Unit 05

一、進行式的用法

文法口訣輕鬆記

◀ *Track 011*

> 1. 進行式：be 動詞和一般動詞一起用
> 2. be 動詞放前頭，一般動詞加上「ing」

1. 進行式：be 動詞和一般動詞一起用

   一般動詞的進行式：同時需要 be 動詞和一般動詞。

2. be 動詞放前頭，一般動詞加上「ing」

   be 動詞放在一般動詞前面，而一般動詞需加上「ing」，也就是：be 動詞＋V-ing。

文法觀念說給你聽

一、進行式需用 be 動詞＋ V-ing，be 動詞跟著人稱、時態作變化，並注意 V-ing 的變化原則。

例如：

I am watching TV. / She is watching TV. / He was watching TV then. / They were watching TV then.

二、進行式的使用時機如下：

1. 現在進行式常配用 now（現在）

2. 過去進行式常配用

   1) then / at that time（那時候）

   2) at...（點鐘）+ 過去時間

   例：at 7:00 yesterday evening 昨晚7:00

   3) while（正當……時候）

三、數線解析：

   現在、過去或未來某個時刻正在發生、進行中，就要用 be 動詞＋ V-ing 形成進行式。

過去進行	現在進行	未來進行
was/were+V-ing	am/are/is+V-ing	will+be+V-ing

❝ 圖解文法一看就懂 ❞

一般 V. 找 be V. 來幫忙，變成：

be V. ＋ V–ing（現在分詞） 正在～

V-ing 變化原則：

常見	需注意
1. V.＋ing [ɪŋ]	1. 短母音＋子音字尾 ➜ 重複字尾＋ing
2. 字尾 e 不發音 ➜ 去 e＋ing，不可去 y ＋ ing（勿與去y ➜ ies / ied混淆）	2. 特例

搖身一變試試看：

V + ing			
一般動詞	進行式	一般動詞	進行式
do（做）	doing	help（幫忙）	helping
wash（洗）	washing		
特例	sing（唱）➜ singing（需再＋ing）		

去 e 加 ing			
一般動詞	進行式	一般動詞	進行式
come（來）	coming	have（吃；玩得）	having
ride（騎）	riding	write（寫）	writing
close（關）	closing		

重複字尾			
一般動詞	進行式	一般動詞	進行式
cut（切）	cutting	put（放）	putting
run（跑）	running	sit（坐）	sitting
plan（計畫）	planning	swim（游泳）	swimming
shop（購物）	shopping	stop（停止）	stopping
begin（開始）	beginning	mop（拖地）	mopping
特例	eat（吃）[it] 長母音 ➜ eating（不必重複字尾）		

不可去 y + ing			
一般動詞	進行式（y+ing）	現在式（去y+ies）	過去式（去y+ied）
study（研讀）	studying	studies	studied
cry（哭）	crying	cries	cried
try（試著）	trying	tries	tried

Unit
05

動詞時態──進行式

Unit
05

動詞時態——進行式

特殊單字			
一般動詞	進行式	一般動詞	進行式
(1) c + king			
picnic（野餐）	picnicking	mimic（模仿）	mimicking
(2) ie ➜ 去 ie 為 y + ing			
tie（打結）	tying	die（死）	dying
lie（躺 / 說謊）	lying	vie（競爭）	vying
(3) 字尾 ee / ye + ing（注意：不可去 e）			
agree（同意）	agreeing	dye（染色）	dyeing

例句現身說法好清楚

一、現在進行式（am / are / is+V-ing）

1. The boy **is running** and play**ing** in the park.

   這個男孩**正在**公園裡邊**跑**邊**玩**。

2. My brother **is watching** TV in the living room.

   我弟弟**正在**客廳**看**電視。

3. He **is standing**, not sit**ting**.

   他**正站**著，不是**坐**著。

4. We're **having** fun. **Are** you com**ing**?

   我們**正玩得**開心。你要**來**嗎？

二、過去進行式（was / were+V-ing）

1. He **was playing** computer games at 10:00 last night.

   昨晚十點他**正在玩**電腦遊戲。

2. He **was watching** TV then(=at that time).

   那時候他**正在看**電視。

3. While Mom **was cooking** dinner, Dad **was reading** the newspaper.

   正當媽媽**煮**晚餐時，爸爸**正在看**報紙。

三、未來進行式（will+be V.+V-ing）

1. This time next year, Jack and I **will be traveling** through France.

   明年此時，我和傑克**將正在**法國**旅遊**。

2. When you come back, he **will be having** dinner.

   當你回來時，他**將正在吃**晚餐。

補充： 進行式相關重要觀念

觀念一：以下表示「存在、所有、感覺」之動詞通常不用進行式：have（有）、know（知道、認識）、remember（記得）、see（看見）、hear（聽）、feel（感覺）、forget（忘記）、love（愛）、like（喜歡）、hate（討厭）、seem（似乎）、wish（希望）、want（想要）

比較	
不用進行式	可用進行式
see（看見）	be watching（正在觀賞～）
	be looking (at)（正看著～）
hear（聽見）	be listeining (to)（正在聽～）

觀念二：往返動詞如 come（來）、go（去）、leave（離開）、leave for（動身前往）、start（出發、開始）……，通常用進行式 be V.＋V-ing 表示「未來」（請參考動詞時態——未來式）。例如：Christmas is coming.　聖誕節快來了。

今日重點回顧筆記

一定要練習寫下來！才能確定自己真的會了喔！

1. 進行式是用be動詞+現在分詞所形成，也就是將一般動詞加上
   _____。
2. 過去進行式是用_____/_____+V-ing。
3. V-ing需特別注意:1. 去_____ +ing / 2. 短母音需_____+ing。

試判斷以下句子是否正確？錯誤的請更正為正確句子。

A. They are playing on-line games at that time.

....

B. She is runing to the police station.

....

C. We are hearing music now.

....

正確答案：

1. ing 　2. was/were 　3. e / 重複字尾

A. They were playing on-line games at that time.

因為出現了at that time（當時），表示是發生在過去的事，所以用were。

B. She is running to the police station.

run是短母音，後面要加-ing前，要記得重複字尾。

C. We are listening to music now.

hear是「聽見」的意思，「聆聽音樂」要用listen to。

二、進行式否定句&疑問句

❝ 文法觀念說給你聽 ❞

進行式的否定句和疑問句用法與 be V. 之用法相同：

一、**疑問句：be V. 搬到句首**

二、**否定句：be V. ＋ not ＋ V-ing**

❝ 圖解文法一看就懂 ❞

Unit
05

動詞時態──進行式

否定句

～ be not V-ing ～
（不是在～）

疑問句

be V. ～ V-ing ～？
（～正在～嗎？）
What ＋ be V. ～ doing?
（～正在做什麼？）

❝ 例句現身說法好清楚 ❞

1. The boy **is** study**ing** English.　　這男孩正在唸英文。

否定 → The boy **is not (=isn't)** study**ing** English.

這男孩沒有在唸英文。

疑問 → **Is** the boy study**ing** English?

這男孩正在唸英文嗎？

否定疑問 → **Isn't** the boy study**ing** English? ＝ **Is** the boy **not** study**ing** English?

這男孩不正在唸英文嗎？

Unit 05

動詞時態──進行式

2. **Are(n't)** the students writ**ing?** 這些學生（不是）正在寫字嗎？

Yes, they are. ➜ **肯定簡答** 是的，他們正在。

No, they aren't. ➜ **否定簡答** 不，他們沒有。

Yes, they are writing. ➜ **肯定詳答** 是的，他們正在寫字。

No, they are not writing. They are reading. ➜ **否定詳答**
不，他們不是在寫字。他們在讀書。

3. What **are** you **doing?** ➜ **問句** 你正在做什麼？

　I'm closing the door. ➜ **答句** 我正在關門。

🎙️ 馬上演練好實力 🎙️

選選看：請從選項中選出符合題目的答案

(　) 1. They_____ dinner now.

　　(A) eating 　　(B) are eating 　　(C) are eatting 　　(D) eat

(　) 2. Tom is _____, not _____.

　　(A) run; sit 　(B) running; sit 　(C) runing; siting 　(D) running; sitting

(　) 3. _____ your father reading newspaper in the living room?

　　(A) Are 　　(B) Do 　　(C) Is 　　(D) Does

(　) 4. The boys _____ reading now. They are playing.

　　(A) aren't 　　(B) isn't 　　(C) don't 　　(D) doesn't

(　) 5. What's your mother doing? She's _____.

　　(A) cook 　　(B) cooking 　　(C) cooks 　　(D) cooked

(　) 6. When David came to my home, I _____ TV.

　　(A) am watching 　(B) watch 　(C) was watch 　(D) was watching

( ) 7. They _____ computer games at 10:00 yesterday morning.
　　　(A) playing　　(B) were play　　(C) were playing　(D) are playing

( ) 8. _____ are you doing? I'm writing e-mails.
　　　(A) How　　　(B) Where　　　(C) What　　　(D) Why

Solution 公佈答案

解答：1. (B)　2. (D)　3.(C)　4. (A)　5. (B)　6. (D)　7. (C)　8. (C)

Unit 05

動詞時態——進行式

Note 筆記手札

有沒有不太熟悉的文法觀念呢？有的話就把它們寫在這裡，之後多做幾次複習吧！加油！

Unit 06 連綴動詞

文法口訣輕鬆記

🔊 *Track 012*

1. be 動詞有 am / are / is 三個字，一般動詞那麼多
2. 連綴動詞過來幫我做形容
3. 看起來；聽起來；聞起來；嚐起來；感覺
4. 似乎；變得；還不錯

1. be 動詞有 am / are / is 三個字，一般動詞那麼多

動詞分成兩大類：be V. 與一般 V.

be V. 為 am / are / is，其他動詞皆為一般 V.。

2. 連綴動詞過來幫我做形容

由一般 V. 借用幾個動詞過來幫助 be V. 做形容，稱為連綴動詞。

3. 看起來；聽起來；聞起來；嚐起來；感覺

常見的連綴動詞（五個感官）：
look（看起來）/ sound（聽起來）/ smell（聞起來）/ taste（嚐起來）/ feel（感覺）

4. 似乎；變得；還不錯

seem（似乎）/ become（變得）/ get（變得）都是很實用的連綴動詞。

文法觀念說給你聽

連綴動詞： 能轉介來幫助be V. 做形容的一般V.（如畫底線之動詞），因為be V. 只表示狀態，透過連綴動詞，便能使句子變得生動。但需注意：

一、其後不可加副詞，例如： She is happy. 她很快樂。

　　　　　　　→ She feels happy. 她覺得很快樂。

　　　　　　　→ She becomes happy. 她變得很快樂。

二、其否定句／疑問句仍須依一般 V. 之原則用助動詞來形成；不可直接像 be V. 直接加 not，

例如： She feels happy. 她覺得快樂。

　　→ She doesn't feel happy. 她覺得不快樂。

三、另外，連綴動詞＋ like ＋名詞……，用來表示「像……」，like 在這裡當介系詞（像……），

例如： It looks rainy. 好像要下雨了。（rainy 為形容詞）

　　→ It looks like rain.（rain 為名詞）

Unit
06

連綴動詞

🔖 圖解文法一看就懂 🔖

一、be 動詞和形容詞的關聯用法：

be V.　＋　形容詞 like（像）＋名詞

二、形容詞和副詞的關聯用法

一般V.　＋　副詞

＊ look at＋副詞

look at 為一般**動詞**，勿混淆。意思為注視／看著，需用副詞修飾。

三、連綴動詞和形容詞的關聯用法

連綴動詞
look / sound / smell / taste / feel /
seem / become /
get（看起來 / 聽起來 / 聞起來 /
嚐起來 / 感覺 / 似乎 / 變得 / 變得）

＋

形容詞

Unit
06

連綴動詞

例句現身說法好清楚

1. He **looks** happy.　他看起來很快樂。

He **looks at** me happ**ily**.　他快樂地看著我。

注意：look 為連綴 V. 所以＋形容詞 / look at 為一般 V. 所以＋副詞

2. The cake **tastes** delicious.　這塊蛋糕嚐起來很美味。

注意：連綴動詞沒有被動語態，所以不用寫成被嚐起來。

3. He **became** busy last year.　他去年變得很忙。

4. She **felt** proud of her son.　她為感到兒子驕傲。

5. She feels good.　她覺得舒服。

否定 → She **doesn't** feel good.　她覺得不舒服。

注意：否定句不可寫成「She feels not good.」，須用助 V.：「She
doesn't feel good.」

疑問 → **Does** she feel good?　她覺得不舒服嗎？

6. The music sounds noisy.　這音樂聽起來很吵。

原問句→**How** does the music sound?　這音樂聽起來怎麼樣？

7. The music sounds like noise.　這音樂聽起來像噪音。

原問句→**What** does the music sound like?　這音樂聽起來像什麼？

馬上演練好實力

選選看:請從選項中選出符合題目的答案

(   ) 1. The girl looks _____.
(A) happy　　(B) happily　　(C) sadly　　(D) beautifully

(   ) 2. The juice _____ sweet.
(A) feels　　(B) tastes　　(C) looks　　(D) sounds

(   ) 3. The music _____ pleasing to the ear.
(A) smells　　(B) sounds　　(C) looks　　(D) tastes

(   ) 4. The sky became _____.
(A) clearly　　(B) darkly　　(C) dark　　(D) like dark

(   ) 5. _____ he feel better?
(A) Is　　(B) Was　　(C) Do　　(D) Does

(   ) 6. The milk _____ sour.
(A) is smelt　　(B) smells　　(C) sounds　　(D) looks

(   ) 7. _____ does the flower look like?
(A) How　　(B) What　　(C) Where　　(D) When

(   ) 8. He _____ very happy with the new job.
(A) sounds　　(B) smells　　(C) seems　　(D) tastes

Unit 06

連綴動詞

Solution 公佈答案

1. (A)　2. (B)　3. (B)　4. (C)　5. (D)　6. (B)　7. (B)　8. (C)

Unit 06

連綴動詞

今日重點回顧筆記

一定要練習寫下來！才能確定自己真的會了喔！

1. 連綴動詞後面需加上_____詞。
2. 連綴動詞加上like，後面再加_____詞。
3. 原問句用_____開頭。

試判斷以下句子是否正確？錯誤的請更正為正確句子。

A. The girls looked happily.

....

B. The cheese cake tastes delicious.

....

C. What does the music sound?

....

正確答案：

1. 形容　2. 名　3. How

A. The girls looked happy.
　連綴動詞後面加的是形容詞，不是副詞喔！

B. 正確

C. How does the music sound?
　「音樂聽起來什麼？」不是很奇怪嗎？所以要改成「音樂聽起來如何？」（How does the music sound?）才合理。一定要用What開頭的話，可以說What does the music sound like?（「音樂聽起來像什麼？」）

Test

我是驕傲的動詞——綜合測驗篇

動詞觀念選選看

( ) 1. _____ Tom and Mary at school?

　　(A) Be　　　　(B) Am　　　　(C) Are　　　　(D) Is

( ) 2. Their father _____ exercise every morning.

　　(A) do　　　　(B) does　　　　(C) to do　　　　(D) doing

( ) 3. _____ your sister _____ the dishes after dinner?

　　(A) Do; wash　(B) Do; washes　(C) Does; washes　(D) Does; wash

( ) 4. She was late for work this morning, but I _____ .

　　(A) was　　　　(B) didn't　　　　(C) wasn't　　　　(D) weren't

( ) 5. She _____ a cup of black tea for me.

　　(A) brought　　(B) bring　　　　(C) give　　　　(D) buy

( ) 6. Will you go out with us tonight? No, I _____.

　　(A) willn't　　(B) won't　　　　(C) will　　　　(D) wasn't

( ) 7. Was her brother _____ dinner at that time?

　　(A) eatting　　(B) ate　　　　(C) eating　　　　(D) eats

( ) 8. The cake _____ delicious.

　　(A) taste　　　(B) is tasted　　(C) tasting　　　(D) tastes

劃線錯誤處，請改成正確文法

1. Did she at home last night? _____

2. Do your friend often plays on-line games? _____

3. Will you going to a concert with us tomorrow? _____

4. The coffee is smelled good. _____

5. How does the skirt look like? _____

6. Did they bought the house last year? _____

7. He falled down and getted hurt. _____

8. There will have a good movie on TV tonight. _____

66 閱讀測驗 99

Mei-ting **is** from a small village in Nantou. Last week she and her brother **came** to Kaohsiung to **stay** with their grandparents. Their house in Nantou **fell down** in a terrible typhoon. Their parents **had** to stay in Nantou to take care of their little sister in the hospital. She **was** seriously hurt when the house **fell down**.

Mei-ting and her brother now **go** to a new school in Kaohsiung. Everyone in the school is nice to them, but Mei-ting **feels** sad because they **have** to stay in Kaohsiung for a long time, until their new house is built. She **misses** her classmates in Nantou very much. They **are** wonderful friends, and their letters have made her feel much better. Mei-ting also **misses** her parents and her little sister. She **hopes** she can **see** them again soon.

【基測 95-1】

(   ) 1. Why did Meiting leave her home?

    (A) Her parents sold their house.

    (B) Her family lost the house in a typhoon.

    (C) She got hurt and needed a better doctor.

    (D) She wanted to go to a bigger school in the city.

(   ) 2. Where are Mei-ting's parents?

    (A) In Taipei.   (B) In Nantou.

    (C) In Kaohsiung.   (D) In a foreign country.

(　　) 3. Who are <u>They</u>?

    (A) Mei-ting's grandparents.

    (B) Mei-ting and her brother.

    (C) Mei-ting's friends in Kaohsiung.

    (D) Mei-ting's classmates in Nantou.

句子重組測驗

1. was / Tommy / dinner / at Bill's home / eating / then

_____

2. last / party / last / the / at looks / happy / Mary

_____

3. restaurant / take / will / you / to / the / tomorrow / I

_____

4. school / did not / yesterday / Tina / a bus / to / take

_____

5. live / Jenny / in / last year / Taipei / Did / ?

_____

6. pay / is / Wendy / to / the / going / bill

_____

7. walks / dog / John / morning / his / every

_____

8. not / He / like / chocolate / does

_____

9. singer / our / is / favorite / Jay

_____

10. will / go / tomorrow / Who / with / Hans / ? / shopping

_____

66中翻英測驗 99

1. 這頓晚餐嚐起來相當美味。

   This dinner _____ delicious.

2. 他每天打籃球。

   He _____ basketball every day.

3. 媽媽明天將開車送你去圖書館。

   Mother _____ _____ you to the library tomorrow.

4. Tina 昨天在沙發上看報紙。

   Tina _____ newspaper on the sofa yesterday.

5. Vincent 上個星期飛去了日本。

   Vincent _____ to Japan last week.

6. 這主意聽起來很棒。

   _____

7. Jerry 昨天下午很忙。

   _____

8. 你覺得如何？

   _____

9. Tina 正在廚房煮早餐。

   _____

10. 我們那時候正在寫功課。

    _____

Solution

我是驕傲的動詞——解答篇

66 動詞觀念選選看 99

1. (C)　　2. (B)　　3. (D)　　4. (C)
5. (A)　　6. (B)　　7. (C)　　8. (D)

66 劃線錯誤處，請改成正確文法 99

1. Was　　2. Does / play　　3. Are　　4. smells
5. What　　6. buy　　7. fell / got　　8. be

66 閱讀測驗 99

1. (B)　2. (B)　3. (D)

　　美婷來自於一個南投的小村莊。上星期她跟她哥哥來高雄和他們的祖父母住在一起。她們在南投的家因為一個嚴重的颱風而倒塌。她父母必須要留在南投照顧在醫院的妹妹。她妹妹因為房子倒塌而受了很嚴重的傷。

　　美婷跟她的哥哥現在在高雄就讀新的學校。每個人在學校對她們都很好，但美婷覺得很難過，因為她必須待在高雄好一段時間，直到新家蓋好為止。她非常想想念她在南投的同學。她們是很棒的朋友，而她們寄給她的信讓她覺得開心許多。美婷同時也很想念她的父母與她的妹妹。她希望能快點見到她們。

66 句子重組測驗 99

1. Tommy was eating dinner at Bill's home then.
   （湯米那時候正在比爾的家吃晚餐。）
2. Mary looked happy at the party last night.
   （瑪莉昨晚在派對上看起來很快樂。）

3. I will take you to the restaurant tomorrow.
（我明天會帶妳去那間餐廳。）

4. Tina did not take a bus to school yesterday.
（提娜昨天沒有搭公車去學校。）

5. Did Jenny live in Taipei last year?（去年珍妮住在台北嗎？）

6. Wendy is going to pay the bill.（溫蒂正要去付帳。）

7. John walks his dog every morning.（約翰每天早上都遛狗。）

8. He does not like chocolate.（他不喜歡巧克力。）

9. Jay is our favorite singer.（傑是我們最喜愛的歌手。）

10. Who will go shopping with Hans tomorrow?
（明天誰要和漢斯去購物？）

中翻英測驗

1. tastes

2. plays

3. will drive

4. read

5. flew

6. The idea sounds great.

7. Jerry was busy yesterday afternoon.

8. How do you feel?

9. Tina is cooking breakfast in the kitchen.

10. We were doing homework then (at that time).

Chapter02 / Question

有了我才能跟美女
搭訕的疑問句

本篇疑問句的學習重點如下：

Unit 01 疑問句 基本觀念

文法口訣輕鬆記

◀ *Track 013*

> 1. W / H 疑問句，Bye-bye 不說 yes / no
> 2. be V.、助 V. 開頭，come on 來個 yes / no

1. **W / H 疑問句，Bye-bye 不說 yes / no**
   W / H 開頭之問句直接回答要說的內容，不須說 Yes / No。

2. **be V.、助 V. 開頭，come on 來個 yes / no**
   be V. 或 助 V. 開頭之問句，須回答 Yes / No。

文法觀念說給你聽

問句可以分成兩大類：

一、**W / H 疑問句**：以 W 或 H 開頭之疑問句，這種疑問句的回答方式不需要說 yes / no，例如：How are you? → I'm fine, thanks. 而 W 或 H 開頭的疑問詞有 What（什麼）、Who（誰）、Which（哪一個）、How（如何）、Where（哪裡）、Why（為什麼）、When（何時）。

二、**Yes / No 疑問句**：以 be 動詞或助動詞開頭之問句，需回答 Yes / No
例1：Am / Are / Is...?（～是嗎？）
例2：Do / does / Did...?（～嗎？）

例3：Can...?（會～嗎？）

例4：Will...?（將要～嗎？）

例5：Are you a teacher? → Yes, I am.

例6：Do you like shopping? → No, I don't.

圖解文法一看就懂

W／H 疑問句和 Yes／No 疑問句開頭的比較

W／H 疑問句

疑問代名詞（what／who／which）開頭

疑問副詞（how／where／why／when）開頭

Yes／No 疑問句

be V.（am／are／is）開頭

助V.（do／does／did／can／will）開頭

例句現身說法好清楚

1. **Who** is that girl? → She is Mary.
   那女孩是誰？ → 她是瑪麗。

2. **Where** are you going? → We are going to the library.
   你們要去哪裡？ → 我們要去圖書館。

3. **Are** you from Singapore? → **No,** I am from Canada.
   你是新加坡人嗎？ → 不，我是加拿大人。

4. **Does** he live with his parents? → **Yes,** he does.
   他和父母親住在一起嗎？ → 是的，住在一起。

高分小撇步

「Do you like coffee or tea? I like coffee.」像這種選擇性的疑問句，也不需回答 Yes / No ！

馬上演練好實力

Unit 01

疑問句基本觀念

請從下列對話中，判別畫底線的句子為 W / H 疑問句或 Yes / No 疑問句

Dialogue 1

Dolly: <u>Where's Mark, Cathy? Did you see him?</u>

Cathy: Yes, I just met him at the entrance of the restroom five minutes ago.

Dolly: But <u>where is the restroom?</u>

Cathy: Oh! It's near the fountain. Some of our classmates are over there. Well, <u>did you mind if I take you there?</u>

Dolly: Not at all. You are so considerate.

Dialogue 2

Dolly: <u>Why did you go to the hospital?</u>

Cathy: Because I had a terrible headache.

Dolly: <u>Are you OK? Did the doctor give you any medicine?</u>

Cathy: Yes, I already took some.

Dolly: <u>How do you feel now?</u>

Cathy: It still hurts. I need to stay in bed, so I can't go to the party with you.

Dolly: That's OK. Take good care!

Solution 公佈答案

中譯：

Dialogue 1

多莉：凱西，馬克在哪裡呢？你有看到他嗎？

凱西：有的，我剛剛五分鐘前在洗手間的入口遇見他。

多莉：但是洗手間在哪裡？

凱西：喔！它是在噴水池附近。有一些我們的同班同學也在那裡。嗯，你介意我帶你去那兒嗎？

多莉：一點也不。你真是體貼。

Dialogue 2

多莉：你為什麼去醫院呢？

凱西：因為我的頭好痛。

多莉：你還好嗎？醫生給你藥了嗎？

凱西：有，我已經吃了一些。

多莉：那現在你覺得怎樣？

凱西：還是很痛。我需要待在床上休息，因此我不能和你一起去聚會。

多莉：沒關係。好好保重！

Yes / No 問句有「Did you see him? / do you mind if I take you there? / Are you OK? / Did the doctor give you any medicine?」

其他則為 **W / H 疑問句**。

Unit
01

疑問句基本觀念

Unit 02 W / H 疑問句

文法觀念說給你聽

W／H 疑問句開頭的疑問詞，可以分為兩種：

一、疑問代名詞：

1. what：問事物、姓名、職業、年齡

(1) **What's** this? It's a notebook.

　　這是什麼？這是一本筆記本。

(2) **What's** your name? My name is Peter.

　　你叫什麼名字？我叫彼得。

(3) **What** does she do? She's a nurse.

　　她是做什麼的？她是護士。

(4) **What's** your age? I'm fifteen (years old).

　　你幾歲？我十五歲。

2. who：問姓名、關係、人

(1) **Who's** that man? He's Mr. Chen. / He is my teacher.

　　那個男人是誰？他是陳先生。/ 他是我的老師。

(2) **Who** are you waiting for? My brother.

　　你在等誰？我哥哥。

3. which：問選擇性事物

(1) **Which** do you like, fishing or swimming? I like both.

　　釣魚或游泳，你喜歡哪一種？我兩種都喜歡。

(2) **Which** team do you root for, the Lions or the Elephants?

　　I root for the Elephants.

　　獅隊或象隊，你支持哪一隊？我支持象隊。

(3) **Which** store do you prefer, this one or that one? I prefer this one.

　　你比較喜歡哪間店，這間或那間？我喜歡這間。

二、 疑問副詞：

1. how：問狀況、程度、方法⋯⋯

(1) **How** are you? Fine, thanks.

　　你好嗎？我很好，謝謝。

(2) **How** do you like the book? Very much.

　　你有多喜歡這本書？非常喜歡。

(3) **How** do you go to school? By MRT.

　　你怎麼去上學？搭捷運。

2. where：問地方（哪裡？）

(1) **Where**'s my bag? It's under the table.

　　我的包包在哪裡？在桌子下面。

(2) **Where**'s your father? He's in the living room.

　　你的父親在哪裡？他在客廳。

(3) **Where**'s the post office? It's on the corner.

　　郵局在哪裡？在轉角。

注意：如果想問「這是哪裡？」可以說Where am I? / Where are we? 但不
　　　　可寫成 Where is this?

3. why：問原因 / 理由（為何？）

(1) **Why** do you go to work late? Because I get up late.

　　你為什麼上班遲到？因為我睡過頭了。

(2) **Why** can't you go out with us this afternoon? Because I have piano
　　lessons.

　　你為什麼今天下午不能跟我們出去？因為我要上鋼琴課。

4. when：問時間（何時？）

(1) **When** did you come here? I came here yesterday.（問過去）

　　你什麼時候來這裡的？我昨天來的。

(2) **When** is your flight? Next Sunday.（問未來）

　　你的班機是什麼時候？下禮拜日。

(3) **When** will you come back? Tomorrow night.（問未來）
你什麼時候會回來？明天晚上。

「「 圖解文法一看就懂 」」

Unit
02

W / H 疑問句

一、what / who 之比較

What

問職業

回答時用a / an

What's that man?
→ He's a teacher.

Who

問關係

回答時用所有格 my, your...

Who's that man?
→ My teacher.

二、which / who 之比較

which（哪個？）　　**who（誰？）= which one（哪個人？）**

問事物，不可問人

問人

例如： Which one do you like, Harry or Tony? 哈利或湯尼你喜歡哪一個？
= Who do you like, Harry or Tony? 哈利或湯尼你喜歡誰？

三、what / how 的相似用法比較

what 疑問代名詞

問年齡
問天氣
問人、事、物如何
感嘆句（多麼！）

how 疑問副詞

問年齡
問天氣
問人、事、物如何
感嘆句（多麼！）

❝ 例句現身說法好清楚 ❞

1. **How old** are you? ＝ **What's** your **age**? 　你幾歲？
   I'm thirteen years old. 　我十三歲。
2. **How** is the weather? ＝ **What's** the weather **like**? 　天氣如何？
   It's hot. 　很熱。
3. **How** does the girl look? She looks **beautiful**. → **形容詞**
   這個女生看起來怎麼樣？她看起來很漂亮。
   ＝ **What** does the girl look **like**? She looks like a doll. → **名詞**
   這個女生看起來像什麼？她看起來像洋娃娃。
4. **How beautiful** a girl! ＝ **What a** beautiful girl! 　多麼漂亮的女生啊!

補充：其他延伸疑問句

一、 what ＋名詞：what 從疑問代名詞 → 疑問形容詞

1. 問時間：幾點、星期、日期、月份、季節、年……

例1：**What time** is it? It's seven o'clock.
　　　現在幾點？現在是七點鐘。

例2：**What day** is it? It's Monday.
　　　今天是星期幾？今天是星期一。

例3：**What date** is it? It's January 1st.
　　　今天是幾月幾日？今天是一月一日。

2. 問顏色

例如：**What color** is it? It's blue.
　　　這是什麼顏色？這是藍色。

3. 問種類、型式

例如：**What kind** of music do you like? I like popular music.
　　　你喜歡哪一種音樂？我喜歡流行樂。

Unit 02

W／H疑問句

Unit
02

W / H 疑問句

二、 how＋形容詞 / 副詞：

1. 問年齡

例如：**How old** are you? I'm twenty eight (years old).

你幾歲？我二十八歲。

2. 問數量

＊ **how many ＋可數名詞**

例1：**How many** dolls do you have?　你有幾個洋娃娃？

＊ **how many ＋不可數名詞**

例2：**How much(money)** is the hamburger?　這個漢堡多少錢？

3. 問頻率

例如：**How often** do you go to a movie? Every month.

你多久看一次電影？每個月。

4. 問時間

例1：**How long** does it take to the park? It takes about ten minutes.

到公園要多久？大約十分鐘。

例2：**How soon** can we have dinner? In ten minutes.

我們多快可以吃晚餐？再過十分鐘。

5. 問速度、長度

例1：**How fast** can you run?

你可以跑多快？

例2：**How long** is the table?

這張桌子多長？

⟪ 馬上演練好實力 ⟫

選選看：請從選項中選出符合題目的答案

(　　) 1. _____ old is your sister?

(A) What　　　(B) How　　　(C) Who　　　(D) Where

( ) 2. _____ are the boys? They are my cousins.

    (A) What   (R) How   (C) Who   (D) Where

( ) 3. _____ a cute little girl!

    (A) What   (B) How   (C) Why   (D) When

( ) 4. _____ are you going? To the park.

    (A) Where   (B) What   (C) How   (D) Why

( ) 5. _____ were you late this morning? I got up late.

    (A) Where   (B) What   (C) How   (D) Why

( ) 6. _____ do you feel now? I feel much better.

    (A) Where   (B) What   (C) How   (D) Why

( ) 7. _____ did you go to Taipei? Last Sunday.

    (A) What   (B) When   (C) Which   (D) Why

( ) 8. _____ does your brother like, rice or bread?

    (A) What   (B) When   (C) Which   (D) Why

Unit 02

W / H 疑問句

Solution 公佈答案

1. (B)   2. (C)   3. (A)   4. (A)   5. (D)   6. (C)   7. (B)   8. (C)

Unit 03 Yes / No 疑問句

文法觀念說給你聽

Yes / No 問句可分為以下兩種：

一、be 動詞問句：

1. 現在式：Am / Are / Is 開頭的問句，例如：

   Are you a student? Yes, I am.

   你是學生嗎？是的，我是。

2. 過去式：Was / Were 開頭的問句，例如：

   Were you at home last night? No, I wasn't.

   你昨晚在家嗎？不，我不在。

二、助動詞問句：

1. 現在式：Do / Does 開頭的問句，例如：

   Do you have a pencil? No, I don't.

   你有鉛筆嗎？不，我沒有。

2. 過去式：Did 開頭的問句，例如：

   Did you get up late this morning? Yes, I did.

   你今天晚起了嗎？是的，我是。

3. 未來式：Will 開頭的問句，例如：

   Will you go to a movie tonight? No, I won't.

   你今晚會去看電影嗎？不，我不會。

4. 完成式：Have / Has 開頭的問句，例如：

   Have you washed the dishes? Yes, I have.

   你洗碗了嗎？是的，我洗了。

5. 其他助動詞：Can / Should... 開頭的問句，例如：

Can you ride a bike? Yes, I can.

你會騎腳踏車嗎？是的，我會。

提醒：可以參考 Chapter1 基礎動詞之疑問句用法，並再次練習。

圖解文法一看就懂

Yes / No 問句有兩大類

be 動詞問句	助動詞問句

Am / Are / Is / Was / Were 開頭之問句

Do / Does / Did / Can / Will... 開頭之問句

例句現身說法好清楚

一、be V. 開頭之問句：

1. **Are** you from Taiwan? Yes, I am.　　你來自台灣嗎？是的，我是。

2. **Is** she busy? No, she isn't.　　她很忙嗎？不，她不是。

3. **Was** Tom late this morning? Yes, he was.

湯姆今天早上遲到了嗎？是的，他是。

二、助 V. 開頭之問句

1. **Do** you like sports? Yes, I do.　　你喜歡運動嗎？是的，我喜歡。

2. **Would** you like to join us? Yes, I'd like to.

你想加入我們嗎？是的，我想。

3. **Can** you go out with me on the weekend? No, I can't.

週末你可以和我出去嗎？不，我不行。

4. **Will** you play basketball tomorrow? No, I won't.

明天你要打籃球嗎？不，我沒有。

高分小撇步

可用Sure. / Of course. / Why not? 代替 Yes

Unit 03

Yes / No 疑問句

Unit
03

Yes
/
No
疑
問
句

❝ 馬上演練好實力 ❞

選選看：請從選項中選出符合題目的答案

(　　) 1. _____ you usually busy in the afternoon?

　　　(A) Do　　　(B) Are　　　(C) Does　　　(D) Is

(　　) 2. _____ she go to school by bicycle?

　　　(A) Do　　　(B) Is　　　(C) Does　　　(D) Are

(　　) 3. _____ he play the piano? No. he can't.

　　　(A) Does　　(B) Are　　　(C) Will　　　(D) Can

(　　) 4. _____ you go shopping with me tomorrow?

　　　(A) Are　　　(B) Will　　　(C) Did　　　(D) Does

(　　) 5. _____ you late for work this morning? Yes, I was.

　　　(A) Were　　(B) Did　　　(C) Was　　　(D) Are

(　　) 6. _____ you get up early yesterday morning?

　　　(A) Were　　(B) Was　　　(C) Do　　　(D) Did

(　　) 7. Did you go to Taipei last Sunday? No, I _____.

　　　(A) can't　　(B) didn't　　(C) don't　　(D) wasn't

(　　) 8. Mom, can I watch TV now? _____

　　　(A) Yes, you can't.　　　　(B) No, you can.

　　　(C) Why not?　　　　　　 (D) Sure, you can't.

Solution 公佈答案

1. (B)　2. (C)　3. (D)　4. (B)　5. (A)　6. (D)　7. (B)　8. (C)

今日重點回顧筆記

一定要練習寫下來！才能確定自己真的會了喔！

1. W/H 開頭之疑問句不須回答＿＿＿＿＿。
2. ＿＿＿＿/＿＿＿＿須回答Yes/No。
3. 問原因理由用＿＿＿＿。

試判斷以下句子是否正確？錯誤的請更正為正確句子。

A. Can she play the drums? She can.

....

B. What is that man? He is my teacher.

....

C. Were you busy then? No, I wasn't.

....

Unit
03

Yes
/
No
疑
問
句

正確答案：

1. Yes/No　2. Be動詞/助動詞　3. Why

A. Can she play the drums? Yes, she can.
　　既然是由助動詞（can）開頭的問句，回答時就要有個Yes/No比較好喔！這裡可以看出是肯定的回答，所以選擇Yes。

B. What is that man? He is a teacher.
　　問句是問那個人的職業，而不是問他「是誰」，所以說他是「一個老師」而非「我的老師」。

C. 正確

Chapter 02 Test

有了我才能跟美女搭訕的疑問句
──綜合測驗篇

❝ 疑問句觀念選選看 ❞

( ) 1. _____ do you like, coffee or tea?

    (A) When   (B) where   (C) Which   (D) Who

( ) 2. _____ were you late for work today? Because of a traffic jam.

    (A) What   (B) Which   (C) Why   (D) How

( ) 3. _____ are you going? To the restaurant.

    (A) Who   (B) How   (C) When   (D) Where

( ) 4. _____ beautiful a lady she is!

    (A) Who   (B) How   (C) What   (D) Which

( ) 5. _____ does it take to the theater? It takes about half an hour.

    (A) How long   (B) How often   (C) How fast   (D) How many

( ) 6. _____ food do you prepare for the picnic?

    (A) How many   (B) How much   (C) How soon   (D) How long

( ) 7. _____ you washed the clothes? No, not yet.

    (A) Did   (B) Do   (C) Were   (D) Have

( ) 8. Can she play the violin? No, she _____.

    (A) can   (B) doesn't   (C) didn't   (D) can't

❝ 劃線錯誤處，請改成正確文法 ❞

1. How a lovely girl she is!_____

2. How fast does it take from here to Taipei? Three hours._____

3. Which do you want, pork or beef? Yes, pork._____

4. How <u>much</u> comic books do you buy?_____

5. How <u>long</u> do you go shopping? Once or twice a month._____

6. <u>Were</u> you lend him the money?_____

7. <u>Were</u> you late this morning? Yes, <u>you were</u>._____

8. <u>Do</u> you play tennis? Yes, I can._____

🔳 閱讀測驗 🔳

Billy：Roger and I are going to have dinner at Silver Hut. **Do you want to join us?**

Carl：**When are you going?**

Billy：Saturday.

Carl：I'd like to, but my sister and I are going biking in Rose Park this Saturday. Maybe next time.

Billy：Oh, OK. But you've been to Silver Hut, right? I always hear people say good things about it. **Is it really that good?**

Carl：Oh, yes. They have great tea, great snacks, and great music. Lots of high school students like to go there. Oh, don't forget to order the nomisini.

Billy：Nomisini? **What's that?**

Carl：It's a bag of chocolate balls with butter inside, and it tastes good with tea.

Billy：It sounds great. I can't wait for Saturday to come.

【基測 95-1】

(   ) 1. Which is true about Silver Hut?

    (A) It is inside a park.   (B) It is a bicycle shop.

    (C) It is closed on Sundays.   (D) It is popular with teenagers.

(　　) 2. What is nomisini?

      (A) A song.   (B) A drink.

      (C) A game.   (D) A snack.

(　　) 3. Why isn't Carl going to Silver Hut?

      (A) He doesn't like the place.

      (B) He has never heard of the place.

      (C) He and his sister already have plans.

      (D) He does not want to go there with Billy.

〝〝句子重組測驗〞〞

1. you / Where / going? / are

_____

2. it / long / How / park / to / does / take / the / ?

_____

3. your / What / favorite / is /food?

_____

4. you / or / do / prefer / Which / , / chicken / steak / ?

_____

5. your / borrow / Can / I / pen / ?

_____

6. teacher / Who / talking / to / was / the / ?

_____

7. you / What / do / get / time / home / ?

_____

8. are / many / there / classroom? / in / books / How / the

_____

9. father / factory / Does / in / your / the / work / ?

_____

10. day / is / What / today / ?

_____

〝中翻英測驗〞

1. 他明天何時會來？

   _____ will he come tomorrow?

2. 你妹妹幾歲？

   _____ old is your sister?

3. 哪一只是我的手錶？

   _____ is my watch?

4. 誰明天將會去派對？

   _____ will go to the party tomorrow?

5. Jenny 昨天在百貨公司買了一本書嗎？

   _____ Jenny buy a book in the department store yesterday?

6. 你會騎腳踏車嗎？

   _____

7. 你為何上學遲到？

   _____

8. 他是做什麼工作的？

   _____

9. Bill 喜歡哪一種水果？

   _____

10. 那個高個子的男孩是誰？

   _____

Chapter 02

Solution

有了我才能跟美女搭訕的疑問句
——解答篇

66 疑問句觀念選選看 99

1. (C)　　　2. (C)　　　3. (D)　　　4. (B)
5. (A)　　　6. (B)　　　7. (D)　　　8. (D)

66 劃線錯誤處,請改成正確文法 99

1. What　　　2. long　　　3. Yes 去掉　　4. many
5. often　　　6. Did　　　7. I was　　　8. Can

66 閱讀測驗 99

1. (D)　2. (D)　3. (C)

比利:羅傑和我要去銀屋吃晚餐。你想要加入我們嗎?

卡爾:你們什麼時候要去?

比利:星期六。

卡爾:我想去,可是我的妹妹和我這星期六要去羅斯公園騎腳踏車。或許下次再跟你們一起去吧。

比利:喔,好吧。但你已經去過銀屋了對不對?我總是聽人們說那邊很不錯。它真的有那麼棒嗎?

卡爾:喔,對啊,他們有好喝的茶、好吃的點心還有很棒的音樂。有很多高中生喜歡去那裡。喔,別忘了要點 nomisini.

比利:那是什麼?

卡爾:那是一包裡面有奶油的巧克力球,而且它跟茶配在一起吃超棒的。

比利:聽起來不錯耶,我等不及禮拜六的到來了。

句子重組測驗

1. Where are you going?（你要去哪兒？）
2. How long does it take to the park?（到公園花費多久時間？）
3. What is your favorite food?（你的最喜愛的食物是什麼？）
4. Which do you prefer, chicken or steak?
   （你比較喜歡哪一個，雞肉還是牛排？）
5. Can I borrow your pen?（我能借你的鋼筆嗎？）
6. Who was talking to the teacher?（誰正在和老師交談？）
7. What time do you get home?（你什麼時候到家？）
8. How many books are there in the classroom?（教室裡有多少書？）
9. Does your father work in the factory?（你的父親在工廠工作嗎？）
10. What day is today?（今天星期幾？）

中翻英測驗

1. When
2. How
3. Which
4. Who
5. Did
6. Can you ride a bicycle?
7. Why do you go to school late?
8. What does he do?
9. What kind of fruit does Bill like?
10. Who is that tall boy?

Chapter 03 / Noun
每天你都看到的名詞

本篇名詞的學習重點如下：

Unit 01　名詞基本觀念

文法觀念說給你聽

名詞可以分成兩大類：

一、可數名詞：可數名詞有單／複數之分，且前面可加數量詞或冠詞，例如：a pen（一支筆）、three pens（三支筆）。

二、不可數名詞：沒有複數形式，恆為單數，所以前面不能加冠詞 a／an，只有特定指稱的時候能在前面加定冠詞 the，例如：the money（那筆錢）。

圖解文法一看就懂

可數名詞

1. 普通名詞：具體的事物，有單、複數之分
2. 集合名詞：本身就是複數

不可數名詞

1. 物質名詞
2. 專有名詞
3. 抽象名詞
* 這三種名詞恆為單數，都不可以加 a～／～s，但可以加 the

例句現身說法好清楚

1. **Who** is that girl? → She is Mary.
   那女孩是誰？ → 她是瑪麗。

2. **Where** are you going? → We are going to the library.
   你們要去哪裡？ → 我們要去圖書館。

3. **Are** you from Singapore? → **No,** I am from Canada.

你是新加坡人嗎？ → 不，我是加拿大人。

4. **Does** he live with his parents? → **Yes,** he does.

他和父母親住在一起嗎？ → 是的，住在一起。

Unit 01

名詞基本觀念

馬上演練好實力

請判斷劃底線的名詞為可數名詞還是不可數名詞：

There are four <u>seasons</u> in a <u>year</u>. They are spring, summer, fall and <u>winter</u>. The <u>weather</u> in spring and fall is not very hot in Taiwan. It is not very cold, either. In summer, the <u>temperature</u> is even over thirty five <u>degrees</u>. It is so hot that a lot of <u>people</u> enjoy going to the beach or going swimming in the pool. In winter, it is dry and cold. People usually have a cold in this season, so most people don't like winter.

I like spring best. Sometimes it rains a lot in spring. After a dry season, we just need the <u>rain</u> very much. The rain comes at the right <u>time</u> because it is important for <u>farmers</u>.

Solution 公佈答案

可數名詞：season(s) / year / degree(s) / people / farmer(s)
不可數名詞：winter / weather / temperature / rain / time

Unit 02 可數名詞

一、普通名詞的複數變化

文法口訣輕鬆記　🔊 *Track 014*

> 1. 可數規則 s / es，還有同形不會變
> 2. 不規則中有規則，技巧幫忙變一變

1. 可數規則 s / es，還有同形不會變

可數名詞通常在字尾加上 s 或 es，但也有一些是單複數同形。

2. 不規則中有規則，技巧幫忙變一變

雖然有一些名詞的複數是不規則變化，但也可利用技巧找出一些規則。

文法觀念說給你聽

可數名詞之複數變化方式：

一、 通常於字尾加 s 或 es

例如： pen → pens / watch → watches

二、 單複數同形不變

例如： a fish → two fish / a Chinese → two Chinese

三、 不規則變化，需特別以技巧熟記

1. 字尾變成 en 或 ren，例如：man → men / ox → oxen

2. 字中有 oo → ee，例如：foot → feet

3. 字尾有 ouse → ice，例如：mouse → mice

🔤 圖解文法一看就懂 🔤

一、普通名詞的複數變化

規則變化	不規則變化
1. 字尾＋s	需熟記，有技巧不規則中有規則 字尾變：en / ren / ice 字中變：ee
2. 字尾 x / o / s / z / sh / ch＋es	
3. 子音＋y ➡ 去 y＋ies	
4. 字尾 f / fe ➡ 去 f / fe＋ves	
5. 單複數同形	

二、搖身一變試試看——規則變化

1. 字尾＋s，唸成有聲的[z]或無聲的[s]

單字	＋s	發音	單字	＋s	發音
pen（筆）	pens	[z]	book（書）	books	[s]
apple（蘋果）	apples	[z]	desk（書桌）	desks	[s]
chair（椅子）	chairs	[z]	cat（貓）	cats	[s]
sister（姐妹）	sisters	[z]	ticket（票）	tickets	[s]
boy（男孩）	boys	[z]	lip（嘴唇）	lips	[s]
girl（女孩）	girls	[z]	month（月）	months	[s]

2. 字尾 x / o / s / z / sh / ch＋es 唸成 [ɪz]

box（盒子）➡ boxes	tomato（蕃茄）➡ tomatoes
glass（玻璃杯）➡ glasses	buzz（嗡嗡聲）➡ buzzes
dish（碗盤）➡ dishes	watch（手錶）➡ watches

注意：
以下字尾的複數變化比較特別，請多加留意：
字尾是子音字母＋o ➡ 通常＋es / 字尾是母音字母＋o ➡ 只需＋s
字尾是 ch 發[tʃ]的音 ➡ 通常＋es /字尾是 ch 不發[tʃ]的音 ➡ 只需＋s。
例如：zoos（動物園）/ bamboos（竹子）/ radios（收音機）/ stomachs
（胃）（ch發[k]，不發[tʃ]）；例外：pianos（鋼琴）/ photos（照片）。

Unit
02

可數名詞

3. 子音＋y ➡ 去 y＋ies [ɪz]

單字	去y＋ies	發音	單字	去y＋ies	發音
baby（嬰孩）	babies	[ɪz]	family（家庭）	families	[ɪz]
city（城市）	cities	[ɪz]	story（故事）	stories	[ɪz]

4. 字尾 f / fe ➡ 去f / fe＋ves [vz]

單字	去f / fe＋ves	發音
wife（太太）	wives	[vz]
knife（刀子）	knives	[vz]
leaf（葉子）	leaves	[vz]
knife（刀子）	knives	[vz]
例外：roof（屋頂）➡ roofs [s]、chef（主廚）➡ chefs [s] chief（首領）➡ chiefs [s]		

5. 單複數同形

fish（魚）	sheep（綿羊）	deer（鹿）
Chinese（中國人）	Japanese（日本人）	Swiss（瑞士人）

補充：習慣用複數的字有 glasses （眼鏡）、shoes （鞋子）、trousers （褲子）、scissors （剪刀）、stockings（長襪）……等。

三、搖身一變試試看──不規則變化

1. 字尾有en / ren

單字	不規則變化	單字	不規則變化
man（男人）	men	woman（女人）	women
policeman（警察）	policemen	ox（公牛）	oxen
child（小孩）	children		

2. oo ➡ ee

單字	不規則變化	單字	不規則變化
foot（腳）	feet	tooth（牙齒）	teeth

| goose（鵝） | geese | | |

3. ouse ➡ ice

單字	不規則變化	單字	不規則變化
mouse（老鼠）	mice	louse（跳蚤）	lice

4. 特殊字（外來字）：

bacterium（細菌）➡ bacteria

phenomen**on**（現象）➡ phenomen**a**

paparazz**o**（專門偷拍名人照片的攝影師，俗稱「狗仔」）➡ paparazz**i**

例句現身說法好清楚

1. There are three **dogs** in the yard.　有三隻狗在院子裡。
2. Can you help me move the **boxes**?　你可以幫我搬這些箱子嗎？
3. Their **wives** are beautiful.　他們的老婆都很漂亮。
4. **Women** like shopping.　女人喜歡購物。
5. Angela bought ten **tomatoes** yesterday.　安琪拉昨天買了十顆蕃茄。
6. They caught five **fish** in the river.　他們在河裡抓了五隻魚。
7. These **policemen** caught two **thieves**.　這些警察抓到了兩名小偷。
8. Thomas raises two **children**.　湯瑪士扶養兩名小孩。
9. I brush my **teeth** twice a day.　我每天刷牙兩次。

二、集合名詞

文法觀念說給你聽

集合名詞就是本身不需要做任何變化，就已是複數的名詞，常見的有以下幾種：

一、people（人們）（＝ person ＋ s → persons）

二、the police（警方）（the police 指某一地區的警察）

三、the class（全班同學）（class(es) 可數 → 課程、班級）

四、the family（全家人）（a family / families 可數 → 家庭）

五、the ＋形容詞，例如：the rich（有錢人）、the poor（窮人）

Unit 02

可數名詞

圖解文法一看就懂

普通名詞

需在字尾做變化，才能表示複數

集合名詞

不需做任何變化即表示複數

例句現身說法好清楚

1. **Young people** like pop music.　年輕人喜歡流行音樂。

2. **The police** are looking for the bad man.　警方正在尋找這個壞人。

3. **The class** are studying English in the classroom.
   全班同學正在教室讀英文。

4. **The Lin family** are having dinner.　林家人正在吃晚餐。

5. **The rich** are not always happy.　有錢人並非都快樂。

6. He likes to help **the poor**.　他喜歡幫助窮人。

馬上演練好實力

選選看：請從選項中選出符合題目的答案

(　　) 1. I saw some _____ play baseball at school.

(A) boy　　　(B) boys　　　(C) boies　　　(D) boyes

(　　) 2. I picked three maple _____.

    (A) leaf   (B) leafs   (C) leave   (D) leaves

(　　) 3. Many _____ crowded into the department store.

    (A) people   (B) peoples   (C) the people   (D) the peoples

(　　) 4. The couple has three _____.

    (A) child   (B) children   (C) childs   (D) childrens

(　　) 5. There are three _____ dancing in the park.

    (A) woman   (B) womans   (C) women   (D) womens

(　　) 6. Let's help _____.

    (A) poors   (B) the poors (C) the poor   (D) a poors

(　　) 7. Joanna is _____.

    (A) a Japanese (B) Japanese (C) the Japanese (D) Japaneses

(　　) 8. The poor dog only has three _____.

    (A) foot   (B) tooth   (C) feet   (D) food

Unit 02

可數名詞

Solution 公佈答案

1. (B) 2. (D) 3. (A) 4. (B) 5. (C) 6. (C) 7. (A) 8. (C)

Unit
02

可
數
名
詞

今日重點回顧筆記

一定要練習寫下來！才能確定自己真的會了喔！

1. 可數名詞複數規則變化，通常在字尾加上_____。
2. f/fe結尾之名詞，複數需變成_____。
3. s/sh/ch結尾之名詞，複數需加上_____。

試判斷以下句子是否正確？錯誤的請更正為正確句子。

A. The womans are talking to each other.

....

B. The leafs are green.

....

C. There are many children in the park.

....

正確答案：

1. s　　2. ves　　3. es

A. The women are talking to each other.
　　woman的複數是women才對。

B. The leaves are green.
　　leaf的複數是leaves。

C. 正確

不可數名詞

📝 文法觀念說給你聽 📝

不可數名詞可以分為以下三大類：

一、物質名詞：通常是材料、食品、飲料以及液體和氣體的名稱，例如：

wood（木頭）	gold（金）	silver（銀）	paper（紙）
meat（肉）	pork（豬肉）	beef（牛肉）	fish（魚肉）
water（水）	tea（茶）	coffee（ 咖啡）	milk（牛奶）
juice（ 果汁）	wine（酒）	ink（墨水）	food（食物）
bread（ 麵包）	rice（米飯）	sugar（糖）	salt（鹽）
money（ 錢）	air（ 空氣）	gas（氣體／瓦斯）	

＊物質名詞可加可數的單位詞，但物質名詞仍為單數
例如：a glass of **water**（一杯水）→ two glasses of **water**（兩杯水）
a cup of **coffee**（一杯咖啡）→ two cups of **coffee**（兩杯咖啡）

常用的單位詞：

a bowl of ～（一碗的）	a plate of ～（一盤的）
a bag of ～（一袋的）	a box of ～（一盒的）
a loaf of ～（一條的）	a piece of ～（一片／張／塊的）
a bottle of ～（一瓶的）	a spoon of ～（一匙的）
a pair of ～（一雙／副的）	a package of ～（一包的）

Unit 03

不可數名詞

二、**專有名詞：**字首需大寫

1. 人名：Tom（湯姆）、Mary（瑪莉）、Mr. Lin（林先生）……
2. 國名：Taiwan（台灣）、America（美國）、Japan（日本）……
3. 地名：Taipei（台北）、New York（紐約）……

三、**抽象名詞：**

art（藝術）	life（人生）	wisdom（智慧）
time（時間）	news（消息）	physics（物理學）
hope（希望）	friendship（友誼）	knowledge（知識）
homework（家庭作業）		

高分小撇步

time ＋ s 表示次數 → 可數名詞

news / physics 本身已有 s，非外加 → 不可數名詞

❝圖解文法一看就懂❞

不可數名詞有三大類

1. 物質名詞
wood, paper...

2. 專有名詞
Taipei, Japan...

3. 抽象名詞
hope, life...

例句現身說法好清楚

1. She cooked some **beef** this morning.　她今天早上煮了一些牛肉。
2. My father has some **coffee** every morning.　我爸爸每天早上會喝一些咖啡。
3. She drinks some **tea**.　她喝一些茶。

注意：以上 beef / coffee / tea 為不可數之物質名詞，不可加 a 或 s。

4. My uncle lives in **America**.　我叔叔住在美國。
5. We will move to **Taipei** next month.　我們下個月將搬到台北。
6. This is my friend, **Mary**.　這是我朋友瑪麗。

注意：以上 America / Taipei / Mary 為不可數之專有名詞，不可加 a / the 或加 s。

7. **Time** is money.　時間就是金錢。
8. No **news** is good news.　沒消息就是好消息。

注意：time / news 為不可數之抽象名詞，不可加 a 或 s，其恆為單數。

馬上演練好實力

選選看：請從選項中選出符合題目的答案

( ) 1. The news _____ true.

(A) is 　　　　(B) be 　　　　(C) are 　　　　(D) were

( ) 2. We have _____ and _____ for breakfast.

(A) bread；milks 　　　　(B) breads；milks

(C) breads；milk 　　　　(D) bread；milk

( ) 3. My mom bought some _____.

(A) breads 　(B) egg 　　　(C) pork 　　　(D) apple

( ) 4. My brother studies in _____.

(A) Japans 　(B) a Japan 　(C) Japan 　　(D) the Japan

Unit

03

不可數名詞

(   ) 5. He spent lots of _____ on the painting.

      (A) times   (B) moneys   (C) dollar   (D) time

(   ) 6. I would like to cook _____ for dinner.

      (A) fish   (B) porks   (C) beefs   (D) noodle

(   ) 7. I bought _____ milk in the supermarket yesterday.

      (A) two bottles   (B) two bottles of

      (C) bottles of   (D) two bottle of

(   ) 8. He is drinking some _____ in the living room.

      (A) waters   (B) milks   (C) juice   (D) teas

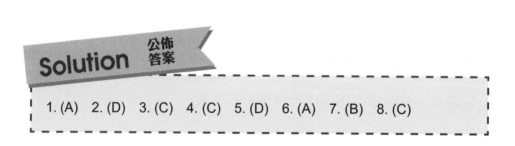

Solution 公佈答案

1. (A)   2. (D)   3. (C)   4. (C)   5. (D)   6. (A)   7. (B)   8. (C)

今日重點回顧筆記

一定要練習寫下來！才能確定自己真的會了喔！

1. 不可數名詞包括:物質名詞／_____名詞／_____名詞。
2. 不可數名詞有為_____數。
3. 不可數之物質名詞可在前面加上_____詞。

試判斷以下句子是否正確？錯誤的請更正為正確句子。

A. Time is money.

....

B. We need some breads.

....

C. They bought three bottles of juices.

....

正確答案：

1. 專有／抽象　2. 單　3. 單位
A. 正確
B. We need some bread.
　　bread不可數，不加s。
C. They bought three bottles of juice.
　　juice不可數，不加s。

Unit
03

不可數名詞

Unit 04 名詞的修飾語

一、常見的修飾語

66 文法口訣輕鬆記 99

> 1. many, few, several, both, every 必須數一數
> 2. much, little 不可數
> 3. a lot, some, any, all, no 隨你數不數

1. many, few, several, both, every 必須數一數

many, few, several, both, every 後面必須加「可數名詞」。

2. much, little 不可數

much, little 後面必須加「不可數名詞」。

3. a lot, some, any, all, no 隨你數不數

a lot, some, any, all, no 後面加「可數 / 不可數名詞」皆可。

66 文法觀念說給你聽 99

名詞修飾語主要可用來：

一、修飾「可數名詞」：如 many, a few, few, several, both, every... 等，注意！ every 的後面恆為可數單數名詞。例：several weeks（好幾個星期）、every week（每星期）

二、修飾「不可數名詞」：如 much, a little, little... 等，例：much money（很多錢）、a little water（一些水）

三、修飾「**可數／不可數名詞**」皆可：如 a lot of, lots of, some, all, any, no... 等，例：some weeks（幾個星期）、some money（一些錢）

📣 圖解文法一看就懂 📣

名詞修飾語和修飾對象：

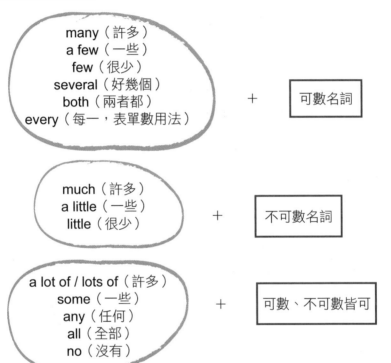

```
┌─────────────────────┐
│  many（許多）        │
│  a few（一些）       │
│  few（很少）         │          ┌──────────┐
│  several（好幾個）   │    +     │ 可數名詞 │
│  both（兩者都）      │          └──────────┘
│  every（每一，表單數用法）│
└─────────────────────┘

┌─────────────────────┐
│  much（許多）        │          ┌────────────┐
│  a little（一些）    │    +     │ 不可數名詞 │
│  little（很少）      │          └────────────┘
└─────────────────────┘

┌──────────────────────────┐
│  a lot of / lots of（許多）│      ┌──────────────────┐
│  some（一些）             │  +   │ 可數、不可數皆可 │
│  any（任何）             │      └──────────────────┘
│  all（全部）             │
│  no（沒有）              │
└──────────────────────────┘
```

📣 例句現身說法好清楚 📣

1. I have **many** friends here.（many ＝ a lot of ＝ lots of）
   我這裡有許多朋友。

2. I have **much** homework today.（much ＝ a lot of ＝ lots of）
   我今天有很多家庭作業。

Unit 04

名詞的修飾語

3. She has **a few** friends here.　她在這裡有一些朋友。

　　She has **few** friends here.　她在這裡幾乎沒有朋友。

4. I drink **a little** water.　我喝一些水。

　　I drink **little** water.　我幾乎沒喝水。

5. Do you have any friends here? Yes, I have **some**.

　　你在這裡有任何朋友嗎？是的，有一些。

6. I don't have any money. ＝ I have **no** money.（not any ＝ no）

　　我沒有任何錢。＝ 我沒有錢。

Unit 04

名詞的修飾語

二、易混淆的修飾語

🔊 文法觀念說給你聽 🔊

　　修飾語除了分成修飾可數、不可數名詞外，還有些可以分成肯定、否定，例如：a little（一些→肯定）、little（很少→否定），需小心使用並分辨其差異。

🔊 圖解文法一看就懂 🔊

易混淆的修飾語

肯定 　　　　　　　　　　　　否定／疑問

一些
a few（＝some）
a little（＝some）
some（一些）

很少；幾乎沒有
few（＝not many）
little（＝not much）
any（任何）

兩者都

both（都）

三者以上全部都

all（全部）

加可數、不可數皆可

some（一些）

必須加可數

several（數個）

Unit 04

名詞的修飾語

例句現身說法好清楚

1. I have **several** comic books. → **可數**

我有一些漫畫書。

注意：several 可用 some 代替

2. I have **some** money. → **不可數**

我有一些錢。

注意：some 不可用 several 代替

3. **Both** my brothers are doctors.　我兩個哥哥都是醫生。

4. **Not both** my brothers are doctors. → **部份否定**

我兩個哥哥並非都是醫生。

＝ One is a doctor; the other one is not.　一個是醫生；一個不是。

5. **All** my classmates are in the gym.　我的同學全都在體育館。

6. **Not all** my classmates are in the gym. → **部份否定**

我的同學並非都在體育館。

＝ Some are in the gym; some are not.　有些在體育館；有些不是。

7. **Every girl** and (every) boy is happy at the party.

每個男孩女孩在派對上都快樂。

8. **Not every** girl likes shopping. → **部份否定**

並非每個女孩都喜歡購物。

Unit
04

名詞的修飾語

= **Some** like shopping; some don't.

有些喜歡；有些不喜歡。

注意：every 後面恆為可數單數名詞。

> **66 馬上演練好實力 99**

(   ) 1. How _____ oranges do you have?

     (A) many   (B) much   (C) any   (D) lot

(   ) 2. How _____ money did you get?

     (A) many   (B) much   (C) any   (D) lot

(   ) 3. He has _____ time.

     (A) many   (B) several   (C) some   (D) a lot

(   ) 4. They have _____ homework.

     (A) a lot   (B) lots   (C) a lot of   (D) many

(   ) 5. She drank _____ water.

     (A) a few   (B) a little   (C) many   (D) a lot

(   ) 6. I don't have _____ brothers.

     (A) no   (B) all   (C) any   (D) much

(   ) 7. We have _____ friends here.

     (A) not   (B) not a   (C) no a   (D) no

(   ) 8. Every boy and girl at the party _____ happy.

     (A) is   (B) are   (C) am   (D) be

Solution 公佈答案

1. (A)   2. (B)   3. (C)   4. (C)   5. (B)   6. (C)   7. (D)   8. (A)

今日重點回顧筆記

一定要練習寫下來！才能確定自己真的會了喔！

1. many/few/several是用來修飾_____名詞。
2. much/little是用來修飾_____名詞。
3. both/all/every加上not可形成_____否定。

試判斷以下句子是否正確？錯誤的請更正為正確句子。

A. She made a lot friends here.

....

B. They spent many money on it.

....

C. They bought three bottles of juice.

....

**Unit
04**

名詞的修飾語

正確答案：

1. 可數　2. 不可數　3. 部分
A. She made a lot of friends here.
　 a lot後面一定要有個of，才能用來修飾名詞。
B. They spent much money on it.
　 money不可數，所以用much。
C. 正確

Chapter 03 Test

每天你都看到的名詞——綜合測驗篇

名詞觀念選選看

(　　) 1. There are three _____ on the table.

(A) watchs　　(B) glasses　　(C) boxs　　(D) tomatos

(　　) 2. The _____ were dancing in the park.

(A) mans　　(B) childs　　(C) women　　(D) wifes

(　　) 3. I saw two _____ in the kitchen.

(A) mice　　(B) juices　　(C) breads　　(D) mouses

(　　) 4. The rich _____ not always happier than the poor.

(A) is　　(B) was　　(C) are　　(D) be

(　　) 5. He bought much _____ yesterday.

(A) beef　　(B) apple　　(C) grapes　　(D) milks

(　　) 6. He has _____ homework to do today.

(A) many　　(B) a lot of　　(C) a few　　(D) several

(　　) 7. We need _____ vegetables for the party tomorrow.

(A) much　　(B) a lot　　(C) a little　　(D) some

(　　) 8. Every girl _____ happy at the dance party.

(A) be　　(B) are　　(C) is　　(D) were

劃線錯誤處，請改成正確文法

1. The <u>childs</u> are playing on the playground. _____

2. They have a <u>little</u> friends here. _____

3. I help mom do <u>many</u> housework yesterday. _____

4. There are <u>lot</u> of sheep on the farm. _____

5. How many <u>peoples</u> are there in your family? Six. _____

6. Lots of fish <u>is</u> in the basket. _____

7. Several <u>policeman</u> are catching the thief. _____

8. No news <u>are</u> good news. _____

66 閱讀測驗 99

（Mrs. Cook arrives home after shopping for **food**.）

Walter: Mom, I can't find my **eraser**.

Mrs. Cook: Again? That's **the fourth time** this month! Have you checked your **pencil box**?

Walter: Yes, but it's not there.

Mrs. Cook: Did you look around in your room?

Walter: Yes, I <u>did</u>.

Mrs. Cook: How about the living room?

Walter: It couldn't be there. I was doing my **homework** in my room and didn't even go into the living room.

Mrs. Cook: Well, then, borrow one from your brother for now. I'll help you find it after I put all the food in the refrigerator.

Walter: OK.

Mrs. Cook: Walter! Look what I've found.

Walter: My eraser!

Mrs. Cook: In the refrigerator?

Walter: Oh, I remember! I got some **juice** from the refrigerator, and...and...

Mrs. Cook: And put the eraser in the refrigerator?

Walter: Well, I don't remember that **part**.

Mrs. Cook: Well, take it, and be more careful next time.

【基測96-2】

(　　) 1. Where did Walter put his eraser?

  (A) In the juice.   (B) In his pencil box.

  (C) In the refrigerator.   (D) In the living room.

(　　) 2. What does <u>did</u> mean in the dialogue?

  (A) To do homework.   (B) To borrow one eraser.

  (C) To go to the living room. (D) To look around in Walter's room.

(　　) 3. What do we know about Walter?

  (A) He is good at cooking.

  (B) He is the only child in the family.

  (C) He has lost his eraser several times.

  (D) He went shopping for food with his mom.

66 句子重組測驗 99

1. bought / I / a / of / from / candy / box / the / store

_____

2. some / Can / bring / you / me / water?

_____

3. and / They / farm / on / some fruit / the / vegetables / grew

_____

4. cooked / yesterday / some / noodles / Mom / morning

_____

5. loaf / man / poor / a / of / bread / to / The / the / gave / guy

_____

6. asks / bag / us / to / her / a / of / Grandmother / buy / sugar.

_____

7. to / sent / two / friend / tickets / Susan / her

_____

8. Please / black tea / me / give / hamburgers / a glass of / and / two

_____

9. How / there / convenient / many / are / in / stores / the town?

_____

10. The / so / TV / is / on / funny / news

_____

「中翻英測驗」

1. 有兩杯果汁在桌上。

   There are two _____ of _____ on the table.

2. 每一位老師和學生都很開心。

   _____ teacher and student _____ happy.

3. 我收到三盒餅乾。

   I got three _____ of cookies.

4. 林太太有三個小孩嗎？

   Does Mrs. Lin have three _____?

5. 冰箱裡有一些水、食物和果汁。

   There is _____ water, _____ and juice in the refrigerator.

6. 台北和高雄是現代化的城市。

   _____

7. 藍色和綠色是不同的色彩。

   _____

8. 請給我一杯熱咖啡。

   _____

9. 他今天有很多家庭作業。

   _____

10. Peter 在速食店點了好幾個漢堡。

    _____

Chapter 03 ⟩Solution

每天你都看到的名詞──解答篇

〔❝ 名詞觀念選選看 ❞〕

1. (B)　　　2. (C)　　　3. (A)　　　4. (C)
5. (A)　　　6. (B)　　　7. (D)　　　8. (C)

〔❝ 劃線錯誤處，請改成正確文法 ❞〕

1. children　　　2. few　　　3. much　　　4. a lot / lots
5. people / persons　6. are　　　7. policemen　8. is

〔❝閱讀測驗❞〕

1. (C)　2. (D)　3. (C)

（庫克太太買完食物後回到家。）

華特　　：媽，我找不到我的橡皮擦。

庫克太太：又來了？這是這個月的第四次了！你有確認過你的鉛筆盒裡面有沒有嗎？

華特　　：有啊，可是沒有在那裡面。

庫克太太：那你有在你的房間裡四處找過嗎？

華特　　：有，我有。

庫克太太：那客廳呢？

華特　　：它不可能在那裡。我一直都在我的房間裡面做我的作業，根本就沒有去客廳。

庫克太太：好吧，那現在去跟你的哥哥借一個吧。等我把所有食物都放進冰箱之後我會幫
　　　　　你找找看。

華特　　：好。

庫克太太：華特！看看我找到了什麼！

華特　　：我的橡皮擦！

庫克太太：怎麼在冰箱裡？

華特　　：喔，我想起來了！我從冰箱裡拿了一些果汁，然後……

庫克太太：然後就把它放進冰箱了？

華特　　：恩，這個我就不記得了。

庫克太太：好吧，拿去，下次注意一點。

🔊句子重組測驗 🔊

1. I bought a box of candy from the store.（我在商店買了一盒糖果。）

2. Can you bring me some water?（你能為我帶來一些水嗎？）

3. They grew some fruit and vegetables on the farm.
   （他們在農場上種了一些水果和蔬菜。）

4. Mom cooked some noodles yesterday morning.
   （媽媽昨天早上煮了一些麵。）

5. The man gave a loaf of bread to the poor guy.
   （那個男人給了這位可憐人一條麵包。）

6. Grandmother asks us to buy her a bag of sugar.
   （奶奶要我們幫她買一袋糖。）

7. Susan sent two tickets to her friend.（蘇珊寄了兩張票給她的朋友。）

8. Please give me a glass of black tea and two hamburgers.
   （請給我一杯紅茶和兩個漢堡。）

9. How many convenient stores are there in the town?
   （這鎮上有多少間便利商店？）

10. The news on TV is so funny.（這則電視上的新聞是如此好笑。）

🔊中翻英測驗 🔊

1. glasses / juice

2. Every / is

3. boxes

4. children

5. some / food

6. Taipei and Kaohsiung are modern cities.

7. Blue and green are different colors.

8. Please give me a cup of hot coffee.

9. He has a lot of homework today.

10. Peter ordered several hamburgers at the fast food restaurant.

Chapter04 / Pronoun
名詞的好麻吉 代名詞

本篇代名詞的學習重點如下：

Unit 01 〈人稱代名詞

一、人稱代名詞基本觀念

文法口訣輕鬆記　🔊 *Track 016*

1. 人稱代名詞分成單複數
2. 你我他：you, he and I
3. 我們你們他們：we, you and they

1. 人稱代名詞分成單複數

　　人稱代名詞，有單數和複數之分。

2. 你我他：you, he and I

　　英文裡的人稱排列順序和中文不同，I（我）要放在最後面。

3. 我們你們他們：we, you and they

　　複數的人稱排列順序和中文相同。

文法觀念說給你聽

「人稱代名詞」可分成兩類：

一、單數：

第一人稱	I	我（恆為大寫）
第二人稱	you	你
第三人稱	he / she / it	他／她／牠；它

三者同時出現的排列順序是：第二人稱、第三人稱、第一人稱（你、他、我）。

例如： You, he, and I are classmates. 我、你和他是同班同學。

二、複數：

第一人稱	we	我們
第二人稱	you	你們
第三人稱共用	they	他們／她們／牠們／它們

排列順序：第一人稱、第二人稱、第三人稱（我們、你們、他們）

例如： We, you, and they are good friends. 我們、你們和他們是好朋友。

圖解文法一看就懂

單數

第一人稱
I（我）

第二人稱
you（你）

第三人稱
he（他）
she（她）
it（牠；它）

複數

第一人稱
We（我們）

第二人稱
you（你們）

第三人稱
they
（他們；她們）
（牠們；它們）

例句現身說法好清楚

◎**單數人稱代名詞**

1. Are **you** a teacher? Yes, I am.　你是老師嗎？是的，我是。

注意：問句用 you（你），答句用 I（我）。

2. This is my brother; **he** is an engineer.　這是我弟弟；他是位工程師。

3. Joanna is my best friend. **She** studies in Harvard now.
喬安娜是我最好的朋友。她現在在哈佛唸書。

4. My mother made a strawberry pie; **it** is very delicious.
我媽媽做了一個草莓派；它很美味。

◎複數人稱代名詞

1. **Tom and I** are classmates. 湯姆和我是同班同學。
We are classmates. 我們是同班同學。

2. Do **you** like traveling? 你們喜歡旅行嗎？
Yes, **we** do. 是的，我們喜歡。

注意：問句用 you，答句用 we。

3. **Ann and Lisa** go shopping together. 安和麗莎一起購物。
They go shopping together. 他們一起去購物。

二、複數人稱代名詞的使用技巧

『文法口訣輕鬆記』 🔊 *Track 017*

1. 我最大，有我（I）就是 we
2. 有你（you），還是 you
3. 沒有 I 或 you，才是 they

1. 我最大，有我（I）就是 we
有 I 和其他人稱，就可合成複數的 we（我們）。

2. 有你（you），還是 you
有 you 和其他人稱，就可合成複數的 you（你們）。

3. 沒有 I 或 you，才是 they
沒有 I 或 you，只有其他人稱，就可合成複數的 they（他們）。

文法觀念說給你聽

一、只要**主詞含有第一人稱 I（我）**，其複數人稱代名詞就是 **we（我們）**

例如：Tom and I → We / You and I → We。

二、**主詞含有第二人稱 you（你），沒有最大的 I**，複數人稱代名詞還是 **you（你們）**，

例如：you and Jack → you。

三、**主詞沒有第一人稱 I 及第二人稱 you**，複數人稱代名詞就用第三人稱 **they（他們）**，

例如：Peter and Ben → they / Mary and Betty → they。

圖解文法一看就懂

人稱代名詞的變化方式

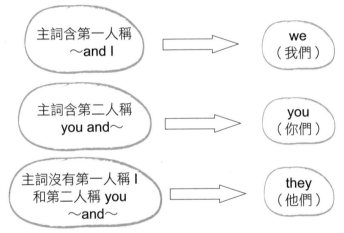

例句現身說法好清楚

1. **John and I** are good friends. → **We** are good friends.

   約翰和**我**是好朋友。 → **我們**是好朋友。

Unit
01

人稱代名詞

2. **You and your father** like hiking. → **You** like hiking.

   你和你爸爸喜歡健行。 → **你們**喜歡健行。

3. Do **you** like hiking? Yes, **we** do.

   你們喜歡健行嗎？是的，**我們**喜歡。

4. **You and I** play on-line games. → **We** play on-line games.

   你和**我**玩線上遊戲。 → **我們**玩線上遊戲。

5. **Coco and Susan** go to a music show together.

   → **They** go to a music show together.

   柯可和蘇珊一起去演唱會。 → **他們**一起去演唱會。

Unit
01

人
稱
代
名
詞

三、人稱代名詞的三格

文法口訣輕鬆記　Track 018

> 1. I、my、me / you、your、you / he、his、him、she、her、her / it、its、it
> 2. we、our、us / you、your、you / they、their、them
> 3. 每天唸一遍，搖身就會變！

1. I、my、me / you、your、you / he、his、him、she、her、her / it、its、it

   以上為「單數人稱代名詞」，主格 / 所有格 / 受格的變化。

2. we、our、us / you、your、you / they、their、them

   以上為「複數人稱代名詞」，主格 / 所有格 / 受格的變化。

3. **每天唸一遍，搖身就會變！**

   所謂熟能生巧，常常唸，自然就記起來其變化了。

📖 文法觀念說給你聽 📖

「人稱代名詞」分為以下三格：

一、**主　格**：當「主詞」用（如上述單元）。

二、**所有格**：當「形容詞」用，像是 **I 變成 my**，其餘代名詞的所有格字尾則皆有 **r** 或 **s**（可觀察中文的變化，是統一加上「的」）。

例 1：**My** bag is new.　我的包包是新的。

例 2：**Her / His** bag is old.　她 / 他的包包是舊的。

三、**受格**：當「受詞」用，**us** 長得最特別，他 / 他們的受格字尾則有個 **m**（可觀察中文的變化，是主詞 / 受詞都相同）。

例 1：**They** like **us**.　他們喜歡我們。

例 2：**We** like **them**.　我們喜歡他們。

Unit
01

人稱代名詞

📖 圖解文法一看就懂 📖

	中文	主格（主詞）	所有格（形容詞）	受格（受詞）
單數	我	I	my	me
	你	you	your	you
	他	he	his	him
	她	she	her	her
	牠（它）	it	its	it
複數	我們	we	our	us
	你們	you	your	you
	他們	they	their	them

📖 例句現身說法好清楚 📖

1. What's **your** name? **My** name is Ted.　　你叫作什麼名字? 我的名字是泰德。

2. **I am his** son.　我是他的兒子。

3. **He is her** brother.　他是她的哥哥。

4. **We like to play with them.**　我們喜歡和他們玩。

四、主格、所有格的使用技巧

〝文法觀念說給你聽〞

一、**所有格不可單獨使用，後面須加上名詞。**

二、以下**主詞加be V. 縮寫**和**所有格**的用法很容易混淆，請特別小心。

（縮寫和所有格右方為KK音標。）

主詞+be V.縮寫	所有格
He's [hiz]	his [hɪz] ＋名詞
You're [jʊr]	your [jʊr] ＋名詞
They're [ðer]	their [ðɛr] ＋名詞

＊注意到了嗎？主詞＋ be 動詞縮寫的母音都是**長母音**，所有格的母音都是**短母音**！

〝圖解文法一看就懂〞

單數

　　　　　　　　主格＋ be V.　　　　　　　　　　　　所有格＋名詞

I am = I'm（我是）
You are = You're（你是）
He is = He's（他是）
She is = She's（她是）
It is = It's（牠／它是）

my ～（我的～）
your ～（你的～）
his ～（他的～）
her ～（她的～）
its ～（牠／它的～）

複數

主格＋ be V.

We are ＝ We're（我們是）
You are ＝ You're（你們是）
They are ＝ They're（他們是）

所有格＋名詞

our ～（我們的～）
your ～（你們的～）
their ～（他們的～）

Unit
01

人稱代名詞

例句現身說法好清楚

1. What's **your** name? → **My** name is Terry. ＝ **I'm** Terry.
   你叫什麼名字？ → 我的名字是泰瑞。/ 我是泰瑞。

2. What's **his** name? → **His** name is Harry. ＝ **He's** Harry.
   他叫什麼名字？ → 他的名字是哈利。/ 他是哈利。

3. What's **her** name? → **Her** name is Lisa. ＝ **She's** Lisa.
   她叫什麼名字？ → 她的名字是莉莎。/ 她是莉莎。

4. **He** is **my** teacher.　他是我的老師。
   ＝ **I** am **his** student.　我是他的學生。

5. **She** is **his** sister.　她是他的妹妹。
   ＝ **He** is **her** brother.　他是她的哥哥。

6. **My** father is a doctor.　我爸爸是醫生。

注意：中文可以說**「我爸爸」**，但英文必須說**My father**，不可寫成
　　　father。

五、主格、受格的使用技巧

文法觀念說給你聽

一、中英文裡的受格差異：

中文裡的主詞和受詞説法上沒有不同，但是英文裡卻需要做變化，並隨著句子中主詞的不同，動詞的變化也跟著主詞有所不同。

例1：I love her. 我愛她。→ She love**s** me.　她愛我。

例2：You love him. 妳愛他。→ He love**s** you　他愛妳。

二、主格和受格的功能：

主格當**主詞**用；受格當動詞或介系詞之後的**受詞**。

Unit 01 人稱代名詞

📖 圖解文法一看就懂 📖

主詞變受詞，受詞變主詞的「交叉相乘法」

主詞（主格）　　　　V.　　　　受詞（受格）

主詞　　　　　　　　　　　　　受詞

V.

跟著新主詞變化

📖 例句現身說法好清楚 📖

1.　I love you.　我愛你。

➡ You love me.　你愛我。

2. They know you.　他們認識你。

➡ You know them.　你認識他們。

3.　We like her.　我們喜歡她。

➡ She likes us.　她喜歡我們。

4. I play baseball with him.　他和我打棒球。

➡ He plays baseball with me.　我和他打棒球。

❝ 馬上演練好實力 ❞

選選看：請從選項中選出符合題目的答案

(   ) 1. Susan is a good girl; she always helps _____ mother.

    (A) she   (B) him   (C) her   (D) he

(   ) 2. _____ are Vivian's classmates.

    (A) Their   (B) We   (C) Our   (D) Them

(   ) 3. The presents are wonderful, and I like _____ all.

    (A) they   (B) us   (C) it   (D) them

(   ) 4. I know that tall boy. _____ Mary's brother.

    (A) She is   (B) His   (C) He's   (D) His is

(   ) 5. They are _____ teacher.

    (A) you   (B) our   (C) we   (D) us

(   ) 6. He sent some books to _____.

    (A) you   (B) our   (C) we   (D) us

(   ) 7. Are Tom and Tim your cousins? Yes, _____ are.

    (A) they   (B) we   (C) you   (D) those

(   ) 8. She helps _____ with the math homework.

    (A) we   (B) he   (C) him   (D) my

Unit 01

人稱代名詞

Solution 公佈答案

解答：1. (C)   2. (B)   3. (D)   4. (C)   5. (B)   6. (D)   7. (A)   8. (C)

Unit
01

人稱代名詞

今日重點回顧筆記

一定要練習寫下來！才能確定自己真的會了喔！

1. 人稱代名詞你、我、他的排列順序為：_____, _____, and _____。

2. he的所有格為_____。

3. they的受格為_____。

試判斷以下句子是否正確？錯誤的請更正為正確句子。

A. She father is a businessman.

....

B. Don't laugh at them.

....

C. The man is he's teacher.

....

正確答案：

1. You / he / I   2. his   3. them

A. Her father is a businessman.

　　she的所有格是her，這裡講的是「她的」爸爸，所以要變換成所有格。

B. 正確

C. The man is his teacher.

　　he的所有格是his才對，不要搞錯了。

指示代名詞

一、指示代名詞基本觀念

❝文法口訣輕鬆記❞ ◀ *Track 019*

> 1. 這叫 this，那叫 that
> 2. 簡答 it 來幫忙
> 3. this 變成 these，that 變作 those
> 4. 簡答就用 they

1. 這叫 this，那叫 that
距離較近的用this（這）；較遠的用that（那）。

2. 簡答 it 來幫忙
在句子中做簡答時，需用代名詞 it 來代替 this / that。

3. this 變成 these，that 變作 those
複數變成 these（這些）和 those（那些）。

4. 簡答就用 they
在句子中做簡答時，需用代名詞 they 來代
替 these / those。

❝文法觀念說給你聽❞

一、距離近的人或物用this（這）/ these（這些）；距離遠的人或物用
　　that（那）/ those（那些）來代替，要特別注意單複數的變化。
　例如：This is a good pen.（單數）/ These are good pens.（複數）

二、簡答須用代名詞 **it（它）**或 **they（它們）**

例1： Is this your pen?

→ Yes, **it** is. 不可寫成 Yes, this is.

例2： Are those your books?

→ Yes, **they** are. 不可回答 Yes, those are.

圖解文法一看就懂

指示代名詞的單複數變化		
	單數	**複數**
近的	this（這）	these（這些）
遠的	that（那）	those（那些）
代名詞	it（它；牠）	they（他們；它們；牠們）
搭配 be 動詞	is	are

例句現身說法好清楚

1. **This** is a book. → **These** are books.　這是一本書。→ 這些是書。

2. **That** is a good watch. → **Those** are good watches.
　　那是一只手錶。→ 那些是手錶。

3. **This** is a pen; **that** is a pencil.　這是一枝鋼筆；那是一枝鉛筆。

4. Is **this** your car?　這是你的車嗎？
　　Yes, **it** is.　對，是的。→ **肯定簡答**
　　No, **it** isn't.　不，不是。→ **否定簡答**
　　Yes, **it** is my car.　對，它是我的車。→ **肯定詳答**
　　No, **it** is not my car.　不，它不是我的車。→ **否定詳答**

5. Are **those** his classmates?　那些是他的同班同學嗎？
　　Yes, **they** are.　對，他們是。→ **肯定簡答**

Unit 02

指示代名詞

No, **they** are not.　个，他們不是。 ➡ **否定簡答**

Yes, **they** are his classmates.　對，他們是他的同學。 ➡ **肯定詳答**

No, **they** are not his classmates.　不，他們不是他的同學。 ➡ **否定詳答**

注意：簡答須用代名詞 **it** 或 **they**。

二、指示代名詞 VS. 指示形容詞的使用技巧

『『 文法觀念說給你聽 』』

一、指示代名詞主要有兩大功能：

1. 當**主詞**，例如：**This** is a book.

2. 當**受詞**，例如：I like **this**.

二、指示形容詞不可與**冠詞**或**所有格**連用。

指示形容詞	
冠詞（a / an / the）	只能任選一種＋名詞
所有格（my / your / his...）	
例如： this pen / a pen / my pen （o） 　　　 this a pen / my this pen / the your pen （x） **注意**：冠詞與所有格也不能連用！	

『『 圖解文法一看就懂 』』

「指示代名詞」和「指示形容詞」的比較

指示代名詞　　　　　　　　指示形容詞

可當主詞
可當受詞　　　　　　　　後面須加名詞

例句現身說法好清楚

1. **This** is a good book.　這是一本好書。→ **指示代名詞**

→ **This** book is good.　這本書是好的。→ **指示形容詞**

不可寫成 This a book is good.

注意：this ＋名詞（book）→ this 為指示形容詞，一定不可以和冠詞 a / an 連用。

2. **This** boy is Tom's brother. → **The** boy is Tom's brother.

這個男孩是湯姆的兄弟。

3. **Those** students are in the gym. → **The** students are in the gym.

這些學生在體育館。

注意：指示形容詞不論遠近 / 單複數，皆可用 the 代替。

4. **This** is a red pen.　這是一支紅筆。

不可寫成 The is a red pen.

注意：This 為指示代名詞，不可用the 代替。

5. Is **that** a short pencil?　那是一枝短的鉛筆嗎？→ **指示代名詞**

→ Is **that** pencil short?　那枝鉛筆是短的嗎？→ **指示形容詞**

馬上演練好實力

選選看：請從選項中選出符合題目的答案

(　　) 1. This is a rose; _____ is a lily.

(A) the 　　(B) those 　　(C) these 　　D) that

(　　) 2. _____ are Mike's grandsons.

(A) The 　　(B) Those 　　(C) That 　　(D) It

(　　) 3. Is this your car? Yes, _____ is.

(A) they 　　(B) that 　　(C) it 　　(D) this

(　　) 4. _____ apple is sweet.

     (A) This　　(B) These　　　　(C) This a　　(D) This an

(　　) 5. _____ people in the village are very nice.

     (A) It　　(B) These　　　　(C) They　　(D) That

(　　) 6. I like _____ skirt very much.

     (A) these　　(B) those　　　　(C) it　　(D) the

(　　) 7. Are those your family? Yes, _____ are.

     (A) they　　(B) we　　　　(C) these　　(D) those

(　　) 8. These are lions and _____ are tigers.

     (A) this　　(B) these　　　　(C) those　　(D) they

Unit 02

指示代名詞

Solution 公佈答案

1. (D)　2. (B)　3. (C)　4. (A)　5. (B)　6. (D)　7. (A)　8. (C)

Unit 02

指示代名詞

今日重點回顧筆記

一定要練習寫下來！才能確定自己真的會了喔！

1. 指示代名詞**this**的複數為：＿＿＿＿＿。
2. 指示代名詞**that**的複數為：＿＿＿＿＿。
3. 簡答時不可用指示代名詞，須改用代名詞，單數＿＿＿＿／複數＿＿＿＿。

試判斷以下句子是否正確？錯誤的請更正為正確句子。

A. Is that your bicycle? Yes, that is.

．．

B. These are their school bags.

．．

C. Are those your clothes? Yes, those are.

．．

正確答案：

1. these　　2. those　　3. it/they

A. Is that your bicycle? Yes, it is.
　　簡答時不用指示代名詞，這裡要改成it（單數）。

B. 正確

C. Are those your clothes? Yes, they are.
　　簡答時不用指示代名詞，這裡要改成they（複數）。

Test

名詞的好麻吉代名詞──綜合測驗篇

🔊 代名詞觀念選選看 🔊

(　　) 1. _____ live on the same street.

　　(A) I, you and he　　　　　　　　(B) He, you and I

　　(C) You, he and I　　　　　　　　(D) You, I and he

(　　) 2. He is my brother. I am _____ sister.

　　(A) he　　　　(B) his　　　　(C) him　　　　(D) her

(　　) 3. _____ name is Tony.

　　(A) She　　　　(B) You　　　　(C) Her　　　　(D) His

(　　) 4. We gave some books to _____.

　　(A) them　　　　(B) they　　　　(C) their　　　　(D) our

(　　) 5. _____ are their cars.

　　(A) That　　　　(B) This　　　　(C) These　　　　(D) The

(　　) 6. Is that your notebook? Yes, _____ is.

　　(A) this　　　　(B) it　　　　(C) that　　　　(D) he

(　　) 7. Tom and Mary are brother and sister. _____ are both my students.

　　(A) We　　　　(B) You　　　　(C) They　　　　(D) That

(　　) 8. Judy and I are classmates. _____ usually go to school together.

　　(A) she　　　　(B) They　　　　(C) You　　　　(D) We

🔊 劃線錯誤處，請改成正確文法 🔊

1. You, we, and they all his students._____

2. Would you like to go with we?_____

3. That boys are from Canada._____

4. Are these pencils red? Yes, these are._____

5. Does Lily like <u>he</u>?_____

6. Peter and you are excellent. <u>They</u> get good grades._____

7. Is <u>that a computer new</u>?_____

8. She is his daughter. He is <u>she</u> father._____

閱讀測驗

Ren-jie:　Hi, Dad, **I**'m back.

Mr. Lin:　How was school?

Ren-jie:　Not bad. **We** played basketball in PE class today. And guess what! **You** won't believe **it**! Our teacher, Miss Chang, can play basketball really well!

Mr. Lin:　Miss Chang? Is **her** name Shu-wen Chang?

Ren-jie:　Yes, **it** is. Do you know **her**? Is **she** famous?

Mr. Lin:　MORE than famous! When **she** was young, **she** was one of the best basketball players on the national team. Thanks to **her**, the team won many games. **You**'re so lucky to be **her** student! Hey, let's go to the park, and you can show me what you learned in class.

Ren-jie:　No, I'm still afraid of **that** big basketball!

【基測 97-1】

(　　) 1. Which is true about Miss Chang?

　　　(A) She is young and beautiful.

　　　(B) She was one of Mr. Lin's students.

　　　(C) She was a famous basketball player.

　　　(D) She helped her students win many games.

(   ) 2. What do we know about Ren-jie?

     (A) He is afraid of his PE teacher.

     (B) He cannot find his basketball.

     (C) He cannot play basketball very well.

     (D) He wants to join the school basketball team.

句子重組測驗

1. is / That / successful / businessman

_____

2. those / basketball / are / boys / Who / over there? / playing

_____

3. That / us / popular / is / singer / with

_____

4. cookies / buy / for them / will / some / Mom

_____

5. asked / her / some / students / Mrs. Huang / questions

_____

6. in / house / is / Taipei / beautiful / Their / very

_____

7. his / He / about / thinking / future / is

_____

8. her / needs to / parents / talk to / Gina

_____

9. room / Tim / cleaning / is / his

_____

10. the / kitchen / usually / We / oven / in / put / the

_____

中翻英測驗

1. 我們昨天去看了一部電影。

_____ went to see a movie yesterday.

2. 他們的老師很仁慈。

_____ teacher is very kind.

3. 她的哥哥們是警察。

_____ brothers are policemen.

4. 我有一隻貓。牠的毛是白色的。

I have a cat. _____ hair is white.

5. 這只手錶是新的。

_____ watch is new.

6. 這些是中文書，不是英文書。

_____

7. 喬治喜歡她。

_____

8. 那些是有趣的書。

_____

9. 那是一朵紅色的花。

_____

10. 這是他的筆嗎？是的，它是。

_____

Solution

名詞的好麻吉代名詞──解答篇

▐▐ 代名詞觀念選選看 ▐▐

1. (C)　　　2. (B)　　　3. (D)　　　4. (A)
5. (C)　　　6. (B)　　　7. (C)　　　8. (D)

▐▐ 劃線錯誤處，請改成正確文法 ▐▐

1. You, we, and they are　　2. us　　　3. Those　　　4. they
5. him　　　　　　　　　　6. You　　7. that　　　8. her

▐▐ 閱讀測驗 ▐▐

1. (C)　2. (C)

仁　傑：嗨！老爸，我回來了。

林先生：今天在學校還好嗎？

仁　傑：還不錯，我們今天體育課打籃球。而且你知道嗎，你絕對不會相信，我們的老師也就是張小姐，竟然能夠打籃球打得這麼好！

林先生：張小姐？她的名字是張淑文嗎？

仁　傑：沒錯。你認識她嗎？她很有名嗎？

林先生：她不只是有名！當她年輕的時候，她可是國家運動代表隊最佳的籃球選手之一，多虧了她，我們的代表隊贏了很多場比賽。你能夠當她的學生真是幸運！嘿，我們去公園吧，然後秀給我看你在課堂上學了些什麼。

仁　傑：不要，我還是很害怕那巨大的籃球！

▐▐ 句子重組測驗 ▐▐

1. That businessman is successful.（那個商人很成功。）

2. Who are those boys playing basketball over there?

（在那裡打籃球的那些男孩是誰？）

3. That singer is popular with us.（那位歌手很受我們歡迎。）

4. Mom will buy some cookies for them.（媽媽將買一些餅乾給他們。）

5. Mrs. Huang asked her students some questions.

（黃老師問她的學生一些問題。）

6. Their house in Taipei is very beautiful.（他們在台北的房子非常漂亮。）

7. He is thinking about his future.（他正在考慮他的未來。）

8. Gina needs to talk to her parents.（吉娜需要和她的父母談談。）

9. Tim is cleaning his room.（提姆正在打掃他的房間。）

10. We usually put the oven in the kitchen.

（我們通常把烤爐放在廚房裡。）

中翻英測驗

1. We

2. Their

3. Her

4. Its

5. This

6. These are Chinese books, not English books.

7. George likes her.

8. Those are interesting books.

9. That is a red flower.

10. Is this his pen? Yes, it is.

Chapter05 / Adjective and Adverb

想大喊小姐好正怎能不學
形容詞和副詞

本篇形容詞和副詞的學習重點如下：

Unit 01 形容詞轉為情狀副詞之規則

一、基本用法

文法觀念說給你聽

情狀副詞的變化方式和用法如下：

一、變化：

情狀副詞表示狀態、性質或方式，一般由**形容詞字尾＋ ly** 構成。

二、用法：

此類形容詞通常放在 **be V. 或連綴動詞之後**（可參考 Chapter 1），而情狀副詞則用來修飾一般動詞或副詞。

圖解文法一看就懂

一、情狀副詞的變化原則：

公式：形容詞＋ ly

常見的	需注意的
1. ＋ ly 2. 字尾是子音 y ➜ 去 y ＋ ily	1. 字尾是 l ➜ ＋ ly 2. 字尾是 ll ➜ ＋ y 3. 字尾是 le ➜ 去 e ＋ y 4. 字尾是 ue ➜ 去 e ＋ ly

二、搖身一變試試看：

常見的	
1. ＋ ly	
slow（慢的）	slowly（慢地）

quick（快的）	quickly（快地）
sad（傷心的）	sadly（傷心地）
cold（冷／冷漠的）	coldly（冷漠地）
bad（壞的）	badly（壞地）

2. 字尾是子音 y ➔ 去 y + ily

happy（快樂的）	happily（快樂地）
heavy（重的）	heavily（重地）
busy（忙的）	busily（忙地）
easy（容易的）	easily（容易地）
noisy（吵鬧的）	noisily（吵鬧地）

需注意的

1. l + ly

careful（小心的、仔細的）	carefully（小心地、仔細地）
beautiful（漂亮的）	beautifully（漂亮地）

2. ll + y

full（滿滿的）	fully（滿滿地）
dull（遲鈍的）	dully（遲鈍地）

3. 字尾 le ➔ 去 e + y

terrible（可怕的）	terribly（可怕地）
possible（可能的）	possibly（可能地）
comfortable（舒服的）	comfortably（舒服地）

4. 字尾 ue ➔ 去 e + ly

true（真的）	truly（真地）

Unit
01

形容詞轉為情狀副詞之規則

66 例句現身說法好清楚 99

1. He **is quick**.　他很快。
→ He **runs** quick**ly**.　他跑得快。
2. We **are happy**.　我們很快樂。
→ We are **singing** happi**ly**.　我們正快樂地唱著。
3. She **looks** cold.　她看起來很冷漠。
→ She **looks** cold**ly at** me.　她冷漠地看著我。
4. **Be careful**, please.　請小心。
→ **Listen to** your teacher careful**ly**.　仔細地聽老師說。
5. The car **is** very **comfortable**.　這車很舒適。
→ She **sits** comfortab**ly** on the chair.　她舒服地坐在椅子上。
6. She **was sad**.　她很傷心。
→ She **talked** about it sad**ly**.　她傷心地談論著這件事。
7. She **was beautiful**.　她很美麗。
→ She **danced** beautiful**ly**.　她跳舞很美。

二、進階用法：形容詞 & 副詞同形

66 文法觀念說給你聽 99

有一些形容詞不需做變化即可當副詞使用，例如：
I am **early** for work.（接在 be 動詞 am 之後，當形容詞）
→ I go to school **early**.（接在一般動詞 go 之後，當副詞）

📖 圖解文法一看就懂 📖

形容詞 & 副詞同形的例子：

形容詞

early（早的）
late（晚的）
fast（快的）
far（遠的）
near（近的）
high（高的）
low（低的）
hard（困難的 / 硬的）

副詞

early（早地）
late（晚地）
fast（快地）
far（遠地）
near（近地）
high（高地）
low（低地）
hard（努力、認真地 / 劇烈地）

📖 例句現身說法好清楚 📖

1. The train is <u>fast</u>. 這火車很快。
   （形容詞）

→ Don't **speak** so <u>fast</u> (=quickly). 不要說這麼快。
   （副詞）

2. Amy **is** <u>late</u> for school. 艾咪上學遲到。
   （形容詞）

→ Amy **goes** to school <u>late</u>. 艾咪上學遲到
   （副詞）

3. The question **is** <u>hard</u>. 這問題很困難。
   （形容詞）

→ The stone **is** <u>hard</u>. 這石頭很硬。
   （形容詞）

Unit
01

形容詞轉為情狀副詞之規則

4. The students **study** <u>hard</u>.　這些學生用功讀書。
　　　　　　　　　　（副詞）

→ It **rains** <u>hard</u> (= heavily).　下大雨。
　　　　　　（副詞）

三、進階用法：例外

❝ 文法觀念說給你聽 ❞

例外字：有些副詞不以 ly 為變化字尾，需特別注意其用法。
像是：**good → well**，不可變成 goodly。

❝ 圖解文法一看就懂 ❞

副詞的例外：

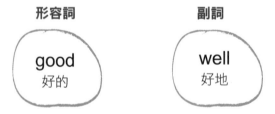

形容詞	副詞
good 好的	well 好地

❝ 例句現身說法好清楚 ❞

1. She can speak very **good** <u>English</u>.　她英語說得很好。（形容詞修飾**名詞**）
→ She can <u>speak</u> English very **well**.　（副詞修飾<u>一般V.</u>）

2. She is a **good** <u>dancer</u>.　她是一位好舞者。（**形容詞修飾名詞**）

→ She can <u>dance</u> very **well**.　她能跳舞跳得很棒。（**副詞修飾一般V.**）

3. "How are you?" "I'm **well**."

　（**well=fine** 可當形容詞，指身體健康狀況）

四、高階用法：特殊字

文法觀念說給你聽

副詞還有以下這些特殊字：

一、字尾+ly 卻衍生成不同意義：

例如：hardly（幾乎不）、lately（最近地 / 近來）、
　　　nearly（幾乎、差不多）

二、字尾+ly 卻只當形容詞：通常由名詞變化而成。

friend（朋友）→ friendly（友善的 / 親切的）

love（愛）→ lovely（可愛的）

三、字尾+ly 卻可同時當形容詞或副詞：通常由名詞變化而成。

time（時間）→ timely（即時的 / 即時地）

week（週）→ weekly（每週的 / 每週地）

month（月）→ monthly（每月的 / 每月地）

year（年）→ yearly（每年的 / 每年地）

圖解文法一看就懂

副詞特殊字的種類:

good(好的)
↓
well(好地)

名詞＋ ly
↓
只當形容詞

時間名詞＋ ly
↓
形容詞／副詞
皆可

Unit 01

形容詞轉為情狀副詞之規則

例句現身說法好清楚

1. He **hardly** works.
   他幾乎不工作。

→ **hardly** 本身已含有否定意味

2. I haven't seen David **lately**.
   我最近沒看到大衛。

3. It's **nearly** (=almost) seven o'clock.
   差不多快七點了。

4. My friend is very **friendly** to me.
   我的朋友對我很友善。

5. The girl looks **lovely**.
   這女孩看起來很可愛。

6. This is a **monthly** ticket.
   這是一張月票。

7. The rent was his biggest **monthly** expense.
   房租是他每月最大的一筆開支。

五、情狀副詞的位置

文法口訣輕鬆記 ◀ *Track 020*

1. **副詞放在句尾最保險！**
2. **動詞直接加受詞不可拆，副詞只好站在動詞前**
3. **動詞加上介系詞還有進行式，副詞就愛把它們拆**

Unit
01

1. **副詞放在句尾最保險！**
   情狀副詞放在句尾準沒錯，最保險！

2. **動詞直接加受詞不可拆，副詞只好站在動詞前**
   動詞＋受詞，是一個不可拆的詞組，副詞置於動詞前面！

3. **動詞加上介系詞還有進行式，副詞就愛把它們拆**
   動詞+介系詞或是 be +V-ing（進行式）副詞可放在中間。例如：
   Listen carefully to me. ➔ 副詞 carefully 將
   listen to 拆開。
   They are happily singing. ➔ 副詞 happily
   將 are singing 拆開。

形容詞轉為情狀副詞之規則

文法觀念說給你聽

情狀副詞的位置，主要以動詞的形式來做區分：

一、沒有受詞，副詞只能放句尾：

主詞＋動詞＋**副詞**

例如：He runs **fast**. 他跑得快。

二、有受詞，副詞除了放句尾，還有其他位置：

1. 主詞＋動詞＋受詞＋**副詞**

→ 主詞＋**副詞**＋動詞＋受詞（動詞／受詞不可拆開）

例如： The man left the room **quietly**.

= The man **quietly** left the room.

這男人安靜地離開了房間。

2. 主詞＋動詞＋介系詞＋受詞＋**副詞**

→ 主詞＋**副詞**＋動詞＋介系詞＋受詞（可放在動詞前）

→ 主詞＋動詞＋**副詞**＋介系詞＋受詞（動詞／介系詞可拆開）

例如：He spoke to the foreigner **slowly**.

= He **slowly** spoke to the foreigner.

= He spoke **slowly** to the foreigner.

他緩慢地對外國人說話。

3. 主詞＋ be 動詞＋分詞（V-ing／p.p.）＋**副詞**

→ 主詞＋ be 動詞＋**副詞**＋分詞（be 動詞／分詞可拆開）

例如：He is reading the newspaper **loudly**.

= He is **loudly** reading the newspaper.

他正大聲地讀報。

三、其他：

1. 放在所修飾的形容詞或副詞前，例如：

It is **really** important.　這真的重要。

The tree grows **wonderfully** fast.　這樹長得快得驚人。

2. 放在句首，加強語氣，例如：

Quickly the soldier picked up the gun.　那士兵迅速拿起槍。

💬 圖解文法一看就懂 💬

情狀副詞的位置：

句中

句尾

S.＋**副詞**＋V.＋O.（受詞）
S.＋V.＋**副詞**＋介系詞＋O.
S.＋ be 動詞＋**副詞**＋V.-ing / p.p.
S.＋V.＋**副詞**（沒有受詞）

S.＋V.＋O.（受詞）＋**副詞**
S.＋V.＋介系詞＋O.＋**副詞**
S.＋ be 動詞＋V.-ing / p.p.＋**副詞**

Unit
01

形容詞轉為情狀副詞之規則

💬 例句現身說法好清楚 💬

1. She sings the songs **happily**.　　她快樂地唱著歌曲。
= She **happily** sings the songs. → **sings 和 the songs 不可拆開**
2. They **listen to** the teacher **carefully**.　　他們仔細地聽老師説。
= They **carefully** listen to the teacher.
= They listen **carefully** to the teacher. → **listen to 可以拆開**
3. The boys are playing baseball **happily**.　　男孩們正快樂地打著棒球。
= The boys are **happily** playing baseball. → **are playing 可以拆開**
4. The boys play **happily**.　　男孩們快樂地嬉戲。
≠ The boys happily play. (x)

💬 馬上演練好實力 💬

選選看：請從選項中選出符合題目的答案

(　　) 1. He learns Japanese _____.
　　　　(A) quick　　(B) quickly　　(C) easy　　(D) happy

(　　) 2. The _____ woman cries _____.

    (A) sad; sadly　(B) sadly; sad　　(C) sad; sad　　(D) sadly; sadly

(　　) 3. This is an _____ question. The student answers it _____.

    (A) easy; easy　(B) easily; easy　(C) easy; easily　(D) ease; easy

(　　) 4. He is sitting _____ on the sofa and reads novels happily.

    (A) comfortable　　　　　　(B) comfortablely

    (C) comfortablly　　　　　　(D) comfortably

(　　) 5. The worker is putting the china into the box _____.

    (A) care　　　(B) carefuly　　(C) careful　　(D) carefully

(　　) 6. He is _____. He received me _____ when I visited him.

    (A) cold ; cold　(B) coldly ; coldly　(C) cold ; coldly　(D) coldly ; cold

(　　) 7. It snowed _____ all night.

    (A) heavily　　(B) heavy　　　(C) safely　　(D) clearly

(　　) 8. He _____ well last night.

    (A) not feel　　(B) didn't feel　　(C) not felt　　(D) didn't felt

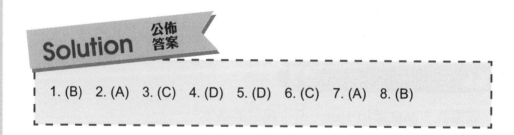

Solution 公佈答案

1. (B)　2. (A)　3. (C)　4. (D)　5. (D)　6. (C)　7. (A)　8. (B)

今日重點回顧筆記

一定要練習寫下來！才能確定自己真的會了喔！

1. 情狀副詞通常在形容詞後面加上_____。
2. good（好的）的副詞型式為特殊變化成_____（好地）。
3. 副詞的位置需特別注意：動詞直接加受詞，需將副詞放在動詞_____或放在句尾。

試判斷以下句子是否正確？錯誤的請更正為正確句子。

A. The foreigner can speak Chinese good.

....

B. He looked cold at us.

....

C. They are carefully moving the desks.

....

Unit 01

形容詞轉為情狀副詞之規則

正確答案：

1. ly　2. well　3. 前面

A. The foreigner can speak Chinese well.
　　這裡的「好」是要形容動詞「speak」，所以用副詞「well」而非形容詞「good」。

B. He looked coldly at us.
　　這裡的「冷」是要形容動詞「look」，所以用副詞「coldly」而非形容詞「cold」。

C. 正確

Unit 02 頻率副詞

一、何謂頻率副詞

文法觀念說給你聽

頻率副詞：

表示事情發生次數之多寡，如：always（總是）、usually（經常）、sometimes（有時）、seldom（不常）、once a week（一週一次）、twice a year（一年兩次）等。

圖解文法一看就懂

肯定

always（總是）
100%
usually（通常）
70 ～ 80%
often（常常）
50%
sometimes（有時候）
20～30%

否定

seldom / rarely
（很少；幾乎不）
10%
never（從未）
0%

例句現身說法好清楚

1. Fred **always** gets up early, so he **never** goes to school late.
   弗雷德總是早起，因此他從未上學遲到。

2. It is **sometimes** warm and **sometimes** cold.　天氣時熱時冷。

3. She **seldom** showed her feelings.　她很少表露感情。

二、頻率副詞的位置與用法

❝ 文法口訣輕鬆記 ❞　◀ *Track 021*

1. **be V. / 助 V. 好可怕，頻率副詞躲後面**
2. **簡答、簡寫，我不怕，頻率副詞跑前面**
3. **打遍天下一般動詞無敵手**

1. **be V.、助 V. 好可怕，頻率副詞躲後面**
   be V.、助 V. 比較大，頻率副詞通常放在它們後面。

2. **簡答、簡寫，我不怕，頻率副詞跑前面**
   若為簡答或簡寫，頻率副詞跑到 be V.、助 V. 的前面。

3. **打遍天下一般動詞無敵手**
   頻率副詞一律放在一般動詞的前面。

❝ 文法觀念說給你聽 ❞

頻率副詞的位置通常如下列：

一、在 be V.、助 V. 之後：

例 1：I am **always** early. 我總是很早到。

例 2：I don't **usually** go to work by bus. 我不常搭公車去上班。

二、簡答、簡寫時，變成在 be V.、助 V. 之前：

例 1：Yes, I **usually** am. 是，我通常是。

例 2：Yes, I **usually** do.　是，我通常是。

三、頻率副詞一律在一般 V. 之前：

例如：I **always** go to school early. 我總是很早去學校。

66 圖解文法一看就懂 99

一般用法　　　　　　　　　　　簡答、簡寫

 +

66 例句現身說法好清楚 99

1. He **is always** happy on weekends.　他週末總是很快樂。

2. She **usually writes** a letter to her parents once a month.
   她通常一個月寫一次信給她的父母親。

注意：頻率副詞不會影響第三人稱單數 V. ＋ s

3. Do you **ever** read this novel?　你曾經看過這本小說嗎？

   No, **never**.　不，從來沒有。

   No, I **never do**.　不，我從沒有看過。

注意：簡答時頻率副詞在助 V. 之前

4. **Are** you **usually** late for school? → Yes, I **usually am**.

＝ **Do** you **usually go** to school late? → Yes, I **usually do**.
   你經常上學遲到嗎？ → 是的，我通常是。

5. **How often** do you go to Taipei?　你多常去台北？

→ Twice a month.　每個月兩次。

注意：問句需用How often ～ ?

補充：頻率副詞的特殊用法

一、sometimes 的用法與位置：

1. She **sometimes** comes to visit us.　她有時來拜訪我們。

＝ **Sometimes** she comes to visit us.

＝ She comes to visit us **sometimes**.

注意：sometimes 放在句中／句首／句尾皆可。

2. 比較有 **and** 和 **but** 時的不同用法

I **sometimes** go to work by bus, and **sometimes** by car.

我有時搭公車上班，有時開車。

I **usually** go to work by bus, but **sometimes** by car.

我通常搭公車上班，但有時開車。

二、not always 為部份否定，不等於 never：

例如： She **doesn't always** go to work by bus; she **sometimes** goes
　　　 there by MRT.　她並非總是搭公車上班；她有時候搭捷運。

三、never、seldom 同為否定：

例如：I **never** go to school by bus, and **seldom** go by bicycle.
　　　　我從未搭公車上學也很少騎腳踏車去。

注意：and 兩邊須連接同樣代表否定的副詞。

四、「祈使句」開頭只可用 Always、Never 這兩個頻率副詞：

例 1.：**Always** be on time.　務必準時。

例 2.：**Never** be late.　絕不可遲到。→ **語氣較 Don't be late. 強烈**

五、very often 只可放句尾：

例如：He goes to Taipei on business **very often**.
　　　　他很常到台北出差。

六、需放在 ought to 之間：

例如：You **ought often to** write to your mother.
　　　　你應該常寫信給你母親。

Unit
02

頻
率
副
詞

Unit
02

率頻副詞

馬上演練好實力

選選看：請從選項中選出符合題目的答案

(　　) 1. He _____ the violin when he is free.
    (A) play usually   (B) plays usually
    (C) usually plays   (D) usually play

(　　) 2. He _____ late for piano class.
    (A) is never   (B) never is   (C) are never   (D) never are

(　　) 3. Does she usually get up early? Yes, she _____.
    (A) usually is   (B) is usually   (C) does usually   (D) usually does

(　　) 4. Are you often busy on weekend? Yes, I _____.
    (A) often do   (B) often am   (C) am often   (D) do often

(　　) 5. We always finish our work on time; we are _____ late.
    (A) always   (B) usually   (C) often   (D) never

(　　) 6. Have you ever traveled to Canada? No, _____.
    (A) always   (B) sometimes   (C) often   (D) never

(　　) 7. We usually have dinner at home, but _____ we eat out.
    (A) always   (B) usually   (C) sometimes   (D) never

(　　) 8. _____ do you visit your grandparents?
    (A) How   (B) How often   (C) How much   (D) How many

Solution 公佈答案

1. (C)   2. (A)   3. (D)   4. (B)   5. (D)   6. (D)   7. (C)   8. (B)

今日重點回顧筆記

一定要練習寫下來！才能確定自己真的會了喔！

1. 頻率副詞的位置通常放在be動詞之＿＿＿＿／一般動詞之＿＿＿＿。
2. 簡答或簡寫時，頻率動詞一律在be動詞和一般動詞之＿＿＿＿。
3. 頻率副詞不會影響到三人稱單數動詞+＿＿＿＿。

Unit 02

頻率副詞

試判斷以下句子是否正確？錯誤的請更正為正確句子。

A. We never are late for work.

....

B. He usually do homework carefully, but I do seldom.

....

C. They don't always get up early.

....

正確答案：

1.後／前　2. 前　3. s

A. We are never late for work.
　頻率副詞放在be動詞的後面比較好。

B. He usually does homework carefully, but I seldom do.
　he是第三人稱單數，相對地後面接的動詞就該用does。而頻率
　副詞總是出現在一般動詞的前面，所以要說I seldom do而非I do
　seldom。

C. 正確

Chapter 05

Test

想大喊小姐好正怎能不學形容詞和副詞──
綜合測驗篇

🔰 形容詞和副詞觀念選選看 🔰

( ) 1. My brother can speak English _____.

    (A) good   (B) well   (C) goodly   (D) friendly

( ) 2. Grandpa is _____ sitting on the armchair.

    (A) comfortable   (B) comfortablely (C) comfortably (D) comfortablly

( ) 3. Listen _____ to me, please.

    (A) carefully   (B) careful   (C) carefuly   (D) care

( ) 4. The tickets to the concert are not _____ bought.

    (A) easy   (B) hardly   (C) difficult   (D) easily

( ) 5. How _____ do you go to a movie? Every month.

    (A) usually   (B) often   (C) always   (D) sometimes

( ) 6. He never goes to school late, but I _____.

    (A) am usually (B) usually do (C) usually am (D) do usually

( ) 7. Sometimes she goes there by bus; and _____ by MRT.

    (A) never   (B) seldom   (C) sometimes (D) always

( ) 8. I don't always get up early; I _____ get up late.

    (A) often   (B) never   (C) usually   (D) sometimes

🔰 劃線錯誤處，請改成正確文法 🔰

1. They are moving slowly the heavy table. _____

2. She seldom go to a ball game. _____

3. He can run very fastly. _____

4. We <u>usually are</u> early to school. _____

5. Do you ever go to that restaurant? No, I <u>do never</u>. _____

6. Never <u>is</u> late. _____

7. How <u>usually</u> does she go to the supermarket? Once a week. _____

8. He <u>goes sometimes</u> to school late. _____

66 閱讀測驗 99

My mother **is always** busy. During the day, she sits in front of the computer and writes stories for children. Mom **always says** that writing is the most important thing in her life. She enjoys it a lot and also gets paid for her writing. <u>That</u> makes her happy because she has three daughters to bring up.

Mom **always tries** to finish her writing before we get back in the evening. By doing so, she has more time to be with us. Mom loves talking and reading with us, but she hates cooking and cleaning. So we have learned how to do housework since we were very young.

Mom **is always** busy writing and taking care of us, but she **is always** smiling. To me, my mother is the most beautiful woman in the world.

【基測 96-1】

(   ) 1. What does the writer try to say in the reading?

    (A) Her mother is a busy but happy woman.

    (B) She hopes to be a writer like her mother.

    (C) She should study harder to make her mother happy.

    (D) Her mother should learn how to use the computer better.

(   ) 2. Which is true about the writer's mother?

       (A) She is seldom at home.

       (B) She usually writes at night.

       (C) She doesn't like to do housework.

       (D) She enjoys playing computer games.

(   ) 3. What does "<u>That</u>" mean in the reading?

       (A) Getting paid for her writing.

       (B) Sitting in front of the computer.

       (C) Having three daughters to bring up.

       (D) Being the most beautiful woman in the world.

〝〝句子重組測驗〞〞

1. to school / Jack / because he / ran / was / late / quickly

_____

2. will / I / do / never / that

_____

3. talks / me / to / seldom / She

_____

4. sad / sadly / and / They / look at / me / are

_____

5. be / questions / Don't / asking / afraid / of

_____

6. usually / I / a cup of / drink / in the morning / coffee

_____

7. shows / Jim / feelings / his / seldom

_____

8. sits / happily / comfortably / He / and watches / TV / on the sofa

_____

9. is / comfortable / This / couch

_____

10. school / ? / usually / you / baseball / after / play / Do

_____

中翻英測驗

1. Melody 常穿紅色洋裝。

   Melody _____ wears a red dress.

2. 他通常戴著一頂棒球帽。

   He _____ wears a baseball cap.

3. 他安靜地走進教室。

   He entered the classroom _____.

4. 他並非總是在家裡吃午餐。

   He _____ _____ eat lunch at home.

5. 有時 Tina 在早上彈鋼琴。

   _____ Tina plays the piano in the morning.

6. 他星期三總是在圖書館裡。

   _____

7. 請仔細確認答案。

   _____

8. 他們在公園裡玩得很開心。

   _____

9. 那些書很重。

   _____

10. 貝蒂唱歌很好聽。

   _____

Chapter 05 〈Solution

想大喊小姐好正怎能不學形容詞和副詞——
解答篇

" 形容詞和副詞觀念選選看 "

1. (B)　　　2. (C)　　　3. (A)　　　4. (D)
5. (B)　　　6. (B)　　　7. (C)　　　8. (D)

" 劃線錯誤處，請改成正確文法 "

1. are slowly moving　　2. goes　　3. fast　　4. are usually
5. never do　　　　　　6. be　　7. often　8. sometimes goes

" 閱讀測驗 "

1. (A)　2. (C)　3. (A)

　　我的母親一直都很忙碌，她每天坐在電腦前面幫小朋友寫故事。我母親一直說寫作在她生命裡是對她來說最重要的事。她樂在其中，並且寫作也是她賺錢的方法之一。那使她很快樂，因為她必須要扶養三個小孩。

　　母親一直試著在我們下課前把她的寫作給完成，因為這樣她就會有比較多的時間來陪伴我們。母親喜歡與我們聊天和跟我一起看書，但她很不喜歡下廚跟打掃家裡。所以在我們年紀非常小的時候我們就一定要學會如何做家事。

　　母親一直忙碌於寫作與照顧我們，但她永遠都保持著微笑。對我來說，我母親是這世界上最美麗的女人。

" 句子重組測驗 "

1. Jack ran to school quickly because he was late.
　（傑克迅速跑向學校，因為他遲到了。）

2. I will never do that.（我絕不會那麼做。）

3. She seldom talks to me.（她很少和我交談。）

4. They are sad and look at me sadly.（他們很悲哀並且傷心地看我。）

5. Don't be afraid of asking questions.（不要害怕問問題。）

6. I usually drink a cup of coffee in the morning.

（我通常早晨喝一杯咖啡。）

7. Jim seldom shows his feelings.（吉姆很少表現他的感情。）

8. He sits on the sofa comfortably and watches TV happily.

（他舒適地坐在沙發上，愉快地看著電視。）

9. This couch is comfortable.（這沙發很舒適。）

10. Do you usually play baseball after school?

（放學後你通常打棒球嗎？）

中翻英測驗

1. often

2. usually

3. quietly

4. doesn't / always

5. Sometimes

6. He is always in the library on Wednesdays.

7. Please check the answer carefully.

8. They played in the park happily.

9. Those books are very heavy.

10. Betty can sing beautifully.

Chapter06 / *Clause*

句子的攣生兄弟叫子句

本篇子句的學習重點如下：

Unit 01 子句基本觀念

❝ 文法口訣輕鬆記 ❞ ◀ *Track 022*

> **1. 你一句，我一句**
> **2. 連接詞，牽紅線，兩句變一句**

1. 你一句，我一句

　　前面一個句子，後面另一個句子，共兩句。

2. 連接詞，牽紅線，兩句變一句

　　兩個句子須透過連接詞當媒人婆牽紅線，才
　　可結合成一句。

❝ 文法觀念說給你聽 ❞

先認識什麼是「子句」？

一、子句的種類：

1. 對等子句：由對等連接詞 and, or, but... 所引導的子句。

2. 從屬子句：由從屬連接詞 when, after, before, who, which, where, that,
　　　　　　　if... 所引導的子句。

＊從屬子句亦稱為次要子句，不能單獨存在；需與另一句子（主要子句）
　共用，以表示完整的意思。

＊本單元討論對等子句和副詞子句，而形容詞子句、名詞子句將後述於
　Part 2 的進階子句。

二、子句的用法：

　　兩個句子結合成一句，必須透過一個連接詞來連結，不可以沒有連接詞。但需注意不可以同時用兩個連接詞，例如：

Because（因為）..., so（所以）... (x) 不可連用

Though（雖然）..., but（但是）... (x) 不可連用

❝ 圖解文法一看就懂 ❞

Unit
01
子句基本觀念

句子＋連接詞＋句子，分成兩大類：

第一類　　　　　　　　　　第二類

從屬子句：
1. 副詞子句
2. 形容詞子句
　（關係子句）
3. 名詞子句

對等子句

❝ 例句現身說法好清楚 ❞

1. I am fifteen**, and** my brother is ten.　　我十五歲，我的弟弟十歲。

→ I am fifteen; my brother is ten. → **在此可用「 ; 」代替「, and」**

2. It is hot in summer here, **but** it is not cold in winter.

　這裡夏天熱，但冬天不冷。

3. I began to learn English **when** I was nine.　　我九歲時開始學英語。

4. The manager was ill, **so** I went in her place.

　因為經理病了，所以我代替她去。

→ **Because** the manager was ill, I went in her place.

注意：不可寫成 **Because** the manager was ill, **so** I went in her place.

Unit 01

子句基本觀念

馬上演練好實力

選選看：請從選項中選出符合題目的答案

( ) 1. Hurry up, _____ we will miss the bus.

    (A) X   (B) or   (C) because   (D) so

( ) 2. He likes jogging _____ I like swimming.

    (A) so   (B) or   (C) after   (D) ；

( ) 3. Get up early, _____ you can catch the first bus.

    (A) and   (B) so   (C) before   (D) X

( ) 4. _____ Tom was sick, _____ he didn't go to school today.

    (A) Because / so   (B) Because / X

    (C) Because / and   (D) X / X

( ) 5. I'm sorry, _____ I can't go shopping with you.

    (A) when   (B) but   (C) so   (D) or

( ) 6. She took a bath _____ she went to bed.

    (A) , so   (B) ,   (C) but   (D) , and then

( ) 7. _____ it is too late, I have to go home.

    (A) X   (B) So   (C) Or   (D) Because

( ) 8. Though he is not clever, _____ he studies hard.

    (A) and   (B) but   (C) X   (D) so

Solution 公佈答案

1. (B)　2. (D)　3. (A)　4. (B)　5. (B)　6. (D)　7. (D)　8. (C)

今日重點回顧筆記

一定要練習寫下來！才能確定自己真的會了喔！

1. 兩個句子需用一個_____詞做連結，不可同時用兩個。
2. 子句通常分成_____子句和從屬子句兩大類。
3. 從屬子句又可分成副詞子句、形容詞子句和_____子句。

試判斷以下句子是否正確？錯誤的請更正為正確句子。

A. He studies hard, but his brother doesn't.

....

B. Because she was late, so she took a taxi there.

....

C. Though he was sick, but he still went to work.

....

Unit
01

子句基本觀念

正確答案：

1. 連接　　2. 對等　　3. 名詞
A. 正確
B. Because she was late, she took a taxi there.
　　Because 和so都是連接詞，不可同時使用。
C. Though he was sick, he still went to work.
　　Though和but都是連接詞，不可同時使用。

Unit 02 對等子句的用法

文法觀念說給你聽

　　「對等子句」就是由對等連接詞（and / or / but...等）連接而成的句子，與主要子句文法功能相當，無主從之分。有些不同的用法須和副詞子句仔細分辨，下個單元會另做詳述。

　　例如： Tina works hard, **and the teacher likes her very much.**

　　→ Tina 很認真，而且老師很喜歡她。

圖解文法一看就懂

對等子句的結構：

例句現身說法好清楚

1. Hurry up, **and** we can catch the train.
   快一點，那麼我們就可以趕上火車。

2. Study hard, **or** you won't pass the exam.
   用功點讀書，否則你將不會通過考試。

3. He had milk this morning, **but** I didn't.

   他今天早上喝了牛奶，但我沒有。

4. Amy can cook, **but** I can't.　　艾咪會煮飯，但我不會。

5. I saw it with my own eyes, **but (yet)** I couldn't believe it.

   我親眼看到，然而我仍不相信。

6. He must be sick, **for** he looks pale.

   他必定是生病了，因為他臉色看起來蒼白。

注意：for 為對等連接詞，前面需有逗號；而 because 則為副詞連接詞。

馬上演練好實力

選選看：請從選項中選出符合題目的答案

(　　) 1. Hurry up, _____ you will be late for school.

　　(A) or 　　　(B) and 　　　(C) but 　　　(D) so

(　　) 2. He likes jogging, _____ I don't.

　　(A) so 　　　(B) or 　　　(C) and 　　　(D) but

(　　) 3. Get up early, _____ you can catch the bus.

　　(A) and 　　　(B) so 　　　(C) but 　　　(D) or

(　　) 4. Get up early, _____ you'll miss the train.

　　(A) so 　　　(B) but 　　　(C) or 　　　(D) and

(　　) 5. I'm sorry, _____ I can't play basketball with you.

　　(A) and 　　　(B) but 　　　(C) so 　　　(D) or

(　　) 6. She did homework, _____ then she watched TV.

　　(A) but 　　　(B) so 　　　(C) or 　　　(D) and

Unit
02

對等子句的用法

(   ) 7. Take a coat, _____ you will get a cold.

       (A) and   (B) but   (C) or   (D) so

(   ) 8. A: Would you like to go swimming with us?

       B: I'd like to, _____ I have a piano class.

       (A) and   (B) but   (C) or   (D) so

Unit 02

對等子句的用法

Solution 公佈答案

1. (A)   2. (D)   3. (A)   4. (C)   5. (B)   6. (D)   7. (C)   8. (B)

Note 筆記手札

有沒有不太熟悉的文法觀念呢？有的話就把它
們寫在這裡，之後多做幾次複習吧！加油！

今日重點回顧筆記

一定要練習寫下來！才能確定自己真的會了喔！

1. 常見表示相反的連接詞為yet /＿＿＿＿＿。
2. 「對等子句」就是由＿＿＿＿＿連接而成的句子。

試判斷以下句子是否正確？錯誤的請更正為正確句子。

A. Hurry up, or you will miss the bus.

....

B. He got up late, so he was late for work today.

....

C. He must be sick, but he looks terrible.

....

Unit
02

對等子句的用法

正確答案：

1. but　2. 對等連接詞
A. 正確
B. 正確
C. He must be sick, for he looks terrible.
　「生病」和「看起來糟糕」兩件事並不衝突，反而有因果關
　係，所以不該用表示「但是」意思的but，而該用表示「所
　以」意思的for。

Unit 03 副詞子句的用法

❝ 文法口訣輕鬆記 ❞　🔊 Track 023

> 1. 副詞子句，動詞跟著主要走
> 2. 你過去，我過去 / 你現在，我現在
> 3. 你未來，我用現在換未來！

1. 副詞子句，動詞跟著主要走

　　副詞子句其動詞時態之使用，須跟著主要子句的動詞做變化。

2. 你過去，我過去 / 你現在，我現在

　　主要子句是過去式，副詞子句即為過去式；
　　主要子句是現在式，副詞子句即為現在式。

3. 你未來，我用現在換未來！

　　主要子句是未來式，注意：副詞子句沒有未
　　來式，須用現在式替代。

❝ 文法觀念說給你聽 ❞

想學會副詞子句的用法，除了學習連接詞之外，最重要的是注意動詞時態的搭配使用。

一、副詞子句中常見的連接詞：

when (as / while)（當……時）	after（……之後）
before（……之前）	if（假如）

because（因為）	although / though（雖然）
until（直到……）	as long as（只要）
as soon as（一……就……）	unless（除非）

二、副詞子句的動詞時態搭配：

副詞子句的時態大都要跟主要子句的時態相同。唯一例外：副詞子句沒有未來式，需用現在式代替，例如：

When he come**s** tomorrow, I **will** tell him the truth.

當他明天來的時候，我將告訴他這個事實。

注意：副詞子句不可因為有 tomorrow 而使用未來式，需用現在式。

圖解文法一看就懂

一、副詞子句和主要子句的差別

副詞子句　　　　　　　主要子句

由副詞連接詞引導　　　不須連接詞

這些都是副詞連接詞： when / after / before / if / because / (al)though / until / unless / as long as / as soon as

二、「副詞子句」和「主要子句」的動詞時態

副詞子句　　　　　　　主要子句

過去（進行）式
現在式
現在式

過去（進行）式
現在式
未來式

Unit
03

副詞子句的用法

〔〔 例句現身說法好清楚 〕〕

1. Vicky usually watches TV **after** she does her homework.
   薇琪寫完功課之後通常會看電視。

= **After** Vicky does her homework, she usually watches TV.

注意： after～此副詞子句前面不須加逗號和主要子句隔開。

2. **After** I had dinner, I washed the dishes.　吃完晚餐後，我去洗碗。

= **After** having dinner, I washed the dishes.

注意： 主詞需是同一人，才可以省略。

3. **Before** we got to the train station, the train left.
   在我們抵達火車站之前，火車開走了。

注意： 前後句主詞不同，不可以省略主詞。

4. **When** I visited Helen yesterday, she was having dinner.
   昨天我拜訪海倫時，她正在吃晚餐。

注意： 也可以用過去進行式來強調當時動作的進行。

5. She did **not** go to bed **until** her daughter came back.
   她一直等到女兒回來才去睡覺。

注意： not...until... 須翻譯成「直到……才……」。

6. **Because** she was sick, she was absent.　因為生病，所以她缺席了。

→ She was sick, **so** she was absent.

注意： 用了 because 就不可再用連接詞 so。

Unit
03

副詞子句的用法

7. **Although** (Though) it rained heavily, they still went out for dinner.

　　雖然下大雨，但他們仍然出去吃晚餐。

→ It rained heavily, **but** they still went out for dinner.

注意：用了 although 就不可再用連接詞 but，但可配用副詞 still。

8. **If** it rains tomorrow, I will stay at home.　　假如明天下雨，我就要待在家。

注意：副詞子句沒有未來式，需用現在式代替；並注意第三人稱單數動詞
　　　　＋ s。

9. **As long as** you study hard, you can get good grades.

　　只要用功，你就可以得到好成績。

馬上演練好實力

選選看：請從選項中選出符合題目的答案

(　　) 1. After he _____ medicine, he felt dizzy.

　　　　(A) is taking　　(B) take　　　(C) takes　　　　(D) took

(　　) 2. After she _____ breakfast, she went to school.

　　　　(A) eat　　　　(B) ate　　　　(C) eats　　　　　(D) is eating

(　　) 3. When he came to my home, I _____.

　　　　(A) was studying　　　　　(B) study

　　　　(C) studies　　　　　　　(D) studying

(　　) 4. She _____ when I called her last night.

　　　　(A) sleep　　(B) sleeps　　(C) was sleeping　(D) slept

(　　) 5. Although she was sick, _____ she still went to school today.

　　　　(A) and　　　　(B) but　　　　(C) or　　　　　(D) X

Unit
03

副詞子句的用法

(   ) 6. Before _____ my uncle, I make a phone call to him.

       (A) visiting   (B) visit   (C) visited   (D) visits

(   ) 7. When spring _____, the snow will melt.

       (A) come   (B) will come   (C) comes   (D) came

(   ) 8. If it _____ tomorrow, we won't go picnicking.

       (A) is raining   (B) rain   (C) rained   (D) rains

Unit 03

副詞子句的用法

Solution 公佈答案

1. (D)   2. (B)   3. (A)   4. (C)   5. (D)   6. (A)   7. (C)   8. (D)

Note 筆記手札

有沒有不太熟悉的文法觀念呢？有的話就把它
們寫在這裡，之後多做幾次複習吧！加油！

今日重點回顧筆記

一定要練習寫下來！才能確定自己真的會了喔！

1. 副詞子句是用＿＿＿＿＿＿＿連結而成。
2. 副詞子句的動詞時式通常須跟著＿＿＿＿＿＿＿做變化。
3. 需特別注意副詞子句沒有＿＿＿＿＿式，需用現在式代替。

試判斷以下句子是否正確？錯誤的請更正為正確句子。

A. Her daughter didn't come back until eleven o'clock.

....

B. If it will rain tomorrow, we will cancel the picnic.

....

C. After did my homework, Mom asked me to go to bed.

....

Unit
03

副詞子句的用法

正確答案：

1. 副詞連接詞　2. 主要子句　　3. 未來

A. 正確

B. If it rains tomorrow, we will cancel the picnic.
　　副詞子句是不能用未來式的，所以要把will rain改成rains。

C. After I did my homework, Mom asked me to go to bed.
　　不說出是誰做了功課可不行，所以別忘了I。

Chapter 06

Test

句子的孿生兄弟叫子句──綜合測驗篇

66 子句觀念選選看 99

( ) 1. She didn't go to work _____ she was very sick.

   (A) so   (B) because   (C) before   (D) but

( ) 2. _____ it rained hard, we still went out.

   (A) Because   (B) Though   (C) Before   (D) Unless

( ) 3. Go down the street, _____ you can see the bakery on your right.

   (A) and   (B) but   (C) yet   (D) or

( ) 4. _____ you help me, I can finish the work on time.

   (A) As soon as (B) Although   (C) As long as (D) Until

( ) 5. _____ I go to bed, I always brush my teeth.

   (A) After   (B) Because   (C) Before   (D) Although

( ) 6. They didn't go to bed _____ their daughter came back.

   (A) because   (B) but   (C) so   (D) until

( ) 7. Get up early, _____ you will miss the first train tomorrow morning.

   (A) or   (B) but   (C) before   (D) so

( ) 8. If it _____ tomorrow, I will stay at home.

   (A) rain   (B) rains   (C) will rain   (D) rained

66 劃線錯誤處，請改成正確文法 99

1. After did my homework, I ate dinner with my family. _____

2. My brother was sick because he didn't go to school this morning. _____

3. Although he is poor, but he works hard. _____

4. When he will come tomorrow, I will tell him the truth. _____

5. Follow the tips, <u>but</u> you can be a good learner. _____

6. <u>Though</u> it is very late, we have to go home now. _____

7. As <u>long</u> as I got home, it started to rain heavily. _____

8. I'm sorry, <u>and</u> I can't help you this time. _____

66 閱讀測驗 99

　　Weight control is very popular these days. People hope to become thin quickly. Some even take medicine without a doctor's prescription. But reports show that **although many of them do lose weight,** they soon gain it back **or** gain even more.

　　So how can you safely control your weight? Diet and exercise are the answers. Eat only **when you are hungry** and eat only food that is good for your health. Never just stop eating; doing so can make you feel even hungrier, **and** you will eat more. Also, it is better to prepare your own food instead of eating out. **And** think about changing your lifestyle. For example, turn off the TV **and** the computer **and** get some exercise every day. **But** remember: Don't be strict with yourself. Give yourself some time to find the best way to control your weight.

【基測 93-1】

(　　) 1. Which is the best title for the reading?

(A) Medicine for Losing Weight.

(B) Tops for Losing Weight Quickly.

(C) Why People Need Weight Control.

(D) Safe Ways to Control One's Weight.

(　　) 2. According to the writer, what happens to people who take medicine to lose weight?

　　(A) They feel unhappy about eating.

　　(B) Many of them put on weight again.

　　(C) They cannot concentrate on their work.

　　(D) Most of them lose too much weight and get sick.

(　　) 3. What does "Don't be strict with yourself" mean in the reading?

　　(A) Eat anything you like when you feel unhappy.

　　(B) Never try to lose weight in a way that is too difficult.

　　(C) Try to relax by watching TV or playing computer games.

　　(D) Don't feel bad if you have spent a lot of money trying to lose weight.

❝句子重組測驗❞

1. father / My / was / busy / went / ,so / I / home / on my own

_____

2. I / with paper / cover my desk / always / I / have / when / lunch

_____

3. will / leave / after / I / they / tell you / the story

_____

4. she / left / she / the light / the room / As / turned off

_____

5. you / come / He / him / if / invite / will

_____

6. man / rich / , but / he / happy / The / is not / old / is

_____

7. he / ill / , / he / Although / hard / was / worked / still

_____

8. was / when / Vivian / her / dancing / saw / I

_____

9. when / It / started to / there / we / rain / got

_____

10. you / As long as / work / , / you / succeed / hard / will

_____

中翻英測驗

1. Sandy 喜歡紅色，但我不喜歡。

   Sandy loves red, _____ I don't.

2. 右轉，你就可以看到一座教堂。

   Turn right _____ you'll see a church.

3. 快一點，否則你會遲到。

   Hurry up, _____ you will be late.

4. Raymond 雖然很聰明但不用功讀書。

   _____ Raymond is clever, he doesn't study hard.

5. Eva 沒有來上學，因為她生病了。

   Eva didn't come to school _____ she was sick.

6. 在妳嘗試之前不要輕易放棄。

   _____

7. 人太多的時候，Fanny 很容易感到頭疼。

   _____

8. 如果明天下雨，我們就會取消野餐。

   _____

9. Jason 生病所以缺席。

   _____

10. Lily 大學畢業之後，她就出國了。

    _____

Chapter 06

Solution

句子的孿生兄弟叫子句——解答篇

66 子句觀念選選看 99

1. (B)   2. (B)   3. (A)   4. (C)
5. (C)   6. (D)   7. (A)   8. (B)

66 劃線錯誤處，請改成正確文法 99

1. doing   2. , so   3. 去掉 but   4. comes
5. and   6. Because   7. soon   8. but

66 閱讀測驗 99

1. (D)   2. (B)   3. (B)

　　近來，體重控制是一件很熱門的事。人們希望能快速地瘦下來，有些人甚至會吃沒經過醫生處方的瘦身藥。但報告顯示，雖然這些人的確體重都變輕了，但他們復胖的速度很快甚至還變得比以前更重了。

　　所以你要怎樣安全地減重呢？控制飲食跟運動是最好的答案。只在你餓的時候進食，此外也只吃對身體有好處的食物。千萬不要不吃東西；如果這樣做的話只會讓你自己更餓，那會讓你吃得更多。還有，自己準備吃的比出去外面吃來的好。更要想一想如何把自己的生活步調改變一下，例如，每天盡量多做些運動而不要看電視或玩電腦。但請記得：別對自己太過嚴格。給自己一點時間來找出控制自己體重的最佳方法吧。

66 句子重組測驗 99

1. My father was busy, so I went home on my own.
（我爸爸在忙，因此我自己回家。）

2. I always cover my desk with paper when I have lunch.
（當我吃午餐時，我總是把紙鋪在桌上。）

3. I will tell you the story after they leave.

（在他們離開後，我將告訴你那個故事。）

4. As she left the room she turned off the light.

（當她離開房間時，她關了燈。）

5. He will come if you invite him.

（如果你邀請他，他將會來的。）

6. The old man is rich, but he is not happy.

（這老年人雖富有，但是他不快樂。）

7. Although he was ill, he still worked hard.

（雖然他生病，但是他仍然努力工作。）

8. Vivian was dancing when I saw her.

（當我看見 Vivian 時，她正在跳舞。）

9. It started to rain when we got there.

（當我們到達那裡時，開始下起雨了。）

10. As long as you work hard, you will succeed.

（只要你努力工作，你將會成功。）

❝中翻英測驗❞

1. but

2. and

3. or

4. Although/Though

5. because

6. Don't give up easily before you try.

7. Fanny usually has a headache when there are too many people.

8. If it rains tomorrow, we'll cancel the picnic.

9. Jason was absent because he was sick. / Jason was sick, so he was absent.

10. After Lily graduated from college, she went abroad.

Part2
進階運用篇

針對英語進階學習者（英檢中級、多益550 分以上程度）特別規劃進階運用說明，學習者們可以了解更深層的文法運用規則及使用範疇。

Chapter07 / Advanced Verbs

動詞進階版——
分詞 PP 很強大

本篇進階動詞的學習重點如下：

Unit 01 過去分詞（p.p.）的變化

Unit 02 動詞時態—現在完成式

Unit 03 被動語態的用法

TEST 動詞進階版—分詞 PP 很強大—
綜合測驗篇

Unit 01 過去分詞（p.p.）的變化

❝ 文法觀念說給你聽 ❞

學習過去分詞有幾個要點：

一、溫故知新： 大多數的過去分詞都是規則變化，且和與過去式的變化相同，因此需複習過去式的變化。

二、知易行易： 一般人把過去分詞想像得太困難了，其實它比 V-ing 還簡單，只需要在動詞原形後面＋ n / en / ne 或母音字母 I → a（過去式）→ u（過去分詞）。

三、整理歸納： 透過下列的分類解析，令人頭痛的過去分詞（p.p.）就能變得容易許多。

四、最終目的： 不要花太多時間去背 p.p.，而應該要學習它的使用方式，例如完成式、被動語態的運用。

❝ 圖解文法一看就懂 ❞

過去分詞（p.p.）的變化方式：

規則變化

不規則變化

1. 與過去式相同
2. 與現在式相同
3. 三代同堂
（三態：現在式、過去式、過去分詞同形）

1. V.＋n
2. 字尾＋ne / en
3. 重複字尾＋en
4. 字中 i → a → u
5. 特殊字
6. 易混淆字

例句現身說法好清楚

1. 過去分詞與過去式相同：

中文	現在式	過去式	過去分詞
結束	end	ended	ended
完成	finish	finished	finished
遵循	follow	followed	followed
避免	avoid	avoided	avoided
邀請	invite	invited	invited
打電話	call	called	called
研讀	study	studied	studied
睡覺	sleep	slept	slept
感覺	feel	felt	felt
花費	spend	spent	spent
建造	build	built	built
說	say	said	said
付帳	pay	paid	paid
發現	find	found	found
聽	hear	heard	heard
贏	win	won	won

2. 過去分詞與現在式相同：

中文	現在式	過去式	過去分詞
跑	run	ran	run
變得	become	became	become
來	come	came	come

Unit
01

過去分詞(p.p.)的變化

3. 三代同堂（三態同形）

中文	現在式	過去式	過去分詞
打賭	bet	bet	bet
切；剪	cut	cut	cut
適合	fit	fit	fit
打擊	hit	hit	hit
放	put	put	put
設定	set	set	set
傷害	hurt	hurt	hurt
戒除；停止	quit	quit	quit
關閉	shut	shut	shut
閱讀	read	read	read
張開；散佈	spread	spread	spread

二、不規則變化（現在式 → 過去式 → 過去分詞）

1. V. + n

(1) 現在式＋n：

中文	現在式	過去式	過去分詞
吹	**blow**	blew	blown
成長；種	**grow**	grew	grown
知道	**know**	knew	known
丟	**throw**	threw	thrown
給	**give**	gave	given
原諒	**forgive**	forgave	forgiven
拿；搭乘	**take**	took	taken
誤解	**mistake**	mistook	mistaken
搖	**shake**	shook	shaken
看見	**see**	saw	seen
上升	**rise**	rose	risen
產生	**arise**	arose	arisen

Unit 01

過去分詞(p.p.)的變化

叫醒	**wake**	woke	waken
注意：過去式的變化可參考基礎篇動詞，過去分詞（p.p.）則大多以現在式字尾＋n。			

(2) 過去式＋n：

中文	現在式	過去式	過去分詞
打破	break	**broke**	broken
說	speak	**spoke**	spoken
偷	steal	**stole**	stolen
＊現在式字尾 k+n / l+n → 無法發音，因此改用過去式+n。			
選擇	choose	**chose**	chosen

2. 字尾＋ ne / en

中文	現在式	過去式	過去分詞
走	go	went	gone
做	do	did	done
吃	eat	ate	eaten
掉落	fall	fell	fallen

3. 重複字尾＋ en

中文	現在式	過去式	過去分詞
得到	get	got	got / gotten
忘記	forget	forgot	forgot / forgotten
注意：字尾是短母音加子音，要重複子音＋en。			
咬	bite [aɪ]	bit	bitten [ɪ]
藏	hide [aɪ]	hid	hidden [ɪ]
寫	write [aɪ]	wrote	written [ɪ]
注意：過去分詞之母音已由長母音 [aɪ] 變成短母音[ɪ]，所以要重複子音＋en。			

Unit

01

過去分詞(p.p.)的變化

Unit 01

過去分詞（p.p.）的變化

4. 字中 i → a → u

中文	現在式	過去式	過去分詞
鈴響	ring	rang	rung
唱歌	sing	sang	sung
游泳	swim	swam	swum
喝	drink	drank	drunk
開始	begin	began	begun

5. 特殊字

中文	現在式	過去式	過去分詞
是	be	was / were	been
出生；孕育	bear	bore	born / borne
撕	tear	tore	torn
穿	wear	wore	wore
發誓	swear	swore	sworn

6. 易混淆字

中文	現在式	過去式	過去分詞
躺	lie	lay	lain
說謊	lie	lied	lied
照耀	shine	shone	shone
擦亮	shine	shined	shined

注意：其規則變化／不規則變化，分別代表不同的意思！

馬上演練好實力

填填看：請填入下列動詞的過去分詞（p.p.）

1. go → _____   2. buy → _____

3. build → _____   4. write → _____

5. eat → _____   6. be → _____

7. drink → _____   8. sing → _____

9. break → _____   10. give → _____

11. take → _____   12. hurt → _____

13. find → _____   14. hear → _____

15. become → _____   16. win → _____

17. study → _____   18. cut → _____

19. see → _____   20. do → _____

Unit
01

過去分詞(p.p.)的變化

Solution 公佈答案

1. gone	2. bought	3. built	4. written	5. eaten
6. been	7. drunk	8. sung	9. broken	10. given
11. taken	12. hurt	13. found	14. heard	15. become
16. won	17. studied	18. cut	19. seen	20. done

Unit 02 動詞時態——現在完成式

文法口訣輕鬆記 🔊 Track 024

> **1. 什麼叫做完成式？完成動作和經驗**
> **2. have 當作助動詞，一般動詞變 p.p.**
> **3. have 真是好幫手，否定疑問就靠它**

1. 什麼叫做完成式？完成動作和經驗

完成式通常表示動作已完成或仍在持續中，以及表示經驗都可以用完成式。

2. have 當作助動詞，一般動詞變 p.p.

完成式：have + p.p.（過去分詞），have 跟著主詞／時間作變化：have/has/had/will have + p.p.。

3. have 真是好幫手，否定疑問就靠它

可藉由助動詞 have 形成否定句：
have not + p.p.；疑問句：Have...+ p.p.?

文法觀念說給你聽

「現在完成式」表示到現在為止，已完成或仍在持續的動作、狀態或表示經歷、經驗，以 have / has + p.p. 來做時態的使用。

例 1：I **have eaten** lunch. → **已完成**
我已經吃了午餐。

例 2：I **have waited** for him for three hours. → **仍在持續**
　　　我已經等他三個小時了。

例 3：I **have been** to Japan. → **經驗**
　　　我曾經去過日本。

圖解文法一看就懂

一、現在完成式的用法：

> have / has
> 助動詞

＋

> p.p.
> 過去分詞

二、現在完成式的使用時機：

句子裡面有　　　　　　　　　　表示的意義

> already 已經
> just 剛才
> yet 尚未

> 剛完成、
> 不久

> for 一段時間
> since 自從
> so far 到目前為止
> How long?
> 多久……？

> 有一段期間、
> 仍繼續至今

> ever 曾經
> once 一次
> twice 兩次
> several times
> 好幾次

> 表經驗、
> 次數

Unit 02

動詞時態—現在完成式

Unit 02

動詞時態──現在完成式

例句現身說法好清楚

一、already（已經）/ yet（尚未）/ just（剛才）

1. I have finished the painting **already**.　我已經完成這幅畫。

＝ I have **already** finished the painting.

注意：already 用在肯定句，可放在句尾或 have 之後。

2. He hasn't read the novel **yet**.　他還沒看這本小說。

3. Have you bought a car yet? No, not **yet**.　你已經買車了嗎？不，還沒。

注意：yet 用在否定 / 疑問句，需放在句尾。

4. I have **just** got an e-mail from my cousin.

　我剛剛收到我表弟的電子郵件。

注意：just 須放在 have 之後。

二、for / since

1. We have lived here **for** ten years.　我們已經住在這裡十年了 。

＝We have lived here **since** ten years ago.

2. She has taught in London **since** 2005.

　自從 2005 年，她就在倫敦教書了。

3. They have moved to New York **since** they married.

　自從他們結婚後，他們就搬到紐約。

注意：since 後面須是過去式。

4. It has been a long time **since** you left Taiwan.

　自從你離開台灣以後，已經有一段時間。

三、經驗 / 次數

1. Have you **ever** been to a baseball game?

→ No, never. / No, I haven't. / No, I never have.

　你曾經去看過棒球比賽嗎？不，從來沒有。

注意：不可回答 No, I never.。

2. This is the most interesting movie that I have **ever** seen.

這是我曾看過最有趣的電影。

注意：ever 通常用於否定／疑問，若用於肯定句常與比較級／最高級連用。

四、have been / have gone 之比較

1. My sister **has been** to Tokyo several times. 　我姊姊**去過**東京好幾次了。

注意：表示「經驗」不可用 gone，要用 been。

2. My sister **has gone** to Tokyo already. She isn't at home now.

我姊姊**已經**去東京了。她現在不在家。

❝ 馬上演練好實力 ❞

選選看：請從選項中選出符合題目的答案

(　　) 1. She _____ the letter already.

    (A) is wrote　(B) is written　(C) has written　(D) has wrote

(　　) 2. Terry _____ breakfast yet.

    (A) eats　　(B) ate　　(C) has eaten　　(D) hasn't eaten

(　　) 3. She _____ ballet for five years.

    (A) learned　(B) has learned (C) is learned　(D) is learning

(　　) 4. We _____ friends since childhood.

    (A) has been (B) have been　(C) are been　(D) were been

(　　) 5. Jo has studied abroad since he _____ from high school.

    (A) graduates (B) graduated the　(C) graduated (D) graduating

(　　) 6. How long _____ the report?

    (A) has he finished　　　　(B) did he finished

    (C) is he finished　　　　　(D) is he finishing

Unit 02

動詞時態—現在完成式

( ) 7. Joanna _____ to Paris twice.

    (A) has gone   (B) is going

    (C) has been   (D) is been

( ) 8. Joanna _____ to Paris. She isn't here now.

    (A) has gone   (B) is going

    (C) has been   (D) is been

Unit 02

動詞時態──現在完成式

Solution 公佈答案

1. (C)   2. (D)   3. (B)   4. (B)   5. (C)   6. (A)   7. (C)   8. (A)

筆記手札 **N**ote

有沒有不太熟悉的文法觀念呢？有的話就把它們寫在這裡，之後多做幾次複習吧！加油！

今日重點回顧筆記

一定要練習寫下來！才能確定自己真的會了喔！

1. 完成式需用have+_____（過去分詞）。
2. have在此為_____詞。
3. 否定句和疑問句以助動詞_____形成。

試判斷以下句子是否正確？錯誤的請更正為正確句子。

A. I have lived here for six years.

....

B. She doesn't have done her homework.

....

C. Has he wrote the letter yet?

....

正確答案：

1. p.p.　2. 助動　3. have
A. 正確
B. She hasn't done her homework.
　這裡的have不是「有」的意思，前面不需要加doesn't。hasn't
　done才是這句正確的用法！
C. Has he written the letter yet?
　write的過去分詞是written，不是wrote喔！

Unit
02

動詞時態──現在完成式

Unit 03 被動語態的用法

一、被動語態的使用時機 & 變化方式

『 文法口訣輕鬆記 』 Track 025

> 1. 主詞／受詞做交換，be V. 來幫忙
> 2. be be be 被 被 被，一般 V. 變 p.p.

1. 主詞／受詞做交換，be V. 來幫忙

被動語態要將主詞、受詞的位置交換，其動詞也要跟著換，且需藉由 be 動詞幫忙。

2. be be be 被 被 被，一般 V. 變 p.p.

形成被動語態，其動詞也要換成 be 動詞＋ p.p.（一般動詞的過去分詞）。

『 文法觀念說給你聽 』

　　「被動」是指主詞是動作的承受者而不是動作的發出者，在此和大家介紹其使用時機以及時態的變化：

一、被動語態的使用時機有：

1. 事物為主詞時，通常為被動。

2. 主詞／受詞位置對調時，此時人稱代名詞的「格」須做變化，像是

I（我）→ by me（被我）

She（她）→ by her（被她）

而且動詞的型態也跟著由主動變成被動：一般 V. → be V. + p.p.

例 1： I saw her → She was seen **by me**. 我看到她。→ 她**被我**看到。

例 2： She laughed at me. → I was laughed at **by her**.

她嘲笑我。→ 我**被她**嘲笑。

二、使用被動語態時，要注意 be V. 的時態變化：

1. 現在式 → am / are / is + p.p.

2. 過去式 → was / were + p.p.

例如：I did the work. → The work was done by me.

3. 未來式 → will（將）be + p.p.

4.

助動詞	can（可以）	+ be + p.p.
	must（必須）	
	should（應該）	

圖解文法一看就懂

主動變被動，用交叉相乘法！

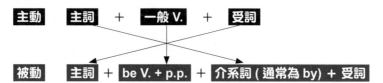

例句現身說法好清楚

1. **People** speak **English** in America.（現在式）

被動 → **English** is spoken (**by people**) in America.

在美國人們講英語。→ 英語在美國被（人們）使用。

注意：by people / by everyone / by someone 通常可省略。

Unit
03
被動語態的用法

2. **He** wrote **the letter** last night.（過去式）

被動　→ **The letter** was written **by him** last night.

他昨晚寫了一封信。　→　一封信昨晚被他寫了。

3. **She** will wash **the dishes** tomorrow.（未來式）

被動　→　**The dishes** will be washed **by her** tomorrow.

她明天將要洗碗。　→　碗明天將會被她洗。

4. Traffic rules **should always be followed**.　　交通規則應該總是被遵守。

5. The computers **can be linked**.　　電腦可以被連結。

注意：助動詞 will / should / can ＋ be ＋ p.p. 形成被動語態。

二、被動語態的否定句 & 疑問句

" 文法口訣輕鬆記 "　　🔊 *Track 026*

> 1. be、be、be，被、被、被，被動語態需要 be
> 2. 否定 / 疑問，也靠 be

1. **be、be、be，被、被、被，被動語態需要 be**
   被動語態需用 be 動詞來幫忙形成，此時 be 需翻譯成「被」，而不再當「是」。

2. **be be be 被 被 被，一般 V. 變 p.p.**
   其否定句、疑問句的造法直接參照 be 動詞的用法即可。

文法觀念說給你聽

被動語態（be V. + p.p.）的否定句和疑問句這樣造：

一、 否定句：be V. + not + p.p.，例如：

Tom did not write the letter.　湯姆沒有寫信。

→ The letter **was not written** by Tom.　信沒有被湯姆寫。

二、 疑問句：直接將 be V. 搬到主詞前，例如：

Did Tom write the letter? 湯姆寫信了嗎？

→ **Was** the letter **written** by Tom? 信被湯姆寫了嗎？

注意：將直述句改成被動句時，須將直述句的助動詞 do / does / did 換成 be 動詞 am / are / is / was / were。

Unit 03

被動語態的用法

圖解文法一看就懂

被動否定句 & 疑問句的架構

否定句

be V.＋not＋p.p.～

疑問句

be V.～＋p.p.～?

例句現身說法好清楚

一、被動否定句

1. He **doesn't write** the letters.　他沒有寫信。

被動　→ The letters **aren't written** by him.　信沒有被他寫。

2. We **didn't win** the game yesterday.　我們昨天沒有贏得比賽。

被動　→ The game **wasn't won** by us yesterday.　比賽昨天沒有被我們贏得。

二、被動疑問句

1. **Does** she clean the room?　她打掃房間嗎？

被動　→ **Is** the room clean**ed** by her?　房間是被她打掃的嗎？

2. **Did** you finish your homework?　你做完你的功課了嗎？

被動　→ **Was** your homework finish**ed** by you?　你的功課被你做完了嗎？

3. Where **did** you **buy** the books?　你在哪裡買這些書的？

被動　→ Where **were** the books **bought** by you?　這些書在哪裡被你買的？

補充：有關被動語態的延伸學習

一、難度較高的被動句型

1. **Who** cleaned the room?　誰打掃了房間？

被動　→ **By whom** was the room cleaned?

注意：Who → By whom / 被動問句 was ＋主詞（the room）＋ p.p.

2. I **saw** her take the money.　我看見她拿了錢。

被動　→ She **was seen** to have taken the money by me.

3. He **made** me wash the car.　他叫我洗車。

被動　→ I **was made** to wash the car by him.

注意：感官 V.（saw）、使役 V.（made）主動時後面省略不定詞 to，被動時須回復成 to V.。（相關用法請參考後續 to V. / V-ing 單元）

二、完成式與進行式的被動

完成式／進行式的被動看似困難，許多人會透過背公式來學習；其實不妨試試下列方法，自己導出公式，自行演練看看，相信會更有趣且有效！

1. 完成被動式

完成：have ＋ p.p.
被動：be V. ＋ p.p. ｝結合→ have ＋ **been** ＋ p.p.（已被……）

例如：My car **has been towed** away many times.

　　　我的車子已被拖吊很多次了。

2. 進行被動式

進行：be V. ＋ **V -ing**

被動：**be V.** ＋ p.p.

結合→ be V. ＋ **being** ＋ p.p.（正被……）

例如：Hurry up! Your car **is being towed** away by the police.

　　　快點！你的車正被警察拖吊。

馬上演練好實力

選選看：請從選項中選出符合題目的答案

(　　) 1. The letter _____ by Rosa.

(A) writes

(B) was written

(C) wrote

(D) is written

(　　) 2. The game _____ by our team.

(A) wins

(B) was winning

(C) was won

(D) won

(　　) 3. The flowers _____ by us.

(A) will plant

(B) planted

(C) plants

(D) will be planted

(　　) 4. Holly's party _____ next Saturday.

(A) will hold

(B) will be held

(C) held

(D) is helding

(　　) 5. The problem _____ easily by us.

(A) solves

(B) can solve

(C) can be solved

(D) solved

Unit

03

被動語態的用法

(   ) 6. The work should _____ by him.
(A) is finished   (B) be finished
(C) finish   (D) be finishing

(   ) 7. Passengers _____ to eat in the MRT system.
(A) aren't allowed   (B) not allowed
(C) didn't allow   (D) wasn't allowed

(   ) 8. _____ the house built by him?
(A) Has   (B) Does   (C) Is   (D) Will

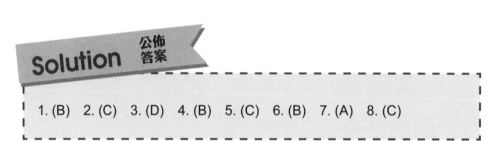

Solution 公佈答案

1. (B)   2. (C)   3. (D)   4. (B)   5. (C)   6. (B)   7. (A)   8. (C)

今日重點回顧筆記

一定要練習寫下來！才能確定自己真的會了喔！

1. 被動語態需用：_____ + p.p.（過去分詞）。
2. 否定句和疑問句以_____形成。
3. 完成式之被動語態形式為have+_____+ p.p.。

試判斷以下句子是否正確？錯誤的請更正為正確句子。

A. She will is taken to the hospital.

....

B. The language isn't spoken anymore.

....

C. The desks have be moved to the second floor.

....

Unit 03

被動語態的用法

正確答案：

1. beV.　2. beV.　3. been

A. She will be taken to the hospital.

別忘了，接在will後面的動詞要打回原形喔！

B. 正確

C. The desks have been moved to the second floor.

記得前面講的過去分詞嗎？這裡要用be的過去分詞been。

Chapter 07

Test

動詞進階版——分詞 PP 很強大
——綜合測驗篇

📖 分詞觀念選選看 📖

(   ) 1. Have you _____ your lunch yet?

     (A) eat   (B) ate   (C) eaten   (D) eating

(   ) 2. They have learned English _____ many years.

     (A) for   (B) since   (C) in   (D) of

(   ) 3. She has been interested in art _____ she was six.

     (A) for   (B) when   (C) before   (D) since

(   ) 4. He _____ to America several times.

     (A) have been   (B) has been   (C) have gone   (D) has gone

(   ) 5. _____ English taught in your school?

     (A) Has   (B) Did   (C) Is   (D) Does

(   ) 6. School rules should _____ by students.

     (A) be following   (B) following   (C) follow   (D) be followed

(   ) 7. Was the trash _____ out by Tiffany?

     (A) take   (B) taking   (C) taken   (D) took

(   ) 8. The sweaters weren't sold _____.

     (A) already   (B) yet   (C) just   (D) for

📖 劃線錯誤處，請改成正確文法 📖

1. Have you done your homework <u>already</u>? _____

2. She has worked <u>since</u> eight hours. _____

3. He isn't here now. He <u>has been</u> to Japan on business. _____

4. We have sang the song many times. _____

5. Traffic rules should are followed by everyone. _____

6. The house was selling to Mr. Lin. _____

7. The game will is played in ten minutes. _____

8. Are the tickets to the game buy yet? _____

🔊 閱讀測驗 🔊

Green Plan in Wonder City
Make new out of the old!

Since 1996, Wonder City **has started** a green plan and **has been** greatly successful in many ways. Places that **were not used** anymore, like railways, factories, and open lands, **have been changed** and brought to new life. They **have now become** parks, restaurants, museums, or shopping centers. They look fresh and clean with trees, flowers, and pieces of art. Olde River, for example, is now a pink belt in the spring with **born-to-smiles** on both of its sides. They are beautiful and smell great. Many people take a walk or go bicycling along the banks of the river. Because of this plan, the city **has become** cleaner and younger. Every year in May, a big green festival is celebrated in Wonder City. People from other cities go to the festival to learn how to make their own cities more beautiful.

【基測 97-1】

( ) 1. What is the reading about?

    (A) An art festival.   (B) vacation plan.

    (C) The change of a city.   (D) The history of a river.

(　　) 2. Which is NOT part of the plan?

      (A) Crowing trees.   (B) Building hotels.

      (C) Making use of art   (D) Using closed factories.

(　　) 3. What are born-to-smiles?

      (A) A belt.   (B) A color.

      (C) A flower.   (D) A piece of art.

66 句子重組測驗 99

1. his / has / Jim / homework / finished

_____

2. them / by / built / the / Was / bridge / ?

_____

3. was / room / asked / to / clean / Tanya / up / the

_____

4. of / English / people / spoken / by / is / millions

_____

5. has / English / taught / for / Terry / ten years

_____

6. was / the hospital / The boy / taken / to

_____

7. you / Have / been / ever / New York / to / ?

_____

8. studied / you / have / ? / How / English / long

_____

9. The / be / one day / will / secret / discovered

_____

10. lived / Raymond / in / years / Taiwan / has / for / twenty

_____

🔠中翻英測驗🔠

1. 自從你離開台灣已經兩年了。

   It has _____ two years _____ you left Taiwan.

2. 我還沒決定。

   I haven't decided _____.

3. Jay 已經在日本住了兩年了。

   Jay has lived in Japan _____ two years.

4. 這封信是用英文寫的。

   The letter was _____ in English.

5. 你去過香港嗎？

   Have you (ever) _____ to Hong Kong?

6. 我姊姊已經到加拿大去了。

   _____

7. 這扇門被他關起來了。

   _____

8. 蛋糕被你妹妹吃掉了。

   _____

9. 她已經學英文三年了。

   _____

10. 這房子已經被我們蓋好了。

   _____

Chapter 07 Solution

動詞進階版──分詞 PP 很強大──解答篇

66 分詞觀念選選看 99

1. (C)   2. (A)   3. (D)   4. (B)
5. (C)   6. (D)   7. (C)   8. (B)

66 劃線錯誤處，請改成正確文法 99

1. yet   2. for   3. has gone   4. have sung
5. should be followed 6. was sold   7. will be played   8. bought

66 閱讀測驗 99

1. (C)   2. (B)   3. (C)

　　灣德城的綠色植物計畫
　　舊物新用！

　　自從 1996 年，灣德城開始實施了綠色植物的計畫，這個計畫非常地成功，許多已經是非常老舊的地方，像是鐵路、工廠和許多空地從此有了很大的改變，它們有了新的生命，變成了公園、餐廳、博物館或是購物中心。它們看起來又新又乾淨，有許多的樹、花跟許多的藝術品。例如，在老舊的河堤兩邊現在種了許多的花草，它們看起來非常地漂亮聞起來也非常香。許多人都在這個河堤邊騎腳踏車欣賞美景。因為這個計畫，這座城市變得乾淨又年輕了許多。在每年的五月，灣德城都會辦一個有關綠色計畫的節日來慶祝。許多人也會從別的城市遠道而來，學習如何讓他們的城市更加美麗。

66 句子重組測驗 99

1. Jim has finished his homework.（吉姆已經完成功課了。）

2. Was the bridge built by them?（橋是他們建造的嗎？）

3. Tanya was asked to clean up the room. （坦雅被要求打掃房間。）

4. English is spoken by millions of people. （數百萬人說英語。）

5. Terry has taught English for ten years. （泰瑞已經教授英語十年了。）

6. The boy was taken to the hospital. （那男孩被帶去醫院了。）

7. Have you ever been to New York? （你曾去過紐約嗎？）

8. How long have you studied English? （你學英文多久了？）

9. The secret will be discovered one day. （這個秘密有一天將被發現。）

10. Raymond has lived in Taiwan for twenty years.

　　（雷蒙已經在台灣住了20年。）

中翻英測驗

1. been / since

2. yet

3. for

4. written

5. been

6. My sister has gone to Canada.

7. The door was closed by him.

8. The cake was eaten by your sister.

9. She has learned English for three years.

10. The house has been built by us.

Chapter08 / Advanced Verbs

動詞進階版──
to V 還是 ing ？

本篇進階動詞的學習重點如下：

Unit 01 不定詞 VS. 動名詞

一、不定詞 & 動名詞基本用法

文法口訣輕鬆記　◀ *Track 027*

1. 動詞前凸（to）、後硬（ing）做變化
2. 前凸（to V.）不定詞
3. 後硬（V-ing）動名詞

1. 動詞前凸（to）、後硬（ing）做變化
　　動詞須做變化才可成為名詞、形容詞、副詞。

2. 前凸（to V.）不定詞
　　在動詞之前加 to 變成「to + V.」稱為不定詞（「to」音似「凸」）。

3. 後硬（V-ing）動名詞
　　在動詞之後加 ing 變成「V-ing」稱為動名詞（「ing」音似「硬」）。

文法觀念說給你聽

　　動詞如果變化為 to + V.（不定詞）或 V-ing（動名詞），可以成為名詞、形容詞或副詞，需分別其差異與用法。

例 1：**Going** to school is boring. → **當名詞**
　　　去上學很無聊。

例 2：I have many things **to buy**. → **當形容詞**
我有很多東西要買。

例 3：I sit down **to talk** to him. → **當副詞**
我坐下來和他說話。

圖解文法一看就懂

不定詞 VS. 動名詞的功能比較

動詞（V.）的變化

不定詞

動名詞

to＋V.
可當成名詞、形容詞或副詞使用。

V-ing
可當成名詞或形容詞使用。

例句現身說法好清楚

一、當名詞：

1. **To see** is to believe. ＝ **Seeing** is believing. 　百聞不如一見；眼見為憑。

2. **To teach** is to learn. ＝ **Teaching** is learning. 　教學相長。

注意：「to ＋ V.」和「V-ing」當主詞，有**名詞**之功能。

二、當形容詞：

1. I have a lot of homework **to do**. 　我有很多功課要做。

2. I can't find a **parking** space near here. 　這附近我找不到停車位。

三、當副詞：

1. He comes **to see** you. 　他來是為了看你。

注意：「to ＋ V.」當作**副詞**用以修飾動詞。

2. **In order to learn** English well, I practice it every day. ＝ **To learn**
English well, I practice it every day.

為了學好英文，我每天練習。

注意：表示目的 in order to V. ～（為了……），常簡寫成 to V. ～，不可用
V-ing 代替；V-ing 沒有表示目的之副詞功能。

四、當介系詞之受詞：

Here are some tips **for learning English well.** 這裡有一些學好英文的秘訣。

注意：介系詞 for 之後須加動名詞當受詞，不可用不定詞。

Unit

01

不定詞 VS. 動名詞

二、不定詞 & 動名詞進階用法

❝ 文法口訣輕鬆記 ❞ ◀ *Track 028*

1. 動詞只能有一個
2. 後面動詞要換裝
3. 加 to、變 ing 分六種

1. 動詞只能有一個

一般而言，一個句子只能有一個動詞，除非有連接詞連結。

2. 後面動詞要換裝

動詞只能有一個，後面的動詞須隨著前面的動詞做變化，才能
與前面的動詞同時存在。

3. 加 to、變 ing 分六種

後面的動詞須加 to 變成 to ＋ V.（不定
詞），或變成 V-ing（動名詞），共有六種
用法。

❝ 文法觀念說給你聽 ❞

　　動詞之後如果還有動詞，主要分成 to + V.（不定詞）或 V-ing（動名詞），可以變化成六種用法：

一、大多數的動詞後面都是加不定詞 → V. + to + V.（不定詞）。

二、有些動詞是後面加動名詞 → V. + V-ing（動名詞）。

三、由第一種用法分化出使役 V. + **to** V.（變成省略 to 之原形不定詞，需注意）。

四、動詞後面是 to + V. / V-ing 皆可，兩種意義相同。

五、動詞後面是 to + V. / V-ing 皆可，但兩種意義不同。

六、感官V. + **to** V.（省略to之原形不定詞，需注意）或感官 V. + V-ing（在此為現在分詞表示進行，而非動名詞）。

❝ 圖解文法一看就懂 ❞

動詞後面接動詞可以這樣接

（一）

V. + to + V.

（二）

V. + V-ing

（三）

使役 V. + **to** V.

Unit
01

不定詞 VS. 動名詞

(四)

任一皆可，意思相同

(五)

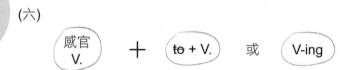

任一皆可，意思不同

(六)

```
感官
V.    ＋    ~~to + V.~~    或    V-ing
```

Unit
01

不定詞 VS. 動名詞

📖 例句現身說法好清楚

一、V. ＋ to ＋ V.

1. He **asked** me **to wash** the car.　他叫我去洗車。

2. She **decided to live** in London.　她決定住在倫敦。

3. I **want to play** basketball with you.　我想和你們打籃球。

＝I would like (love) to play basketball with you.

＝I'd like (love) to play basketball with you.

4. Mary and I **went to see** a movie yesterday.　瑪莉和我昨天去看了一部電影。

好記小撇步

你可以運用記憶口訣來記住下列幾個常在後面加不定詞的動詞：

你總是告訴我，要求我去決定，並非我自願，真是想要吐（to ＋ V.）
ask（要求）/ tell（告訴）/ decide（決定）/ volunteer（自願）/ want
（想要）＝ would like to（'d like）＝ would love（'d love）/ expect
（預期）/ wish（希望；想要）/ hope（希望）/ plan（計畫）/ teach
（教）/ learn（學）

二、使役V. + to V.

1. Mom **had** me **clean** my room yesterday. 　媽媽昨天叫我打掃房間。

2. My sister **made** me **think** of a doll. 　我妹妹使我想到洋娃娃。

3. **Let's go.** 　咱們走。

4. I **help** my brother **(to) do** his English homework.
   我幫我弟弟做他的英文作業。

注意：使役 V. 之特例 help（幫忙）後面加 to + V. 或 V. 皆可。

好記小撇步

> 你也可以用記憶口訣來記住下列幾個需要接原形動詞的使役動詞！
> **使役叫你去做就做，不要吐（to）**
> 使役 V. 的後面不要 to，須直接 + V. 原形（省略 to 之原形不定詞）
> 如：make / have / let（叫、讓、令……）

三、V. + V-ing

1. I **enjoy singing** English songs. 　我喜愛唱英文歌。

2. They **practice playing** baseball after school 　他們放學後練習打棒球。

3. He **spent** two days **reading** the book. 　他花了兩天讀這本書。

4. The child **kept asking** me questions. 　這孩子一直問我問題。

5. We all **avoided mentioning** that name. 　我們都避免提及那個名字。

好記小撇步

> 你可以利用這個口訣，記住 13 個只能接 V-ing 之常用動詞：
> **喜愛練習高爾夫，真的很花錢，雖然好玩但錢花完，真的有麻煩。放棄吧！停止吧！我們該避免繼續浪費。我很介意，所以提出建議。**
> enjoy（喜愛）/ practice（練習）/ spend（花費）/ finish（完成）/
> have fun（好玩）/ have trouble（有麻煩）/ give up（放棄）/ avoid
> （避免）/ waste（浪費）/ quit（停止）/ keep（繼續）/ mind（介意）/
> suggest（建議）

Unit
01

不定詞 VS. 動名詞

Unit
01

不
定
詞

VS.

動
名
詞

四、喜惡 V. / 開始＋ $\begin{cases} \text{to + V. 皆可，意思相同：} \\ \text{V-ing} \end{cases}$

1. I **like to play** tennis. ＝ I **like playing** tennis.　我喜歡打網球。

注意：喜惡動詞有like（喜歡）、love（愛）、hate（恨；討厭）……等。

2. It **begins to rain**. ＝ It **begins raining**.　開始下雨了。

注意：表示「開始」的動詞有 begin、start。

五、特殊V. ＋ $\begin{cases} \text{to + V.} \\ \text{V-ing} \end{cases}$ **任一皆可，但兩種意思不同**

1. remember（記得）／forget（忘記）＋ $\begin{cases} \text{to + V.（未做）} \\ \text{V-ing（已做）} \end{cases}$

(1) I remember **to see** that movie. → **未看**　我記得要去看那部電影。

(2) I remember **seeing** that movie. → **已看**　我記得看過那部電影了。

(3) Don't forget **to turn off** the lights. → **未關**　別忘記關燈。

(4) I forgot **posting** the letter. → **已寄**　我忘了信已寄出。

2. stop（停止）$\begin{cases} \text{to + V.（去做）} \\ \text{V-ing（不要做）} \end{cases}$

(1) They stop **to look** at the beautiful flowers. → **去做**
　　他們停下來看這些漂亮的花。

(2) Please stop **talking**. → **不要做**
　　請不要講話。

3. need（需要）$\begin{cases} \text{to + V.（去做─主動）} \\ \text{V-ing（被做─被動）} \end{cases}$

(1) I need **to wash** my car.→ **主動**　我需要去洗我的車。

(2) My car needs **washing**.→ **被動**　我的車需要被洗。

六、感官 V. + { **to + V.**
　　　　　　　 V-ing

1. I **heard** him **play** the guitar last night. → **不要 to**

   我昨晚聽見他彈吉他。

2. He **saw** a man **running** after a woman. → **表進行**

   他看見一個男人正在追一個女人。

好記小撇步

你可以用這個口訣來判斷感官動詞需要接原形 V. 或 V-ing：

看見了聽見，不要 to

與使役動詞用法相似，須＋ V.（省略 to 之原形不定詞）

正在進行 ing

若表進行（正在發生），則＋ V-ing

而感官動詞有 see（看見）、watch（觀賞）、look at（注視）、hear（聽）、listen to（傾聽）、feel（感覺）

Unit
01

不定詞 VS. 動名詞

❝ 馬上演練好實力 ❞

選選看：請從選項中選出符合題目的答案

(　　) 1. Tony's father told him ＿＿＿＿ hard.

　　　 (A) studies　　(B) to study　　(C) studying　　(D) study

(　　) 2. We decided ＿＿＿＿ a present for Mom.

　　　 (A) buy　　(B) buying　　(C) bought　　(D) to buy

(　　) 3. Don't spend too much time ＿＿＿＿ TV.

　　　 (A) watch　　(B) to watch　　(C) watching　　(D) watches

(　　) 4. Mother makes me ＿＿＿＿ my homework before I play video games.

　　　 (A) finish　　(B) to finish　　(C) finishing　　(D) finished

(   ) 5. The teacher _____ his students study in the classroom.

        (A) asked   (B) wanted   (C) told   (D) had

(   ) 6. Don't forget _____ off the light before you leave.

        (A) turn   (B) to turn   (C) turning   (D) to turning

(   ) 7. It has stopped _____. Let's play baseball outside.

        (A) rain   (B) to rain   (C) raining   (D) rained

(   ) 8. I saw a boy _____ in the park.

        (A) to play   (B) played   (C) to playing   (D) play

Unit
01

不定詞 VS. 動名詞

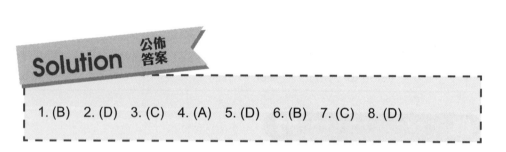

Solution 公佈答案

1. (B)   2. (D)   3. (C)   4. (A)   5. (D)   6. (B)   7. (C)   8. (D)

今日重點回顧筆記

一定要練習寫下來！才能確定自己真的會了喔！

1. 動詞前面加上＿＿＿＿＿＿，則為不定詞。
2. 動詞後面加上＿＿＿＿＿＿，則為動名詞。
3. 不定詞可當名詞、形容詞，還可當＿＿＿＿＿詞。

試判斷以下句子是否正確？錯誤的請更正為正確句子。

A. Sing English songs is fun.

....

B. We decided to visit Canada this summer.

....

C. She heard a boy cried.

....

Unit 01

不定詞 VS. 動名詞

正確答案：

1. to　　2. ing　　3. 副

A. Singing English songs is fun.

　　這裡要用動名詞，所以sing加ing。

B. 正確

C. She heard a boy cry/crying.

　　感官動詞+名詞後面，要加上動詞原形或動詞+ing才行喔！

Unit 02 ▶ 情緒動詞的現在分詞 VS. 過去分詞

❝ 文法口訣輕鬆記 ❞

1. **情緒動詞變分詞，當作形容詞**
2. **人用「ed」感到；事物用「ing」**

1. **情緒動詞變分詞，當作形容詞**
   情緒動詞可變化成過去分詞（V-ed）和現在分詞（V-ing），當形容詞使用。

2. **人用「ed」感到；事物用「ing」**
   通常人用過去分詞（V-ed），事物則用現在分詞（V-ing）來修飾。

❝ 文法觀念說給你聽 ❞

情緒動詞可變化成「現在分詞」和「過去分詞」，當「形容詞」使用。

一、現在分詞（V-ing）： 通常用來修飾事、物，但某些特殊情況也可修飾人，但指的是「特質」而非感覺或情緒。

例 1：The speech was **boring**.　這場演講很無聊。

例 2：The woman hates the **boring** man.　這女人討厭這無聊的男人。

二、過去分詞（V-ed）： 通常用來修飾人，表示人的感覺或情緒，不可用來修飾事物。

例如：We are **excited** about the **exciting** game.
　　　我們對這場刺激的比賽感到很興奮。

圖解文法一看就懂

一、情緒動詞之「過去分詞&現在分詞」用法：

過去分詞　　　　　　　　　　　　　現在分詞

人＋be V.＋V-ed＋介系詞＋物　　　　物＋be V.＋V-ing＋to 人

＊ be V. 可用連綴動詞代替，如 get, feel, become...

Unit 02

二、情緒動詞的過去分詞（V-ed）與介系詞的搭配

人＋be V.＋	過去分詞	介系詞
人＋be V.＋	interested（感到有趣的）	in
	surprised（感到驚訝的）	at
	tired（感到厭煩的）	of
	bored（感到無聊的）	with
	satisfied（感到滿意的）	with
	confused（感到困惑的）	with
	worried（感到擔憂的）	about
	excited（感到興奮的）	about
	embarrassed（感到尷尬的）	about
	scared（感到害怕的）	at / by
	touched / moved（受感動的）	by
	disappointed（感到失望的）	with 人 / at 事

情緒動詞的現在分詞 VS. 過去分詞

Unit 02

情緒動詞的現在分詞 VS. 過去分詞

❝❝ 例句現身說法好清楚 ❞❞

一、基本用法

1. Tom is **interested** in English.　湯姆對英文有興趣。
＝ English is **interesting** to Tom.

2. I am **surprised** at the news.　我對這個消息感到驚訝。
＝ The news is **surprising** to me.

3. They are worried about the **missing** boy.　他們擔憂那個失蹤的男孩。

4. We were deeply **moved / touched** by the movie.
我們深深地被這部電影感動。

5. The movie was **boring**; we felt **bored** with it.
這部電影很無聊；我們覺得它很無聊。

二、特殊用法

1. Tom is **interesting**; we all like him.　湯姆很風趣；我們全都喜歡他。

2. John is **boring**, so nobody likes him.　約翰很無聊，所以沒人喜歡他。

❝❝ 馬上演練好實力 ❞❞

選選看：請從選項中選出符合題目的答案

(　　) 1. New and _____ things are always happening.

(A) surprise　　(B) surprises　　(C) surprising　　(D) surprised

(　　) 2. He didn't understand his homework. He became _____.

(A) exciting　　(B) troubling　　(C) confused　　(D) satisfied

(　　) 3. Mrs. Watt is interested in _____.

(A) watch TV　　　　　　(B) to watch TV

(C) watching TV　　　　　(D) look at TV

(   ) 4. School work makes them _____ and they don't enjoy learning.

     (A) bored   (B) burned   (C) boring   (D) confusing

(   ) 5. Tom is _____. No one in the class likes him.

     (A) bore   (B) boring   (C) bored   (D) bores

(   ) 6. I like to talk to John because he is very _____.

     (A) interested   (B) interests   (C) interesting   (D) interest

(   ) 7. I was _____ to hear the _____ news.

     (A) surprised; surprised   (B) surprising; surprised

     (C) surprising; surprising   (D) surprised; surprising

(   ) 8. Is math _____ him?

     (A) interest   (B) interest to   (C) interested in   (D) interesting to

Unit 02

情緒動詞的現在分詞 VS. 過去分詞

Solution 公佈答案

1. (C)   2. (C)   3. (C)   4. (A)   5. (B)   6. (C)   7. (D)   8. (D)

Unit
02

情緒動詞的現在分詞VS.過去分詞

今日重點回顧筆記

一定要練習寫下來！才能確定自己真的會了喔！

1. 情緒動詞通常以_____形式來形容人。
2. 情緒動詞通常以_____形式來形容事物。
3. 需特別注意過去分詞後面配用之_____詞。

試判斷以下句子是否正確？錯誤的請更正為正確句子。

A. I am worrying about the test.

....

B. They are interested of science.

....

C. We were excited about the exciting game.

....

正確答案：

1. V-ed　　2. V-ing　　3. 介系

A. I am worried about the test.

　worrying是「令人感到擔憂」的，接在I am 後面，表示「我這個人很令人擔憂」，不是這句想要表達的意思。

B. They are interested in science.

　interested後面要接in才是正確的介系詞！

C. 正確

Test

Chapter 08

動詞進階版—to V 還是 ing？
——綜合測驗篇

🔶 動詞觀念選選看 🔶

( ) 1. Eating vegetables _____ good for you.

    (A) are   (B) is   (C) were   (D) be

( ) 2. They made him _____ the garbage out.

    (A) take   (B) took   (C) takes   (D) taking

( ) 3. She is very interested _____ English.

    (A) for   (B) in   (C) on   (D) of

( ) 4. We are tired _____ doing the same work.

    (A) for   (B) in   (C) on   (D) of

( ) 5. Playing computer games _____ a lot of fun.

    (A) has   (B) have   (C) is   (D) are

( ) 6. We saw a thief _____ into the house.

    (A) ran   (B) runs   (C) running   (D) to run

( ) 7. They practice _____ the words and sentences with the CD.

    (A) say   (B) saying   (C) said   (D) to say

( ) 8. She decided _____ on a diet.

    (A) going   (B) to go   (C) went   (D) goes

🔶 劃線錯誤處，請改成正確文法 🔶

1. Were they surprised <u>on</u> the news? _____

2. She heard the boy <u>sang</u> a love song. _____

3. She enjoys <u>to play</u> the guitar. _____

4. They wanted me <u>go</u> with them. _____

5. He was <u>boring</u> with his work. _____

6. Doing the dishes <u>are</u> easy for me. _____

7. Let's <u>waiting</u> for Tom. _____

8. Don't forget <u>bring</u> me a cup of coffee when you come back to the office. _____

閱讀測驗

Bill and Jill were going to visit Da-wei and Li-hua Wu in Taiwan for several days. Before they left America, Bill and Jill **tried to learn** about Chinese food and Taiwanese ways of **doing** things. They **wanted to be** polite. They learned that most people in Taiwan eat rice, drink tea, and take off their shoes when they go into a friend's apartment. Bill and Jill even **learned to use** chopsticks.

At the same time, Da-wei and Li-hua learned about American food and American ways of doing things. <u>They</u> **wanted to be** friendly. When Bill and Jill came to the Wu's house, Da-wei and Li-hua **told them to keep** their shoes on. Later they went out for dinner. They ate pizza and drank Coke. The next few days, they had breakfast in a coffee shop and ate hamburgers in a fast-food restaurant.

On their way back to America, Bill and Jill were thinking about why they never ate rice or drank tea or ate with chopsticks. They never took off shoes when they visited the Wu family. They thought that **living** in Taiwan was just like **living** in America.

【基測 96-2】

(　　) 1. How did Bill and Jill prepare for their trip to Taiwan?

    (A) They learned to speak Chinese.

    (B) They prepared a new pair of shoes.

    (C) They bought a lot of American food.

    (D) They learned to do things the way Taiwanese people do.

（　　）2. Which made Bill and Jill think that Taiwan was just like America?

      (A) The Wu family often ate fast food.

      (B) The Wu family drank tea after dinner.

      (C) The Wu family could speak good English.

      (D) The Wu family took off their shoes in the house.

（　　）3. What does <u>They</u> mean in the reading?

      (A) Bill and Jill.

      (B) Da-wei and Li-hua.

      (C) Most people in Taiwan.

      (D) American ways of doing things.

66 句子重組測驗 99

1. wanted / She / to / noticed / be

_____

2. to / We / out / today / decided / eat

_____

3. Gina / job / bored / is / very / her / with

_____

4. interesting / computer / is / games / very / Playing

_____

5. really / books / Sandy / reading / enjoys / comic

_____

6. is / us / good / Eating / for / vegetables

_____

7. We / at / surprised / the / are / report

_____

8. speaking / They / English / each other / practice / with

_____

9. more / he / hard / make / To / money, / works

_____

10. has / raining / stopped / It

_____

🔖**中翻英測驗** 🔖

1. 每天喝足夠的水對我們的健康很重要。

_____ enough water every day is important for our health.

2. 你想加入我們嗎？

Would you like _____ join us?

3. Peter 的父母親很擔心他。

Peter's parents are worried _____ him.

4. 我們對這場棒球比賽感到很興奮。

We are _____ about the baseball game.

5. 我花了一星期在日本旅行。

I spent a week _____ in Japan.

6. 你昨晚忘記關燈了。

_____

7. Lisa 對數學感到無趣。

_____

8. 老師要求我們用功一點。（ask）

_____

9. Rick 對電影很感興趣。

_____

10. 媽媽昨天叫我打掃房間。（make）

_____

Solution

動詞進階版—to V 還是 ing？——解答篇

🔊 動詞觀念選選看 🔊

1. (B)　　　2. (A)　　　3. (B)　　　4. (D)
5. (C)　　　6. (C)　　　7. (B)　　　8. (B)

🔊 劃線錯誤處，請改成正確文法 🔊

1. at　　　　2. sing/singing　　3. playing　　4. to go
5. bored　　　6. is　　　　　　7. wait　　　　8. to bring

🔊 閱讀測驗 🔊

1. (D)　　2. (A)　　3. (B)

　　比爾跟茱兒來台灣的這幾天拜訪了大衛跟吳麗華。在他們離開美國之前，他們有學著如何品嚐台灣的食物與台灣的習俗。他們希望他們是有禮貌的。他們學到，台灣人大部分的時間都是吃飯、喝茶，且當進入朋友家的時候會先把鞋子給脫掉。比爾跟茱兒也學習如何使用筷子。

　　同時，大衛跟麗華也學習如何品嚐美國的食物與美國的習俗。他們想呈現出友善的一面。當比爾跟茱兒來到吳家的房子時，大衛跟林華跟他們說可以不用脫鞋。之後，他們一起去吃晚餐。他們吃披薩跟喝可樂。之後的幾天，他們在一家咖啡廳用早餐，也在一家速食店吃漢堡。

　　在他們要回去美國的路上，比爾跟茱兒在想他們怎麼沒吃到白飯或喝到中國茶或是用到筷子。當他們參觀吳家的時候也不需要把鞋子給脫掉。他們覺得，居住在台灣其實跟美國是一樣的。

🔊 句子重組測驗 🔊

1. She wanted to be noticed.（她想被大家注意。）

2. We decided to eat out today.（我們決定今天出去吃飯。）

3. Gina is very bored with her job.（吉娜對她的工作感到厭煩。）

4. Playing computer games is very interesting.（玩電腦遊戲很有趣。）

5. Sandy really enjoys reading comic books.（珊蒂很喜歡看漫畫書。）

6. Eating vegetables is good for us.（吃蔬菜對我們很好。）

7. We are surprised at the report.（我們對這個報導感到驚訝。）

8. They practice speaking English with each other.（他們彼此練習説英語。）

9. To make more money, he works hard.（為了賺更多的錢，他認真工作。）

10. It has stopped raining.（雨已經停了。）

❝❝中翻英測驗❞❞

1. Drinking

2. to

3. about

4. excited

5. traveling

6. You forgot to turn off the lights last night.

7. Lisa feels bored with Math.

8. The teacher asks us to study harder.

9. Rick is interested in movies.

10. Mom made me clean my room yesterday.

Chapter09 / Advanced Pronoun

代名詞進階版— 我還是我

本篇進階代名詞的學習重點如下：

Unit 01 反身代名詞的用法

文法口訣輕鬆記　🔊 *Track 030*

> 1. 反身代名詞，反過來說自己
> 2. 自己不落單，跟著主詞走

1. 反身代名詞，反過來說自己

反身代名詞是指：～自己（我自己、你自己、他自己……），須由人稱代名詞加上自己（單數＋ self / 複數＋ selves）。

2. 自己不落單，跟著主詞走

其使用方法必須跟著主詞做變化而不可單獨使用。

文法觀念說給你聽

一、反身代名詞的變化方式：

通常用所有格＋ self（單數）/ ＋ selves（複數）

例1：my → my**self**（我自己）/ our → our**selves**（我們自己）

例2：you → your**self**（你自己）/ you → your**selves**（你們自己）

注意：需留意第三人稱是由**受格**變成，如：he → him**self**（他自己）/ they → them**selves**（他們自己）

二、反身代名詞的使用方式： 必須跟著主詞一起出現，形成加強語氣之功能，不可單獨使用。例如：

例1：I do it (by) my**self**. 　我自己做的。

不可寫成： Myself do it.

例2：**He** went there (by) **himself**. 他自己去那裡。

不可寫成： Himself went there.

注意： 祈使句會省略主詞 you，故會單獨看見反身代名詞 yourself / yourselves，如：Do it yourself.（自己做—DIY。）

圖解文法一看就懂

	主詞	所有格	反身代名詞
單數	I	my	myself（我自己）
	you	your	yourself（你自己）
	he	his	himself（他自己）
	she	her	herself（她自己）
	it	its	itself（牠自己）
複數	we	our	ourselves（我們自己）
	you	your	yourselves（你們自己）
	they	their	themselves（他們自己）

例句現身說法好清楚

一、基本用法

1. **I** cook dinner (by) **myself**. 我自己煮晚餐。

2. **Sam** washed the car (by) **himself**. 山姆他自己洗車。

3. **Jack and Lily** paid the bill (by) **themselves**. 傑克和莉莉他們自己付帳。

4. **We** have to love **ourselves**. 我們必須愛自己。

Unit 01 反身代名詞的用法

二、特殊用法

1. **Mary** went shopping **herself**.　瑪莉自己去購物。

→ Mary **herself** went shopping.→ **加強語氣，強調主詞**

2. I saw Michael **himself**.　我看見麥可他本人。→ **加強語氣，強調受詞**

3. We just did that **for** ourselves.　我們那樣做只是**為了**我們自己。

注意：表示「目的」要用 **for** 不用 **by**

三、好好用的生活用語

1. D.I.Y. = Do it **yourself**.　自己動手做。

2. Help **yourself** to some snacks.　自己去取用點心吧。

3. Make **yourself** at home.　別客氣，當作自己家一樣。

4. Enjoy **yourself**! = Have fun! = Have a good time!
　好好享受，祝你玩得愉快！

注意：祈使句省略主詞 you，所以反身代名詞必須用 yourself（或 yourselves）

5. Heaven helps **those** who help **themselves**.　天助自助者。

Unit 01

反身代名詞的用法

馬上演練好實力

選選看：請從選項中選出符合題目的答案

（　）1. Help _____, students.
　　(A) yourself　(B) yourselfs　(C) yourselves　(D) themselves

（　）2. Sally went to a movie _____ yesterday.
　　(A) sheself　(B) by herself　(C) himself　(D) by her

（　）3. He's talking to _____.
　　(A) heself　(B) hiself　(C) by him　(D) himself

(　　) 4. The boys cleaned the room _____.

(A) himself　　(B) themselves　(C) yourselves　(D) ourselves

(　　) 5. Tom and I go to Taipei _____.

(A) ourselves　(B) himself　　(C) myself　　(D) themselves

(　　) 6. We all enjoyed _____ at the party last night.

(A) ourself　　(B) weselves　(C) ourselves　(D) myself

(　　) 7. John and Jerry stayed at home _____.

(A) ourselves　(B) himself　　(C) yourselves　(D) themselves

(　　) 8. I did it for _____.

(A) yourself　(B) herself　　(C) myself　　(D) himself

Unit 01

反身代名詞的用法

Solution 公佈答案

1. (C)　2. (B)　3. (D)　4. (B)　5. (A)　6. (C)　7. (D)　8. (C)

Unit
01

反身代名詞的用法

今日重點回顧筆記

一定要練習寫下來！才能確定自己真的會了喔！

1. 反身代名詞的形式為：one/some/all...+_____+名詞（受詞）。
2. 反身代名詞通常用_____格+self/selves形成。
3. 需特別注意：第三人稱是由_____格變化成。

試判斷以下句子是否正確？錯誤的請更正為正確句子。

A. I did the work by herself.

....

B. They usually cook by theirselves.

....

C. He went to a movie by hiself.

....

正確答案：

1. of　　2. 所有　　3. 受

A. I did the work by myself.
　主詞是「我」，反身代名詞就不能變成「她自己」啊！

B. They usually cook by themselves.
　they的反身代名詞是themselves才對喔！

C. He went to a movie by himself.
　he的反身代名詞是himself才對喔！

不定代名詞的用法

Unit 02

「 文法觀念說給你聽 」

不定代名詞是指數量不定之代名詞。

一、常見的不定代名詞：

1. 代替可數名詞： one（一個）、each（每一個）、both（兩者）、several（好幾個）、many（許多）

2. 代替不可數名詞：much（許多）

3. 可數、不可數皆可： some（一些）、most（大部份）、any（任何）、all（全部）

二、用法：

1. one / ones 代替前面使用過的名詞，單數用 one 複數用 ones

例1：I don't like the big apple. Please give me the small **one**.
　　　我不喜歡這個大蘋果。請給我那個小的。

例2：I don't like the big apples. Please give me the small **ones**.
　　　我不喜歡這些大蘋果。請給我那些小的。

2. 不定代名詞＋ of ＋ the ＋名詞

或不定代名詞＋ of ＋所有格（my / your / his / her / their...）＋名詞

或不定代名詞＋ of ＋受格（us / you / them / it）

例1：**One** of the (my) students **was** late this morning.
　　　我其中一個學生今天早上遲到了。

注意：不定代名詞若當主詞，動詞須跟著不定代名詞做變化！

例2：**Some** of the (my) students **were** late this morning.
　　　我的一些學生今天早上遲到了。

例3：**All** of the meat **is** fresh. 所有的肉都是新鮮的。

注意：不可數名詞 meat 恆為單數，所以需配用單數動詞！

Unit 02

不定代名詞的用法

圖解文法一看就懂

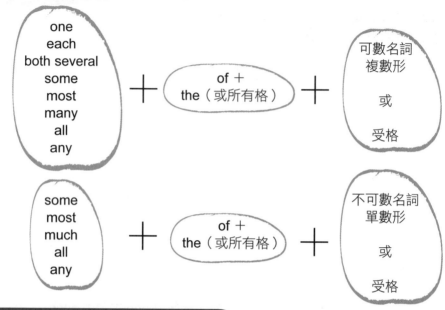

例句現身說法好清楚

一、可數的

1. **One** of the students is sick.　這些學生的其中一個生病了。

2. **Both** of my parents love me very much.　我的父母親兩個人都很愛我。

3. **Some** of the boys are my good friends.　這些男孩其中一些是我的好朋友。

4. **Most** of the books are good.　這些書大多數都不錯。

5. **All** of the girls are beautiful.　這些女孩全部都很漂亮。

6. I don't know **any of them**（受格）.　我不認識他們之中任何一個。

7. Richard is taller than **any of us**（受格）.　理查比我們當中任何人都高。

二、不可數的

1. **Some** of the water **is** clean.　這水其中一些是乾淨的。

2. **All** of the money on the desk **is** Tom's.　書桌上的這些錢全部是湯姆的。

3. **Most** of the paper **is** white.　這些紙大部份是白色的。

馬上演練好實力

選選看：請從選項中選出符合題目的答案

( ) 1. _____ of the students was sick.
    (A) One   (B) Both   (C) Some   (D) Many

( ) 2. _____ of his parents are doctors.
    (A) One   (B) Both   (C) Some   (D) Most

( ) 3. Some of the money in the boxes _____ Tom's.
    (A) are   (B) is   (C) am   (D) be

( ) 4. _____ of the water is clean.
    (A) Several   (B) Many   (C) All   (D) Your

( ) 5. Do you know any of _____?
    (A) them   (B) we   (C) the boy   (D) they

( ) 6. One of _____ is a fake.
    (A) watches   (B) the watch   (C) the watches   (D) watch

( ) 7. _____ of the girls at the party is happy.
    (A) Every   (B) Both   (C) All   (D) Each

( ) 8. Much of _____ is fresh.
    (A) fruit   (B) the fruit   (C) the fruits   (D) the apples

Unit 02

不定代名詞的用法

Solution 公佈答案

1. (A)   2. (B)   3. (B)   4. (C)   5. (A)   6. (C)   7. (D)   8. (B)

不定代名詞的用法

今日重點回顧筆記

一定要練習寫下來！才能確定自己真的會了喔！

1. 不定代名詞必須跟著_____詞做變化。
2. several為_____數之不定代名詞。
3. much為_____數之不定代名詞。

試判斷以下句子是否正確？錯誤的請更正為正確句子。

A. Both of they are my friends.

　　＿＿＿＿＿＿＿＿＿＿＿＿＿＿＿＿＿

B. One of the student was sick.

　　＿＿＿＿＿＿＿＿＿＿＿＿＿＿＿＿＿

C. Much of the water is clean.

　　＿＿＿＿＿＿＿＿＿＿＿＿＿＿＿＿＿

正確答案：

1. 主　2. 可　3. 不可

A. Both of them are my friends.
　 both of後面要接受詞，所以該用them而不是they。

B. One of the students was sick.
　 既然要說的是「學生們」中的其中一個，那當然就要用students
　 而不是student了。

C. 正確

272

所有代名詞的用法

Unit 03

❝ 文法口訣輕鬆記 ❞

🔊 *Track 031*

> 1. 所有代名詞，看誰所擁有
> 2. s 好心腸，幫了大家忙
> 3. my 就自己來，轉身變成 mine
> 4. his 很神奇，不變也厲害

1. 所有代名詞，看誰所擁有

　　所有代名詞是指「……人的……」，用以代替前面所用過的名詞。

2. s 好心腸，幫了大家忙

　　通常在主詞後面加上 s 就能變成所有格代名詞。

3. my 就自己來，轉身變成 mine

　　「我的～」需將 my → mine，自己做不同的變化。

4. his 很神奇，不變也厲害

　　his 字尾已有 s，所以不需做變化。

❝ 文法觀念說給你聽 ❞

所有代名詞由**所有格**變化而成，用來代替前面使用過的單數或複數名詞。

一、所有代名詞的變化方式：

1. **所有格代名詞 → 所有代名詞：**

須特別熟記 mine，其餘則＋ s；而 his 已有 s，所以不需變化。例如：

my → **mine** / your → **yours** / his → **his** / her → **hers** / our → **ours** / their → **theirs**

Unit 03

所有代名詞的用法

2. **一般名詞 → 所有代名詞**：

所有格本身是單數則加 **'s**，例如：Tom's／本身是複數則變成 **s'**，例如：the boys'

二、所有代名詞的使用方法：如果所有代名詞的後面接動詞，則必須注意單複數的動詞變化，特別要注意 mine / his / hers / ours / theirs 代替的有可能是複數名詞也有可能是單數名詞。

例1：My shoes are red; **hers** are white.

我的鞋子是紅的，她的是白的。

例2：Our teacher is Mr. Lin; **theirs** is Mr. Wang.

我們的老師是林先生，他們的是王先生。

❝ 圖解文法一看就懂 ❞

搖身一變試試看

一、所有格 ➜ 所有代名詞

	所有格	所有代名詞
我的	my	mine
你／你們的	your	yours
他的	his	his
她的	her	hers
我們的	our	ours
他們的	their	theirs

二、一般名詞 ➜ 所有代名詞

一般名詞	所有代名詞（和所有格相同）
Tom	Tom's（湯姆的）
my brother	my brother's（我弟弟的）

Mr. Lin	Mr. Lin's（林先生的）
the Lins	the Lins'（林家人的）
the boys	the boys'（這些男孩的）

例句現身說法好清楚

1. Her house is red; **mine** is white. → **mine ＝ my house**，單數
   她的房子是紅的；我的是白的。

2. Her shoes are red; **mine** are white. → **mine ＝ my shoes**，複數
   她的鞋子是紅的；我的是白的。

3. Our teacher is from Taipei; **theirs** is from Tainan.
   → **theirs ＝ their teacher**，單數
   我們的老師來自台北；他們的老師來自台南。

4. The two books are **his**, not **hers**. → **his** 不變；**her** 變 **hers**
   這兩本書是他的；不是她的。

5. Jack's sister is fourteen years old, and **Tom's** is, too.
   → **Tom's ＝ Tom' sister**，單數
   傑克的妹妹 14 歲；湯姆的妹妹也是。

6. This is your car; that is **Mr. Lin's**. → **Mr. Lin's ＝Mr. Lin's car**
   這是你的車；那是林先生的。

馬上演練好實力

選選看：請從選項中選出符合題目的答案

(　　) 1. A: Is that your car?
　　　　B: Yes, it's _____.
　　　　(A) my　　　　(B) yours　　　　(C) mine　　　　(D) your

Unit
03

所有代名詞的用法

Unit
03

所有代名詞的用法

(   ) 2. That pen is _____ .

    (A) your   (B) her   (C) my   (D) yours

(   ) 3. Is the house _____?

    (A) theirs   (B) your   (C) her   (D) our

(   ) 4. Our house is bigger than _____.

    (A) your   (B) hers   (C) their   (D) him

(   ) 5. My car is red; _____ is black.

    (A) her   (B) his   (C) their   (D) our

(   ) 6. One of the watches is _____.

    (A) Jack's   (B) him   (C) my   (D) our

(   ) 7. My shoes are white; hers _____ yellow.

    (A) is   (B) was   (C) are   (D) be

(   ) 8. Your teacher is from Tainan; _____ is from Taipei.

    (A) the boys'   (B) the boy   (C) our   (D) my

Solution 公佈答案

1. (C)   2. (D)   3. (A)   4. (B)   5. (B)   6. (A)   7. (C)   8. (A)

今日重點回顧筆記

一定要練習寫下來！才能確定自己真的會了喔！

1. 所有代名詞是由_____格+名詞所變化而成。
2. my的所有代名詞為_____。
3. 人稱代名詞之唯一和所有格一樣的是_____。

試判斷以下句子是否正確？錯誤的請更正為正確句子。

A. This is not mine; it's your.
_____

B. Tom's sister is a doctor; Judy's is, too.
_____

C. That is your pen, not my.
_____

Unit 03

所有代名詞的用法

正確答案：

1. 所有　　2. mine　　3. his

A. This is not mine; it's yours.
　　your的所有代名詞是yours，別忘了這個s喔！

B. 正確

C. That is your pen, not mine.
　　my的所有代名詞是mine才對喔！

Chapter 09

Test

代名詞進階版——我還是我——綜合測驗篇

66 代名詞觀念選選看 99

( ) 1. One of the students _____ late this morning.

    (A) are   (B) were   (C) was   (D) be

( ) 2. _____ of the food is not fresh.

    (A) Many   (B) Some   (C) Several   (D) Both

( ) 3. My shoes are white, and his _____ black.

    (A) is   (B) was   (C) are   (D) be

( ) 4. Both of _____ are good students.

    (A) they   (B) them   (C) we   (D) your

( ) 5. Your house is bigger than _____.

    (A) theirs   (B) our   (C) my   (D) her

( ) 6. That car is his, and this one is _____.

    (A) her   (B) mine   (C) their   (D) your

( ) 7. My brother usually cleans his room by _____.

    (A) himself   (B) hiself   (C) herself   (D) heslef

( ) 8. They did the work by _____.

    (A) theirselves   (B) themself   (C) themselves   (D) theyselves

66 劃線錯誤處，請改成正確文法 99

1. Is that new apartment their? _____

2. All of the food are fresh and delicious. _____

3. Some of boys enjoy jogging. _____

4. Help themselves to the snacks, boys and girls. _____

5. She has to cook dinner by yourself. _____

6. The digital camera is not mine; it's your. _____

7. One of the <u>girl</u> is his classmate. _____

8. Is that your birthday present? Yes, it's <u>my</u>. _____

66 閱讀測驗 99

Katie wrote a letter to her English teacher and got a reply from him. Read their letters and answer the question.

Dear Mr. Hu,

My family moved here from England three months ago. I can't speak Chinese well, and it's difficult for people to understand me. I'm losing confidence.

Could you please tell me what I should do?

Katie

Dear Katie,

I'm glad that you let me know about your problem. Here are some things you can do:

1. Your class is going to have a Story Time this month. **All of you** should tell stories. You should tell **one**, too. I'm sure you can learn a lot from doing so.

2. Try to practice speaking with your teachers and classmates. Don't be afraid.

3. Talk to Nanako and Yu-kim. Nanako is from Japan, and Yu-kim is from Korea. They might be able to give you some advice.

4. Some foreign students told me that watching *Happy Times* on TV can help. The language is easy.

Please try these ideas and see if you can do better. Don't worry too much. I have confidence in you.

Mr. Hu

【基測 95-2】

(   ) 1. What is Katie's problem?

(A) She is taking too many classes.

(B) She misses her parents in England.

(C) She is not good at the new language.

(D) She thinks the teachers are too serious.

(   ) 2. Mr. Hu tries to help Katie in many ways. Which is NOT said in his letter?

(A) Writing a letter every day.

(B) Watching a TV program.

(C) Telling stories in class.

(D) Talking to other foreign students.

(   ) 3. What language is used in Happy Times?

(A) Chinese   (B) English   (C) Japanese   (D) Korea

66句子重組測驗 99

1. and / Maria / the / I / ourselves / tree / decorated / Christmas

_____

2. the yellow dress / Lily / than / pink / in / prettier / looks / in the / one

_____

3. students / Both of / junior high school / are / my / brothers

_____

4. mine / The / not / bike / green / is

_____

5. English / Is / the / text book / ? / yours

_____

6. bathroom / Can / go to / the patient / ? / the / herself

_____

7. is / This cap / mine / his / the black / is / , and / one

_____

8. the / Some of / by / cookies / are / Tim / made

_____

9. to / Harry / go / the / will / himself / party

_____

10. babies' / Most / food / natural / the / is / of

_____

中翻英測驗

1. 這部新電腦看起來像舊的。

   The new computer looks like an old _____.

2. 紅色的花比粉紅色的漂亮。

   Red flowers are more beautiful than pink _____.

3. 我的同學其中之一是從加拿大來的。

   _____ of my classmates is from Canada.

4. 我的車子是藍色的，但他們的是綠色的。

   My car is blue, but _____ is green.

5. 這些書是 Nancy 的，不是我們的。

   These books are Nancy's, not _____.

6. 那部白色的轎車是她的嗎？

   _____

7. 放學後我通常自己回家。

   _____

8. 我的學生之中有一些戴眼鏡。

   _____

9. Kitty 昨晚自己去看電影了。

   _____

10. Hans 今天早上弄傷了自己。

   _____

Chapter 09

Solution

代名詞進階版──我還是我──解答篇

🔊 代名詞觀念選選看 🔊

1. (C)　　　2. (B)　　　3. (C)　　　4. (B)
5. (A)　　　6. (B)　　　7. (A)　　　8. (C)

🔊 劃線錯誤處，請改成正確文法 🔊

1. theirs　　2. is　　　3. the boys　　4. yourselves
5. herself　　6. yours　　7. girls　　　8. mine

🔊 閱讀測驗 🔊

1. (C)　2. (A)　3.(A)

　　凱蒂寫了一封信給她的英文老師並且收到他的回覆。請閱讀他們兩個人的信，並且回答問題。

親愛的胡先生：
　　我家三個月前從英格蘭搬到這裡。我的中文說得不好，所以人們很難了解我。我漸漸地失去了自信，所以你能告訴我該怎麼辦嗎？
凱蒂

親愛的凱蒂：
　　我很高興你讓我知道你的問題。這裡有幾件你能做的事情：
1. 你的班上這個月會有一個「故事時間」。你們所有人都必須說故事，而你也必須說一個故事。我相信你能從說故事當中學到很多事情。
2. 試著和你的老師和同學練習口說，別害怕。
3. 和 Nanako 及 Yu-kim 談談吧。Nanako 從日本來，而 Yu-kim 則來自韓國，他們也許能給你一些建議。
4. 有一些外國學生告訴我，看電視節目「歡樂時光」會很有幫助。裡面的用語非常簡單。
　　請試試這些建議並且看看你能不能越來越進步。別太過擔心，我對你有信心。
胡先生

【句子重組測驗】

1. Maria and I decorated the Christmas tree ourselves.
   （瑪莉亞和我親自裝飾耶誕樹。）

2. Lily looks prettier in the yellow dress than in the pink one.
   （麗莉穿這件黃色洋裝看起來比粉紅色那件更漂亮。）

3. Both of my brothers are junior high school students.
   （我兩個弟弟都是國中生。）

4. The green bike is not mine.（那部綠色的單車不是我的。）

5. Is the English text book yours?（這本英文課本是你的嗎？）

6. Can the patient go to the bathroom herself?（那個病患能自己去廁所嗎？）

7. This cap is his, and the black one is mine.
   （這頂帽子是他的，而黑色的是我的。）

8. Some of the cookies are made by Tim.（這餅乾其中一些是提姆做的。）

9. Harry will go to the party himself.（哈利將自己去派對。）

10. Most of the babies' food is natural.（大多數嬰兒的食品是天然的。）

【中翻英測驗】

1. one

2. ones

3. One

4. theirs

5. ours

6. Is that white car hers?

7. I usually go home by myself after school.

8. Some of my students wear glasses.

9. Kitty went to a movie herself last night.

10. Hans hurt himself this morning.

超級比一比就靠我
比較級

本篇比較級的學習重點如下：

Unit 01 比較級的用法

文法口訣輕鬆記 ◀ *Track 032*

> 1. 前加長，短延後
> 2. 好壞多少不規則
> 3. 最高級最棒了，前面加個「the」

1. 前加長，短延後

多音節的單字，通常已夠長了，所以比較級要另外加 more / most 在前面。單音節或雙音節的單字則通常較短，可直接在字尾＋ er / est。

2. 好壞多少不規則

不規則的變化很少，常用的有四個字：好（good）、壞（bad）、多（many；much）、少（little）。

3. 最高級最棒了，前面加個「the」

最高級是指特定的「最……」，須在最高級前加上定冠詞 the。

文法觀念說給你聽

一、比較級和最高級的變化方式：

1. 規則變化：

	比較級	最高級
長音節	**more＋adj.** 如：more beautiful	**the most＋adj.** 如：the most beautiful
短音節	**adj.＋er** 如：shorter	**the adj.＋est** 如：the shortest

2. 不規則變化：請參考「圖解文法一看就懂」

二、用法：

1. 比較級＋ than ＋比較的對象：

例1：May is **more beautiful than I.** 梅比我漂亮。

例2：Ted is **shorter than Tim.** 泰德比提姆矮。

2. 最高級通常是表示某一範圍內，「最……」：

例1：She is **the most beautiful** girl in my class.
　　　她是我班上最漂亮的女孩。

例2：He is **the shortest** boy in my class. 他是我班上最矮的男孩。

**Unit
01**

比
較
級
的
用
法

圖解文法一看就懂

一、比較級和最高級的變化原則

	規則變化	不規則變化
長音節	more～/ the most～	需熟記，有口訣
短音節	～er / the ～est	好壞多少，不規則

二、搖身一變試試看

1. 規則變化（長音節）

原級	比較級	最高級
interesting （有趣的）	**more** interesting （較有趣）	**most** interesting （最有趣）
expensive （貴的）	**more** expensive （較貴的）	**most** expensive （最貴）
beautiful （漂亮的）	**more** beautiful （更漂亮）	**most** beautiful （最漂亮）
important （重要的）	**more** important （更重要）	**most** important （最重要）
comfortable （舒服的）	**more** comfortable （更舒服）	**most** comfortable （最舒服）

convenient （便利的）	**more** convenient （更便利）	**most** convenient （最便利）
delicious （美味的）	**more** delicious （更美味）	**most** delicious （最美味）
famous （有名的）	**more** famous （更有名）	**most** famous （最有名）
difficult （困難的）	**more** difficult （更困難）	**most** difficult （最困難）

Unit
01

比較級的用法

2. 規則變化（短音節）

(1) **+ er / est**

原級	比較級	最高級
tall（高的）	taller（較高）	tallest（最高）
short（矮的）	shorter（較矮）	shortest（最矮）
small（小的）	smaller（較小）	smallest（最小）
cold（冷的）	colder（較冷）	coldest（最冷）
cheap（便宜的）	cheaper（較便宜）	cheapest（最便宜）
new（新的）	newer（較新）	newest（最新）

(2) 字尾 e **+ r / st**

原級	比較級	最高級
large（大的）	larger（較大）	largest（最大）
nice（好的）	nicer（較好）	nicest（最好）
safe（安全的）	safer（較安全）	safest（最安全）
brave（勇敢的）	braver（較勇敢）	bravest（最勇敢）

(3) 短母音加子音字尾，需**重覆字尾＋ er / est**

原級	比較級	最高級
big（大的）	bigger（較大）	biggest（最大）
hot（熱的）	hotter（較熱）	hottest（最熱）
wet（濕的）	wetter（較濕）	wettest（最濕）
thin（瘦的）	thinner（較瘦）	thinnest（最瘦）

(1) 字尾子音＋ y 需去 y ＋ ier / iest

原級	比較級	最高級
dry（乾的）	drier（較乾）	driest（最乾）
easy（容易的）	easier（較容易）	easiest（最容易）
early（早的）	earlier（較早）	earliest（最早）
busy（忙的）	busier（較忙）	busiest（最忙）
heavy（重的）	heavier（較重）	heaviest（最重）
happy（快樂的）	happier（較快樂）	happiest（最快樂）
pretty（漂亮的）	prettier（較漂亮）	prettiest（最漂亮）

3. 不規則變化：

原級	比較級	最高級
good / well（好）	better（較好）	best（最好）
bad（壞）	worse（較壞）	worst（最壞）
many / much（多）	more（較多）	most（最多）
little（少）	less（較少）	least（最少）

Unit 01

比較級的用法

例句現身說法好清楚

一、比較級：

1. The blue car is **more expensive** than that red one.
   這部藍色的車比那部紅色的貴。

2. English is **more interesting** than math.　英文比數學有趣。

3. Tom is **taller** than John.　湯姆比約翰高。

→ John is **shorter** than Tom.　約翰比湯姆矮。

4. Daniel is **heavier** than David.　丹尼爾比大衛重。

5. David is **thinner** than Daniel.　大衛比丹尼爾瘦。

6. Peter is **the better** of the two boys.　彼得是這兩個男孩之中比較好的那一個。

注意：因為有 of the... 之限定，所以必須在比較級前＋the，為特殊用法。

Unit
01

比較級的用法

二、最高級：

1. Mary is **the most beautiful** girl at the party.　瑪莉是派對上最漂亮的女孩。

2. Who is **the tallest**, Tom, Tim, or Jim?　湯姆、提姆或吉姆，誰最高？

3. Peter is **the best** of the three boys.　彼得是這三個男孩之中最好的那一個。

4. This is **the most interesting** movie that I have ever seen.

這是我曾經看過最有趣的一部電影。

補充：比較級的其他用法

一、比較級的進階用法

1. 特殊變化字：有一些單字的比較級和最高級變化比較特殊，可能是完全
   長得不一樣，也可能是變化後意思完全不同，特別在這裡補充。

(1) 表親屬關係：**old**（老的）→ **elder**（較年長）→ **eldest**（最年長）

例如：Her eldest daughter is in college.　她的長女在上大學。

(2) 表時間：**late**（晚的）→ **later**（稍後）→ **latest**（最新的）

例如：See you later.　待會兒見。

(3) 表順序：**late**（晚的）→ **latter**（較後面的）→ **last**（最後的）

例1：This is the latest movie.　這是最新的電影。

例2：He was the last person to leave.　他是最後離開的人。

2. 特殊用法：

(1) as ＋原級＋ as，不可用比較級或最高級，例如：

His car is **as new as** mine.　他的車子和我的一樣新。

(2) as ～ as，可用副詞之原級，修飾一般動詞，例如：

He drives **as carefully as** you.　他開車像你一樣小心。

(3) prefer（較喜歡）本身已有比較級之意，不需配用 than，需用介系詞
   to，例如：

He **prefers** playing computer games **to** watching TV.

他喜歡玩電腦遊戲勝過看電視。

(4) junior（較年幼的）/ senior（較年長的）本身也有比較級之意，但不需
   配用 than，需用介系詞 to，例如：

Sally is **junior to** me.　莎莉比我年幼。

I am **senior to** Sally.　我比莎莉年長。

(5)「The ＋比較級,... the ＋比較級」表示「愈來愈⋯⋯」，例如：

The longer you stay here, **the more** you will like the place.

你在這裡待得愈久，你會愈喜歡這個地方。

二、原級 / 比較級 / 最高級的替換用法：

1. Helen is **the best** student in her class. → **最高級**

　　海倫是她班上最好的學生。

= Helen is **better than** any other student in her class. → **比較級**

　　海倫比她班上任何其他的學生好。

= Helen is **better than** all the other students in her class. → **比較級**

　　海倫比她班上所有其他的學生好。

= No other student in her class is **as good as** Helen. → **原級**

　　海倫她班上沒有其他的學生像她一樣好。

2. Coco is **the most beautiful** girl at the party. → **最高級**

　　柯可是派對上最漂亮的女生。

= Coco is **more beautiful than** any other girl at the party. → **比較級**

　　柯可比派對上其他任何的女生漂亮。

= Coco is **more beautiful than** all the other girls at the party. → **比較級**

　　柯可比派對上其他所有的女生漂亮。

= No other girl at the party is **as beautiful as** Coco. → **原形**

　　派對上沒有其他的女生像柯可一樣漂亮。

Unit
01

比較級的用法

馬上演練好實力

選選看：請從選項中選出符合題目的答案

(　　) 1. Jenny is _____ of the three girls.
　　(A) more beautiful　　　　　(B) beautiful
　　(C) most beautiful　　　　　(D) the most beautiful

(　　) 2. Cindy is _____ than her sister.
　　(A) heavy　　(B) heaviest　　(C) heavier　　(D) very heavier

(　　) 3. He did as _____ as you.
　　(A) good　　(B) well　　(C) better　　(D) best

(　　) 4. The small watch is _____ than that large one.
　　(A) expensive　　　　　(B) expensiver
　　(C) more expensive　　　(D) the most expensive

(　　) 5. Book One is _____ than Book Two.
　　(A) easier　　(B) easyier　　(C) easyer　　(D) more easy

(　　) 6. Who is _____, Jack or Jason?
　　(A) tall　　(B) taller　　(C) tallest　　(D) more

(　　) 7. This is _____ book that I have ever read.
　　(A) better　　(B) the best　　(C) good　　(D) the better

(　　) 8. He is taller than _____ in his class.
　　(A) any student　　　　　(B) all students
　　(C) any other student　　　(D) all the students

Solution 公佈答案

1. (D)　2. (C)　3. (B)　4. (C)　5. (A)　6. (B)　7. (B)　8. (C)

今日重點回顧筆記

一定要練習寫下來！才能確定自己真的會了喔！

1. 長音節的形容詞，其比較級需在前面加上＿＿＿＿＿＿。
2. 短音節的形容詞，其比較級需在後面加上＿＿＿＿＿＿。
3. 最高級需在前加上定冠詞＿＿＿＿＿。

試判斷以下句子是否正確？錯誤的請更正為正確句子。

A. Tony is gooder than his older brother.

....

B. Living in a big city is more convenient.

....

C. She is a most beautiful girl at the party.

....

Unit 01

比較級的用法

正確答案：

1. more　　2. er　　3. the

A. Tony is better than his older brother.

　　good的比較級是better，不是good直接加-er喔！

B. 正確

C. She is the most beautiful girl at the party.

　　既然是「最」，就只有唯一那一個，所以用the當冠詞。

Unit 02 比較級的修飾語

文法口訣輕鬆記
Track 033

1. very 加原級，much 修飾比較級
2. very good / much better

1. very 加原級，much 修飾比較級

原級常用 very 作為修飾語，比較級則用 much 作為修飾語，勿混淆。

2. very good / much better

可利用 very good / much better 來幫助記憶這個原則。

文法觀念說給你聽

一、原級修飾語可用：very / so / quite...，例如：

The weather is **very hot** in Kaohsiung.

高雄的天氣很熱。

二、比較級修飾語可用：much / even / a lot / a little / far / still...，例如：

The weather is **much hotter** in Kaohsiung than in Taipei.

高雄天氣比台北熱得多。

圖解文法一看就懂

原級 & 比較級的修飾語比較

very + 原級
↓
very good

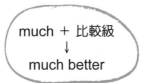

much + 比較級
↓
much better

例句現身說法好清楚

1. Our room is **much bigger** than theirs.　　我們的房間比他們的大多了。
2. This book is **even more** useful than that.　　這本書比那本甚至還更有用。
3. It turned out **far better** than we had expected.　　結果比我們預料的好得多。
4. It's hot today, but it'll be **still hotter** tomorrow.　　今天很熱，但明天會更熱。

馬上演練好實力

( ) 1. I feel _____ better today.
　　(A) very　　　　(B) so　　　　(C) much　　　　(D) many

( ) 2. Judy is _____ beautiful than Susan.
　　(A) much more　(B) much　　　(C) very much　　(D) very more

( ) 3. I like the watch because it is very_____ .
　　(A) gooder　　(B) better　　(C) good　　　　(D) worse

( ) 4. This question is _____ than that one.
　　(A) more easy　(B) more easier　(C) very easier　(D) much easier

( ) 5. The house is _____ more expensive than ours.
　　(A) much　　　(B) very much　(C) so　　　　(D) many

( ) 6. Tom is _____ than his brother.

(A) very good　　(B) very better　(C) even better　　(D) much bad

( ) 7. In Taiwan, summer is _____ than fall.

(A) very hot　　　(B) much hot　　(C) even hottest　(D) a lot hotter

( ) 8. The sick child looks _____ worse today than yesterday.

(A) very　　　　　(B) quite　　　　(C) much　　　　　(D) too

Unit 02

比較級的修飾語

1. (C)　2. (A)　3. (C)　4. (D)　5. (A)　6. (C)　7. (D)　8. (C)

有沒有不太熟悉的文法觀念呢？有的話就把它們寫在這裡，之後多做幾次複習吧！加油！

今日重點回顧筆記

一定要練習寫下來！才能確定自己真的會了喔！

1. very可用來修飾＿＿＿＿級。
2. much可修飾＿＿＿＿級。
3. even可修飾＿＿＿＿級。

試判斷以下句子是否正確？錯誤的請更正為正確句子。

A. I feel very better now.

....

B. Lily is much more beautiful than Sally.

....

C. He looks quite worse today.

Unit

02

比
較
級
的
修
飾
語

正確答案：

1. 原　　2. 比較　　3. 比較
A. I feel much better now.
　　比較級前面不能加very，要加much或even才行。
B. 正確
C. He looks much/even worse today.
　　比較級前面也不能加quite，可用much或even代替。

Chapter 10

Test

超級比一比就靠我比較級──綜合測驗篇

比較級觀念選選看

( ) 1. Terry is _____ than Tony.

    (A) heavy   (B) tall   (C) heavier   (D) tallest

( ) 2. Learning English is _____ now than before.

    (A) important   (B) most important

    (C) more important   (D) the most important

( ) 3. She is _____ than her sister.

    (A) pretty   (B) thinner   (C) beautiful   (D) clever

( ) 4. Sally is _____ of the three girls.

    (A) the happier   (B) the most happy (C) the happiest   (D) happy

( ) 5. Book One is _____ than Book Two.

    (A) very easier   (B) much easy   (C) more easier   (D) much easier

( ) 6. Summer is _____ than any other season.

    (A) hotter   (B) very hotter   (C) much hot   (D) very hot

( ) 7. Danny studies harder than _____ in his class.

    (A) any boy   (B) any other boy (C) all other boys (D) all boys

( ) 8. That book is as _____ as that one.

    (A) better   (B) worse   (C) good   (D) best

劃線錯誤處，請改成正確文法

1. He is <u>most</u> handsome boy in the class. _____

2. Living in Taipei is <u>convenient</u> than living in the country. _____

3. He is <u>most interesting</u> boy I have ever seen. _____

4. We are <u>very</u> faster than you. _____

5. Peter is taller than <u>all the boys</u> in his class. _____

6. The room is bigger than <u>any room</u>. _____

7. She is as <u>prettier</u> as her sister. _____

8. He is <u>more lazier</u> than his brother. _____

66 閱讀測驗 99

Playing computer games is fun. It has become very popular. Young people like to do it in their free time. Here are some important things you have to know when you play computer games.

First, you should learn English well. If your English is good enough, you can understand the computer games **more clearly**. Then you play the games **better than** your friends.

Second, you should not buy illegal software. The fake copies are **much cheaper**, but they will easily hurt your computers.

Third, you should not spend too much time playing the games. That will make your eyes become **weaker**. Take a 10-minute rest after you play 50 minutes every time.

Follow these things and you can be a happy computer game player.

【基測 90-2】

(　) 1. According to the reading, how can you become a good computer game player?

(A) Buy a lot of software.

(B) Follow the game rules.

(C) Spend a long time playing computer games.

(D) Learn English to understand the games better.

(   ) 2. What is the best title for the reading?

    (A) The Most Popular Computer Games

    (B) News About Illegal Computer Games

    (C) Tips for Playing computer Games Well and Safely

    (D) Ways to Find Cheap and Fashionable computer Games

66 句子重組測驗 99

1. one / beautiful / pink skirt / is / more / The / than / the / green

_____

2. English is / easier / much / science / than

_____

3. Tina / better / than John / did

_____

4. boy / is / the / class / best / in / Who / the / ?

_____

5. This box / that / than / heavier / one / is

_____

6. than / expensive / The chair / more / that table / is

_____

7. faster / The / than / is / the / MRT / bus

_____

8. is / important / in the book / most / The part / the

_____

9. than / Jenny / much / feels / better / before

_____

10. Jason / than / is / Tony's / younger / brother

_____

中翻英測驗

1. 誰比較漂亮，Jenny還是Jill?

   Who is _____ beautiful, Jenny or Jill?

2. 這張藍色的椅子比紅色的椅子舒服。

   The blue chair is _____ comfortable _____ the red one.

3. 這本書是書店裡最貴的。

   The book is _____ _____ expensive in the bookstore.

4. 這是全台灣最大的房子。

   This is _____ _____ house in Taiwan.

5. Rick比Tom還矮。

   Rick is _____ than Tom.

6. 這是我看過最刺激的電影。

   _____

7. 加拿大冬天比台北冷多了。

   _____

8. 在我的班上，沒有其他學生像Harry一樣用功。

   _____

9. 你擁有愈多，想要的就愈多。

   _____

10. Cindy是三個女孩中最高的。

    _____

Chapter 10

Solution

超級比一比就靠我比較級——解答篇

比較級觀念選選看

1. (C)　　2. (C)　　3. (B)　　4. (C)
5. (D)　　6. (A)　　7. (B)　　8. (C)

劃線錯誤處，請改成正確文法

1. the most　　2. more convenient　3. the most interesting　4. much
5. all the other boys　6. any other room　7. pretty　　8. (much) lazier

閱讀測驗

1. (D)　2. (C)

　　玩電腦遊戲很有趣。它已經變得很受歡迎。年輕人喜歡在他們的空閒時間玩。當你玩電腦遊戲時，這裡有一些重要的事情你必須知道。

　　首先，你應該學好英語。如果你的英語夠好，你能更清楚理解電腦遊戲，那麼你就會玩得比你的朋友好。

　　其次，你不應該買不合法的軟體。盜版品雖然便宜得多，但是它們將容易損害你的電腦。

　　第三，你不應該花費太多時間玩遊戲，那將使你的眼力變得較弱。每次玩50分鐘後，要休息10分鐘。

　　遵照這些事情，你就可以是個快樂的電玩玩家。

句子重組測驗

1. The pink skirt is more beautiful than the green one.
（這件粉紅色的裙子比綠色那件漂亮。）

2. English is much easier than science.（英文比科學簡單多了。）

3. Tina did better than John.（提娜做得比約翰好。）

4. Who is the best boy in the class?（誰是班上最好的男孩？）

5. This box is heavier than that one.（這個箱子比那個重。）

6. The chair is more expensive than that table.
   （這張椅子比那張桌子貴。）

7. The MRT is faster than the bus.（捷運比公車快。）

8. The part is the most important in the book.
   （這個部份是這本書裡最重要的。）

9. Jenny feels much better than before.（珍妮覺得比之前好多了。）

10. Jason is younger than Tony's brother.（傑森比湯尼的哥哥年輕。）

中翻英測驗

1. more

2. more / than

3. the most

4. the biggest

5. shorter

6. This is the most exciting movie that I have ever seen.

7. Winter is much colder in Canada than in Taipei.

8. No other student studies as hard as Harry in my class.

9. The more you have, the more you want.

10. Cindy is the tallest of the three girls.

Chapter 11 / Advanced Clauses
進階子句的大家族聚會

本篇進階子句的學習重點如下：

Unit 01 形容詞子句

一、形容詞子句的架構

文法口訣輕鬆記　　🔊 *Track 034*

> **1. 關係代名詞擁有雙功用，當作連接詞又是代名詞**
> **2. 前有先行詞，是人、非人，關代跟著走**

1. 關係代名詞擁有雙功用，當作連接詞又是代名詞

關係代名詞(who/which…)可引導形容詞子句，修飾前面的名詞，在句中具有連接詞和代名詞的雙重功用。

2. 前有先行詞，是人、非人，關代跟著走

關係代名詞簡稱為關代，須跟著前面的名詞做變化。前面的名詞稱為先行詞，可分為：人和非人，用不同的關代做連結。

文法觀念說給你聽

　　形容詞子句就是由關係代名詞、關係副詞所引導修飾前面名詞（先行詞）的子句：

一、關係代名詞的功能：兼具連接詞及代名詞之功能

1. 連接詞：連接兩個句子。

2. 代名詞：代替與先行詞相同之人事物。

二、關係代名詞的種類和用法：

1. 關係代名詞分為人（**who**）與非人（事物、動物）（**which**）。

2. 關係代名詞當主格、所有格時不可省略，當受格（**whom / which**）則通常省略，故須仔細判斷句子中是否內含一個形容詞子句。

3. 關係代名詞who / whom / which 一般可由 **that** 代替，但所有格 **whose**（形容詞）不可用 that 代替。

三、先行詞的用法：

1. 先行詞：又叫前置詞，是放置在前的名詞。

2. 先行詞之後通常接著關係代名詞來連接另一子句。

📖 圖解文法一看就懂

一、關係代名詞的種類

	人	非人（事物／動物）	可否用 that 代替	可否省略
主格	who	which	可	不可
所有格	whose	whose 或 of which	不可	不可
受格	whom	which	可	可

二、形容詞子句的基本用法

先行詞 ＋ 關係代名詞連接的子句，即為：形容詞子句

📖 例句現身說法好清楚

一、先行詞是人

1. 當主格（主詞）

The boy who（＝ that）talked to you yesterday is my brother.

（先行詞）（形容詞子句：主詞 who ＋動詞＋ talked；who 不可省略）

昨天和你說話的男孩是我弟弟。

Unit 01

形容詞子句

2. 所有格（形容詞）：

The woman **whose** name is Mary teaches us English.

（先行詞）（形容詞子句：關係代名詞whose（形容詞）＋名詞 name；

不可用 that代替whose）

名叫瑪莉的那位女士教我們英文。

3. 受格（受詞）：

I know the man **(whom ＝ that)** your father is talking to.

　　（先行詞）　　（形容詞子句：受格 whom 可省略）

我認識你爸爸正在跟他說話的那個男人。

二、先行詞非人

1. 當主格（主詞）：

I bought the book **which**（＝ that）has many beautiful pictures.

　　　　（先行詞）（形容詞子句：主詞 which ＋動詞 has；which 不可省

略）

我買了有許多漂亮圖片的那本書。

2. 當所有格（形容詞）：

The house **whose** door is red is Mr. Lin's.

（先行詞）（形容詞子句：關係代名詞whose（形容詞）＋名詞 door；不

可用 that 代替）

門是紅色的那棟房子是林先生的。

→ The house the door of which is red is Mr. Lin's.

＊ of which 已較少使用，大多以 whose 之用法替代之

3. 當受格（受詞）：

I like the skirt （**which ＝ that**）you bought me last week.

　　（先行詞）　　　（形容詞子句：受格 which 可省略）

我喜歡你上星期買給我的那件裙子。

二、形容詞子句的合併技巧

文法觀念說給你聽

如果想將句子合併成形容詞子句，可以利用下面的合併技巧：

一、須先找出先行詞，即為與另一句相同之人事物。

二、先行詞在前很麻煩，第①句須拆成一前一後，中間加入關係代名詞
（簡稱「關代」）連接第②句做為形容詞子句。

三、先行詞在後很簡單，第①句之後直接用關代連接第②句形容詞子句即
可。

圖解文法一看就懂

形容詞子句的合併技巧

先行詞在前

先行詞在後

①句前＋關代＋②句＋①句後

①句＋關代＋②句

例句現身說法好清楚

一、 先行詞在前

① The man is my PE teacher.

（先行詞）

② They are talking about the man.

改成關代 whom，搬至先行詞 the man 之後，因是受詞所以可省略

合併 → The man (whom) they are talking about is my PE teacher.

①句前　　關代　　②句（形容詞子句）　　①句後

他們正在談論的那個男人是我的體育老師。

Unit

01

形容詞子句

注意 不可寫成「The man whom is my PE teacher they are talking about.」因為關代 whom 連接的第②句為形容詞子句,不可拆開。也不可寫成「The man whom they are talking about him is my PE teacher.」因為第②句相同之 the man 已由關代 whom 代替,不可再用代名詞 him,以免重複。

二、先行詞在後

① I know the man .

先行詞

② They are talking about the man .

改成關代 whom,搬至先行詞 the man 之後,因是受詞所以可省略

合併 → I know the man (whom) they are talking about.

①句   關代   ②句(形容詞子句)

我認識他們正在談論的那個男人。

三、形容詞子句的翻譯技巧

文法觀念說給你聽

分辨中英文的修飾語差異:

中 / 英文之差異在於中文不須用「後位修飾」,也就是不論形容詞為單字、片語、子句皆放在名詞之前,但英文裡若以片語、子句作形容,則須放在名詞之後。

🔶 圖解文法一看就懂 🔶

一、中英文修飾語的主要差異

中文	英文	
前位修飾	前位修飾	後位修飾
形容詞＋名詞	形容詞＋名詞	名詞＋形容詞片語
		名詞＋形容詞子句

二、中英文形容詞之位置比較

中文	英文
她是個**可愛的**女孩。	She is a **lovely** girl.
樹下的那個男孩是我的弟弟。	The boy **under the tree** is my brother. （形容詞片語：後位修飾）
她喜歡的<u>那個人</u>是我老師。	<u>The man</u> **(whom) she likes** is my teacher. （形容詞子句：後位修飾）
子句不須連接詞	子句須用連接詞—關係代名詞

🔶 例句現身說法好清楚 🔶

1. 我想要一個**會說笑話的**<u>男朋友</u>。

→ I want a <u>boyfriend</u> **who can tell jokes**.

　　關代 who 連接形容詞子句

2. **他批評的**<u>那個人</u>是我丈夫。

→ <u>The man</u> **(whom) he criticized** is my husband.

　　關代 whom 連接形容詞子句

3. 電腦只是**我們使用的**<u>機器</u>。

→ Computers are just <u>machines</u> **(which) we use**.

　　關代 which 連接形容詞子句

4. **我昨天買的**<u>那本書</u>很有趣。

→ <u>The book</u> **(which) I bought yesterday** is very interesting.

關代 which 連接形容詞子句

5. 昨天我們去了那座**風景很美的**<u>山</u>。

→ Yesterday we went to the <u>mountain</u> **whose scenery is very beautiful.**

關代 whose 連接形容詞子句

Unit
01

形
容
詞
子
句

四、用介係詞片語改寫句子

🔊 文法觀念說給你聽 🔊

　　由 who / which ＋ V. 引導的形容詞子句，可換成介系詞片語（in / with / on...）來修飾前面的名詞，例如：

I know the girl **who wears** a white skirt.

→ I know the girl **in** a white skirt.

不可寫成：

I know the girl **who in** a white skirt.

因為不可同時連用關代＋介系詞，兩者要擇一使用。

🔊 圖解文法一看就懂 🔊

用介系詞改寫形容詞子句

形容詞子句　　　　　　　　　　　　介系詞片語

關代＋V.

介系詞～
（in / with / on...）

❝ 例句現身說法好清楚 ❞

1. 合併 Do you know <u>the girl</u>? ／ <u>The girl</u> is wearing the green sweater.
形容詞子句 → Do you know the girl <u>who is wearing</u> the green sweater?

關代 ＋ V.

介系詞片語 → Do you know the girl <u>in</u> the green sweater?

介系詞（穿）

你認識穿綠色毛衣的那個女孩嗎？

2. 合併 <u>The girl</u> is beautiful. ／ <u>The girl</u> has big eyes and long hair.
形容詞子句 → The girl <u>who has</u> big eyes and long hair is beautiful.

關代 ＋ V.

介系詞片語 →The girl <u>with</u> big eyes and long hair is beautiful.

介系詞（有）

有著大眼睛和長髮的那個女孩很漂亮。

五、that的特殊用法

❝ 文法觀念說給你聽 ❞

一、不可用 that 的情況：

除了前面提到的關代當所有格時不可用 that 代替之外，還有一些情況是絕對不可用 that 的，如補述用法：…,who /,which（即逗點之後，可參考下一個單元），或是下面這兩個情形，也不可用 that：

介系詞之後：to whom...，不可用to that

慣用法：people who...，不用people that

二、一定要用 that 的情況：

有一些情況則不可用一般的關係代名詞 who / which...，而必須用 that

Unit 01

形容詞子句

代替，須特別留意，比方先行詞前有特定修飾語（最高級 / 序數 / the same...）。

例 1：This is **the most** expensive watch **that** I have ever seen. → **必須用 that，而不用which**

例 2：This is **the first** English novel **that** I read. → **必須用 that，而不用 which**

例 3：He is **the first** boy **that** I talked to. → **必須用 that，而不用 whom**

Unit 01

形容詞子句

圖解文法一看就懂

要用 that 和不用 that 的情形

不可用	必須用
1. 逗點「,」之後（補述用法）	1. 先行詞是最高級：the best / the most～
2. 介系詞之後	2. 先行詞有序數：the first～
3. 先行詞是 people / those 等表示人的慣用法	3. 先行詞同時含人、事、物
4. 關代是 whose 時	4. Which / Who 開頭之疑問句為避免重複使用 which / who 時
	5. 其他：先行詞含有 the same / the very / the only / any / no / all...之修飾語

例句現身說法好清楚

一、不可用 that：

1. Your mother, **who** is a teacher, can speak English. → **逗點之後**
   你的母親是位會說英語的老師。

2. That is the house **in which** she lives. → **介系詞之後**
   那就是她住的那棟房子。

3. **People who** use their free time well are usually happy. → **先行詞為 people**

善用空閒時間的人們通常是快樂的。

4. Christmas is a time for friends and family members to see each other again and to send Christmas cards to **those who** live far away.

聖誕節是朋友家人互相再見，以及寄聖誕卡給住在遠方的人的一段時間。

→ **先行詞為 those**

二、必須用 that：

1. This is <u>the best</u> movie **that** I have ever seen. → **最高級**

這是我看過最棒的電影。

2. He is <u>the first</u> man **that** I want to see. → **序數**

他是第一個我想見的人。

3. There are <u>a man and his dog</u> **that** are running in the park.

→ **先行詞同時有人、動物**

有個男人和他的狗，他們在公園裡跑步。

4. <u>Who</u> is the man **that** has long hair? → **Who 開頭**

那個留長髮的男人是誰？

5. She is <u>the very</u> girl **that** Tom likes. → **含修飾語the very**

她正是湯姆喜歡的女孩。

6. He is <u>the only</u> boy **that** talked to me in a friendly way.

→ **含修飾語 the only**

他是唯一一個親切地和我說話的男孩。

7. She is <u>the same</u> woman **that** I met at the theater yesterday.

→ **含修飾語 the same**

她和我昨天在戲院遇見的是同一個女人。

六、補述 & 限定用法的比較

❝ 文法口訣輕鬆記 ❞

◀ *Track 035*

1. 逗點補述，代表唯一，就是這一個
2. 沒有逗點，就不限定，還有其他的

1. **逗點補述，代表唯一，就是這一個**
   關係代名詞之前加上「,」是為了做補充說明，指前面所用的唯一名詞。

2. **沒有逗點，就不限定，還有其他的**
   若沒有「,」是一般限定用法的形容詞子句，除了限定說明前面的名詞外，可能還有其他的。

❝ 文法觀念說給你聽 ❞

形容詞子句分為：

一、限定用法：關代後不需加「,」來補充說明。例如：

Mr. Brown has a son **who** is a doctor. 布朗先生有一個當醫生的兒子。

注意：限定用法一可能還有其他的兒子。

二、補述用法：關代後必須加「,」來補充說明。例如：

Mr. Brown has a son, **who** is a doctor.

布朗先生有一個兒子，他在當醫生。

注意：補述用法一只有一個兒子。

圖解文法一看就懂

補述和限定的比較

補述

先行詞＋關代

意指：代表唯一

限定

先行詞＋關代

意指：不只一個

例句現身說法好清楚

1. His mother, **who** is a teacher, is nice. → **mother 是唯一**
   他的媽媽是位老師，人非常的好。

2. His sister **who** is a teacher went to Taipei yesterday. → **可能還有其他的 sister，但在此限定補充說明當老師的那一個**
   他那個當老師的妹妹昨天去台北了。

3. We went to Japan, **where** we stayed for a week. → **Japan 是唯一**
   我們去了日本，在那邊待了一個星期。

4. We went to the restaurant **where** you met Cindy. → **可能還有其他的餐廳，但在此限定補充說明主詞去過的 restaurant**
   我們去了你遇見辛蒂的那間餐廳。

馬上演練好實力

選選看：請從選項中選出符合題目的答案

( ) 1. Do you know the man _____ at the door?
(A) who standing (B) stands (C) who stand (D) who is standing

Unit 01

形容詞子句

(　　) 2. Susan is reading the letter ＿＿＿＿.

    (A) Peter write   (B) which Peter writing

    (C) Peter wrote   (D) Peter writing

(　　) 3. The girl ＿＿＿＿ big eyes is my sister.

    (A) who having   (B) with   (C) in   (D) has

(　　) 4. They bought a car ＿＿＿＿ color is white.

    (A) whose   (B) that   (C) who   (D) which

(　　) 5. Mary is one of the students ＿＿＿＿ late this morning.

    (A) were   (B) which were   (C) who were   (D) was

(　　) 6. The house ＿＿＿＿ he lives is expensive.

    (A) which   (B) where   (C) in that   (D) that

(　　) 7. I saw the boy and his dog ＿＿＿＿ were sleeping on the floor.

    (A) which   (B) who   (C) that   (D) whose

(　　) 8. They have a daughter, ＿＿＿＿ studies in Taipei.

    (A) that   (B) who   (C) which   (D) whom

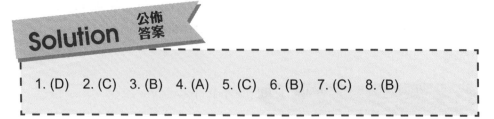

Solution 公佈答案

1. (D)　2. (C)　3. (B)　4. (A)　5. (C)　6. (B)　7. (C)　8. (B)

今日重點回顧筆記

一定要練習寫下來！才能確定自己真的會了喔！

1. 形容詞子句使用的關係代名詞，修飾_____可用who。
2. 先行詞有修飾語一最高級／序數時，必須用_____引導形容詞子句。

試判斷以下句子是否正確？錯誤的請更正為正確句子。

A. The house which has a big yard is Mr. Lin's.

....

B. She is the most beautiful girl who I have ever seen.

....

C. The boy who cap is red is my younger brother.

....

正確答案：

1. 人　　2. that
A. 正確
B. She is the most beautiful girl that I have ever seen.
　 講最高級時，要用that而不是who。
C. The boy whose cap is red is my younger brother.
　 帽子（cap）是屬於弟弟的，所以要用whose。

Unit 02 名詞子句

〝 文法口訣輕鬆記 〞

> 1. 名詞子句分兩類：確定 / 不確定
> 2. 確定有說用 that / 確定沒說用 what
> 3. 不確定就要找 whether
> 4. 間接問句也幫忙問一問

1. 名詞子句分兩類：確定 / 不確定

　　名詞子句分成兩大類，共四種。

2. 確定有說用 that / 確定沒說用 what

　　確定一件事，明確說出來就用 that 引導；未明確說出就用 what 引導。

3. 不確定就找 whether

　　不確定就用 whether（是否）引導，後面常加or not。

4. 間接問句也幫忙問一問

　　或將直接問句改成間接問句，當作名詞子句，放在動詞後面當受詞。

〝 文法觀念說給你聽 〞

名詞子句在句子中當主詞，亦可在動詞之後當補語或受詞，分為四種：

一、由 that 引導，當主詞或受詞（有說出明確具體的內容）。

例1：<u>That you study hard</u> is good. 你用功唸書是好的。→ **明確說出「用功唸書」是好的**

例2：I know <u>that you are a good student</u>. 我知道你是一個好學生。→ **明確說出你是「一個好學生」**

二、由 what 引導，當主詞或受詞（未說出明確具體的內容）。

例1：<u>What he said</u> is true. 他所說的是真的。→ **未明確說出「他所說的」內容是什麼**

例2：Mom bought <u>what I want</u>. 媽媽買了我想要的。→ **未明確說出「我想要的」是什麼**

三、由 whether（是否）引導，當主詞或受詞。

例1：<u>Whether they like it or not</u> is not important to me.
他們喜歡或不喜歡對我來說不重要。

例2：I don't know <u>whether they like it or not</u>. 我不知道他們喜不喜歡。

四、當間接問句，作為動詞之後的受詞（詳述於後，請參考Chapter12）。

例如：Who are you? → I don't know <u>who you are</u>. 我不知道你是誰。

🙰 圖解文法一看就懂 🙲

名詞子句的用法

確定　　　　　　　　　　　　　　不確定

已說出：用 that
未說出：用what

whether～(or not)
間接問句

Unit 02

名詞子句

例句現身說法好清楚

一、that 的用法：

1. **That** he helped me is true. → **在句首不可省略**

   他有幫我忙是真的。

2. The difficult thing <u>is</u> **that** she can't make up her mind to go on a diet.

   → **在 be 動詞 is 之後不可省略**

   困難的是她無法下定決心節食。

3. I <u>think</u> **(that)** it <u>will</u> rain tomorrow.

   → **在一般動詞 think 之後可省略；且名詞子句可有未來式**

   我覺得明天會下雨。

二、what 的用法：

1. This is **what** I need.　這是我所需要的。

2. **What** he told you is true.　他所說的是真的。

3. **What** is yours is mine.　你的就是我的。

三、whether 的用法：

1. We don't know **whether** the news is true or not.

   我們不知道這消息是否真的。

注意： or not 可省略

2. Do you know **whether / if** he likes the present?

   你知道他是否喜歡那個禮物嗎？

3. I wonder **if** she is ill.　不知她是否病了。

注意： 可用 if 當作是否，但後面通常不接 or not

四、間接問句的用法：請參考Chapter 12進階問句

馬上演練好實力

選選看：請從選項中選出符合題目的答案

( ) 1. The most difficult thing is _____ I can't quit smoking.

   (A) what　　　(B) that　　　(C) which　　　(D) this

( ) 2. _____ he is a teacher is true.

   (A) What　　　(B) Who　　　(C) That　　　(D) Whether

( ) 3. _____ you need is to take a rest.

   (A) What　　　(B) Who　　　(C) That　　　(D) Which

( ) 4. Do you know _____ he likes small animals or not?

   (A) that　　　(B) what　　　(C) which　　　(D) whether

( ) 5. I'm not sure _____ he likes dogs or not.

   (A) which　　　(B) what　　　(C) that　　　(D) whether

( ) 6. _____ your father told you is important.

   (A) Which　　　(B) What　　　(C) That　　　(D) Whether

( ) 7. Do you remember _____ Mom asked you to study harder?

   (A) which　　　(B) what　　　(C) that　　　(D) this

( ) 8. 選出一個正確的句子

   (A) I think whether it will not rain tomorrow.

   (B) I remember that Dad told me.

   (C) That is what you need.

   (D) I know if it is true or not.

Unit 02

名詞子句

Solution 公佈答案

1. (B)　2. (C)　3. (A)　4. (D)　5. (D)　6. (B)　7. (C)　8. (C)

Unit 02

名詞子句

今日重點回顧筆記

一定要練習寫下來！才能確定自己真的會了喔！

1. 名詞子句有確定並說出一件事，需用_____引導。
2. 名詞子句不確定可用_____引導，後面常配用的or not可省略。
3. 副詞子句沒有未來式；名詞子句_____未來式。

試判斷以下句子是否正確？錯誤的請更正為正確句子。

A. I'm not sure that she likes the gift or not.

....

B. I remember what my father told me.

....

C. I know that he visits Japan tomorrow.

....

正確答案：

1. that　2. whether　3. 有

A. I'm not sure whether she likes the gift or not.

不確定的事，用whether表示。

B. 正確

C. I know that he will visit Japan tomorrow.

明天以後的事是未來的事情，要用未來式。

Test

Chapter 11

進階子句的大家族聚會——綜合測驗篇

66 子句觀念選選看 99

(　　) 1. The women who _____ wearing hats look pretty.

    (A) is　　　　(B) be　　　　(C) are　　　　(D) was

(　　) 2. The house _____ has six rooms is too big for us.

    (A) where　　(B) which　　(C) who　　　(D) when

(　　) 3. The lady _____ a red dress is my cousin.

    (A) wears　　(B) is wearing　(C) who wear　(D) in

(　　) 4. The girl _____ big eyes looks lovely.

    (A) has　　　(B) who having　(C) with　　(D) in

(　　) 5. I still remember _____ my teacher taught me.

    (A) that　　　(B) what　　　(C) which　　(D) who

(　　) 6. _____ he is an honest boy is true.

    (A) That　　　(B) What　　　(C) Who　　　(D) Which

(　　) 7. I'm not sure _____ she likes cats or not.

    (A) that　　　(B) what　　　(C) whether　(D) which

(　　) 8. The novel _____ she read yesterday is interesting.

    (A) where　　(B) what　　　(C) X　　　　(D) who

66 劃線錯誤處，請改成正確文法 99

1. The dog who you keep is very cute. _____

2. The important thing is what I have already made up my mind. _____

3. Do you know that he finished his work or not? _____

4. She is the only girl who he loves. _____

5. We visited Paris, which we stayed for a few days and had fun. _____

7. I don't know <u>that</u> he said. _____

7. The software <u>who</u> teaches English is very helpful. _____

8. The man <u>with</u> the green sweater is my PE teacher. _____

66 閱讀測驗 99

The Purple Knife

This month's movie for both young and old

The story

Molly Wilson is a shy little girl **who lives in Glass Town.** One day the people in her town get sick in a strange way. The wisest woman in the town says **that Molly is the only person who can save them.** She has to find a purple knife in the Black House of Ice Mountain all by herself. The house is so dark and dangerous that nobody ever went near it before. Experience Molly's exciting trip and find out **if she can save the people of Glass Town.**

The best part

People find joy and hope in the wonderful magic world of The Purple Knife, **where animals talk and people fly.** The burning bridge is the most exciting part of the movie. It looks surprisingly real—no one in the theater can take their eyes off it!

The weak part

The music is not as exciting as it should be during exciting moments. Also, the story ends too soon. People may leave the theater with some questions in their minds.

【基測 98-1】

(   ) 1. What do we know about the story?

    (A) It does not happen in the real world.

    (B) Molly is too shy to save the people in her town.

    (C) The wisest woman is going to get the knife with Molly.

    (D) People in Glass Town get sick after they come back from Black House.

(   ) 2. What does the writer think of the movie?

    (A) The story is not exciting.

    (B) Its music is great for the story.

    (C) Some parts of it are bad for children.

    (D) The writer is unhappy about the way it ends.

❝句子重組測驗❞

1. which / in 1950 / was destroyed / The / was built / bridge / in an earthquake

    _____

2. next to / keeps / The woman / Jane / several cats / who lives

    _____

3. Taipei / a / 2000 / Sam met / to / has / friend / moved / since / who

    _____

4. man / Do / know / the / ? / you / whose / is / son / that boy

    _____

5. large / she / is / a / town / Where / lives

    _____

6. is / I / tell / you / book / the / can't / where

    _____

7. wrong / What / you / is / did

    _____

8. money / The / are / trouble / we / that / short of / is

_____

9. believe / I / yourself / all / that / you / can / do / it / by / can't

_____

10. most / your mind / thing / is / The / you / have to / that / make up / important

_____

「中翻英測驗」

1. 那個穿白色洋裝的女孩是我的同學。

The girl _____ is wearing a white dress is my classmate.

2. 奶奶相信都市裡的孩子比較容易生病。

Grandmother believes _____ children in cities get sick more easily.

3. 我不在乎你怎麼想。

I don't care _____ you think.

4. Helen 希望我們能保持聯絡。

Helen hopes _____ we can keep in touch.

5. 你知道 Rick 是否將去那個派對嗎？

Do you know _____ Rick is going to the party or not?

6. 他在讀一本馬克吐溫寫的書。

_____

7. 老師責備了打壞窗子的男孩。

_____

8. Rose 昨天帶來的布丁很好吃。

_____

9. 她是唯一穿洋裝的女孩。

_____

10. 妳昨天買的那本書很有趣。

_____

Solution

進階子句的大家族聚會——解答篇

🙶 子句觀念選選看 🙷

1. (C)　　　2. (B)　　　3. (D)　　　4. (C)
5. (B)　　　6. (A)　　　7. (C)　　　8. (C)

🙶 劃線錯誤處，請改成正確文法 🙷

1. which　　　2. that　　　3. whether　　　4. that
5. where　　　6. what　　　7. which/that　　8. in

🙶閱讀測驗🙷

1. (A)　2. (D)

紫刀
老少咸宜的本月電影

故事大綱
　　茉莉威爾森是一個住在葛萊斯鎮的害羞小女孩。有一天，住在這個鎮上的人們得了怪病，而這個鎮上最有智慧的女人說，茉莉是唯一一個能夠拯救他們的人。她必須靠自己找到一把紫刀，這把紫刀位於冰山裡的黑暗之屋。黑暗之屋是如此地黑暗及危險，所以以前從來沒有人曾經到過那附近。請體驗茉莉充滿刺激的旅程，並看看她是否能拯救葛萊斯鎮上的人們。

本片最棒的部份
　　觀眾在「紫刀」的完美神奇世界中找到了歡樂與希望，在這部電影裡，動物能說話且人類可以飛翔。橋燃燒起來是電影裡最刺激的部份，因為它看起來就像真的一樣！戲院裡沒有任何人不被這個場景吸引！

本片缺點
　　在刺激的片段，配樂卻不如情節那麼地刺激。此外，故事結束地太快了，觀眾也許會因此而在心中帶著一些疑問離開戲院。

🔖 句子重組測驗 🔖

1. The bridge which was built in 1950 was destroyed in an earthquake.
   （1950 年建的那座橋毀於一場地震。）

2. The woman who lives next to Jane keeps several cats.
   （那個住在珍恩隔壁的女人養了幾隻貓。）

3. Sam met a friend who has moved to Taipei since 2000.
   （山姆遇到一位 2000 年就搬到臺北的朋友。）

4. Do you know the man whose son is that boy?
   （你認識那個兒子是那個男孩的男人嗎？）

5. Where she lives is a large town.（她住的地方是一個大城鎮。）

6. I can't tell you where the book is.（我不能告訴你書在哪裡。）

7. What you did is wrong.（你所做的是錯的。）

8. The trouble is that we are short of money.（麻煩的是我們缺錢。）

9. I can't believe that you can do it all by yourself.
   （我不敢相信你能完全靠你自己來做好它。）

10. The most important thing is that you have to make up your mind.
    （最重要的事情是你必須下定決心。）

🔖 中翻英測驗 🔖

1. who

2. that

3. what

4. that

5. whether

6. He was reading a book which was written by Mark Twain.

7. The teacher scolded the boy who broke the window.

8. The puddings (which / that) Rose brought yesterday were delicious.

9. She is the only girl that is wearing a dress.

10. The book (which / that) you bought yesterday is interesting.

Chapter12 / Interrogative Sentences
問東問西都不能少
的進階問句

本篇疑問句的學習重點如下：

Unit 01 間接問句

🔊 *Track 037*

❝ 文法口訣輕鬆記 ❞

1. 間接問句要小心，不是真的疑問句，改成主詞加動詞

2. who are you，間接變成 who you are

1. 間接問句要小心，不是真的疑問句，改成主詞加動詞

由問句轉變成間接問句，當作一般動詞的受詞，須改成直述句的型態 S+V。

2. who are you，間接變成 who you are

例如將問句 are you，換回直述句 you are。

❝ 文法觀念說給你聽 ❞

在造間接問句時，有幾個地方要注意，如下：

一、大原則：

間接問句已非一般問句，須寫成主詞＋動詞，例如：

Who are you? → I don't know **who you are**.

你是誰 → 我不知道你是誰

Where is he? → I don't know **where he is.**

他在哪裡？→ 我不知道他在哪裡。

二、注意動詞變化：

1. 間接問句中不需一般助動詞 do / does / did，所以要去掉do / does / did，而動詞須＋ s 或改成過去式，例如：

Where **did you** live? → I don't know where **you lived**.

你住在哪裡？→ 我不知道你住在哪裡。

2. 若為有意義之助動詞（can / will...），則需搬回主詞之後，變成「主詞+
   助動詞+ 動詞」，例如：
   What **should I do**? → I don't know what **I should do**.
   我該做什麼？ → 我不知道該做什麼。

🔳 圖解文法一看就懂 🔳

直接問句變成間接問句的方法

直接問句

疑問詞＋V.

疑問詞＋be
V.＋主詞

疑問詞＋do / does /
did＋主詞＋V.

間接問句

疑問詞＋V.

疑問詞＋主詞
＋be V.

疑問詞＋主詞
＋V.

（注意動詞的時態）

直接問句

疑問詞＋有意義之
助V.＋主詞＋V.

間接問句

疑問詞＋主詞
＋助V.＋V.

例句現身說法好清楚

1. I don't know.　我不知道。

   What happened to Tom?　湯姆怎麼了？

→ I don't know **what happened** to Tom.　我不知道湯姆怎麼了。

注意：what happened... 為主詞＋ V.，故不需變化。

2. Do you know?　你知道嗎？

   Who is the boy?　這男孩是誰？

→ Do you know **who** the boy **is**?　你知道這男孩是誰嗎？

3. I'd like to know.　我想知道。

   What **does** Mr. Lin **teach**?　林先生教什麼？

→ I'd like to know **what** Mr. Lin **teaches**.　我想知道林先生教什麼。

4. Do you know?　你知道嗎？

   What **will he** buy?　他會買什麼？

→ Do you know what **he will** buy?　你知道他會買什麼嗎？

5. Do you think?　你認為呢？

   What **did he** buy?　他買了什麼？

→ **What** do you think **he bought**?　你認為他買了什麼？

注意：此為 think / guess 之特殊用法，需將疑問詞 what 搬到句首。

6. I'd like to know.　我想知道。

   What **can he do**?　他能做什麼？

→ I'd like to know what **he can do**.　我想知道他能做什麼。

❝ 馬上演練好實力 ❞

選選看：請從選項中選出符合題目的答案

(   ) 1. Do you know _____ angry?

    (A) why is he   (B) he is why   (C) why he is   (D) why does he

(   ) 2. I don't know _____ .

    (A) who that man is   (B) who is that man

    (C) who that is man   (D) that man is who

(   ) 3. I know _____ .

    (A) what he want   (B) he wants what

    (C) what does he want   (D) what he wants

(   ) 4. Can you tell me _____ ?

    (A) what is his name   (B) what this word means

    (C) when will he come   (D) what should I do

(   ) 5. I can tell you _____

    (A) when will he come?   (B) when he will come.

    (C) when he will come?   (D) when he come.

(   ) 6. Do you remember _____ ?

    (A) who is that boy in red   (B) when will he come back

    (C) what happened in the accident (D) what does he teach

(   ) 7. I'd like to know _____ .

    (A) where does she live   (B) what he teach

    (C) what happened to her   (D) what has she done

(   ) 8. Do you know _____ ?

    (A) why is he late   (B) if it rains tomorrow

    (C) how much tea did he drink (D) where he lives

Unit

01

間
接
問
句

Solution 公佈答案

1. (C) 2. (A) 3. (D) 4. (B) 5. (B) 6. (C) 7. (C) 8. (D)

今日重點回顧筆記

Unit 01

間接問句

一定要練習寫下來！才能確定自己真的會了喔！

1. 間接問句已非一般問句，需改成主詞+_____詞之形式。

2. 直接問句改為間接問句不需助動詞do/does/did，將其去掉後需注意動詞_____。

3. 直接問句改為間接問句，若有意義之助動詞，需改為主詞+_____+動詞。

試判斷以下句子是否正確？錯誤的請更正為正確句子。

A. I don't know what should I do.

....

B. Do you know what happened to him?

....

C. I'm not sure where does she live.

....

正確答案：

1. 動 2. 時式 3. 助動詞

A. I don't know what I should do.
  間接問句要改回主詞＋動詞形式，所以不能用what should I do 這種問句形式。

B. 正確

C. I'm not sure where she lives.
  間接問句要改回主詞＋動詞形式，所以不能用where does she live這種問句形式。

附加問句

文法口訣輕鬆記

🔊 *Track 038*

1. 附加問句唱反調：前肯定，附加問否定
2. 附加否定通常用縮寫 / 主詞只用代名詞
3. be V. / 助 V. 分別幫我問一問

1. 附加問句唱反調：前肯定，附加問否定

附加問句的肯定 / 否定須與前面的直述句相反。

2. 附加否定通常用縮寫 / 主詞只用代名詞

附加問句主詞必須用代名詞，其使用的否定型態則用縮寫（isn't / don't...）。

3. be V. / 助 V. 分別幫我問一問

附加問句也像一般問句，須用 be V. 或助動詞來形成。

文法觀念說給你聽

「附加問句」是一種反義的「疑問句」，其用法如下：

一、前面的直述句是肯定，附加問句則用否定表示。

二、前面的直述句是否定，附加問句則用肯定表示。

三、要參照動詞的問句型態，用 be 動詞或助動詞來形成問句。

例1： **Frank is** from the USA, **isn't he?** 法蘭克來自美國，不是嗎？

例2： **Frank comes** from the USA, **doesn't he?** 法蘭克從美國來，不是嗎？

例3： **Alice was not** at home, **was she?** 艾莉絲不在家，對嗎？

例4： **Alice doesn't** like fries, **does she?** 艾莉絲不喜歡薯條，是嗎？

注意： 附加問句用否定時，通常用縮寫；而主詞必須用代名詞來表示。

『『 圖解文法一看就懂 』』

一、直述句和附加問句的結合

直述句	+	附加問句
主詞＋肯定	+	，否定＋代名詞？
主詞＋否定	+	，肯定＋代名詞？

注意：
1. 附加問句須用代名詞，而且跟著主詞做變化。
2. 附加問句的否定通常是用縮寫。

二、附加問句的基本用法

直述句	附加問句
be V.	，be V.～？
一般 V.	，助 V.（do / does / did）～？
助 V.（can / will / should...）	，助 V.（can / will / should...）～？
完成式 have＋p.p.	，助 V. have～？
被動式 be V.＋p.p.	，be V.～？

Unit
02

附
加
問
句

『『 例句現身說法好清楚 』』

一、**be V. 附加問句**：

1. **Daniel is** a student, **isn't he?** → **現在式**　丹尼爾是學生，不是嗎？

2. **I am** your friend, **am I not?**（＝ aren't I? 縮寫常借用aren't）
   我是你的朋友，不是嗎？

3. **Susan was** tired, **wasn't she?** → **過去式**　蘇珊累了，不是嗎？

4. **There is** a pen on the desk, **isn't there?**　桌上有枝筆，不是嗎？

注意：There is (are)... 之句型，附加問句仍用～ there? 不可寫成 isn't it?

5. **This is** your sister, **isn't it?**　　這是你姊姊，不是嗎？

注意：主詞 this（這）/ that（那）之代名詞為 it；不可因為是 your sister
而寫成 isn't she?

6. **These are** nice watches, **aren't they?**　　這些是不錯的手錶，不是嗎？

注意：主詞 these（這些）/ those（那些）之代名詞為 they；不可寫成
aren't these? 或誤寫為 aren't there?

二、一般 V. 附加問句：

1. **Peter goes** to school by MRT, **doesn't he?** → **現在式**

彼得搭捷運上學，不是嗎？

2. **My father read** in the living room, **didn't he?** → **過去式**

我爸爸在客廳看書，不是嗎？

三、助 V. 附加問句：

1. **You can** get plane tickets, **can't you?** → 助V. can 變can't

你可以拿到機票，不是嗎？

2. **I will** go to church tomorrow, **won't I?** → 助V. will 變won't

我明天將要去教堂，不是嗎？

3. **We should** study hard, **shouldn't we?** → 助V. should 變shouldn't

我們應該用功讀書，不是嗎？

四、完成式（have + p.p.）附加問句：

1. **Tom has studied** English for a long time, **hasn't he?**

湯姆讀英文已經有一段時間了，不是嗎？

2. **Tom has to** go with his brother, **doesn't he?**

湯姆必須跟他哥哥一起走，不是嗎？

注意：has to 不是完成式，而是代表「必須……」，故要用否定助 V.
「doesn't」，不可用完成式「hasn't」。

Unit
02

附
加
問
句

五、被動（be V. + p.p.）附加問句：

1. The glass **was broken, wasn't it?**　這杯子破了，不是嗎？

注意：被動式 be V. ＋ p.p. 可直接用 be V. 做附加問句。

六、特殊的附加問句：附加問句的主詞是指子句中的主詞

1. I think **he can** answer the question, **can't he?**

　　我想他可以回答這個問題，不是嗎？

補充：其他附加問句

一、主要子句內含否定 → 附加問句須用肯定

1. There is <u>no</u> student in the classroom, **is there?**

　　教室裡沒有學生，不是嗎？

2. He <u>seldom</u> goes to the movies, **does he?**　他很少去看電影，不是嗎？

3. Mr. Brown <u>never</u> goes to work by bus, **does he?**

　　伯朗先生從不搭公車上班，不是嗎？

4. I drank <u>little</u> water, **did I?**　我幾乎沒喝水，不是嗎？

注意：no / seldom / never / little 皆為否定之意，後面附加問句用肯定即
　　　可。

＊**特例**：The man is <u>too</u> old <u>to</u> work, **isn't he?**　這男人太老而無法工作，
　　　不是嗎？

too...to...（太～而不能～），雖有否定之意，但其附加問句仍需用否定
表示，需特別注意。

二、祈使句的附加問句

1. Stand up, **will you?**　站起來，好嗎？

2. Don't stand up, **will you?**　不要站起來，好嗎？

> **注意**：祈使句的附加問句不分肯定 / 否定，一律用 will you? 但表示**邀請**
> 時為特例，須用**won't you?**
> ＊特例：Have some tea, **won't you?**　喝點茶，好嗎？——表「邀請」

三、Let's 之附加問句特殊用法

1. Let's go, **shall we?**　咱們走，好嗎？

＊ Let's 是Let us 之縮寫，因為包含自己所以附加問句用 **shall we?**

2. Let's not go, **all right (=OK)?**　咱們不要走，好嗎？

> **注意**：Let us... 是「請求對方讓我們……」，為祈使句，所以附加問
> 句須用 **will you?**
> ＊特例：Let us go, **will you?**　請你讓我們走，好嗎？

Unit
02

附
加
問
句

66 馬上演練好實力 99

選選看：請從選項中選出符合題目的答案

(　) 1. Your mother is very busy, _____ ?
(A) is she　　(B) isn't she　　(C) are you　　(D) aren't you

(　) 2. That's your boyfriend, _____ ?
(A) isn't he　(B) isn't that　(C) isn't it　　(D) is he

(　) 3. There is some water in the glass, _____ ?
(A) is it　　　(B) isn't it　　(C) is there　　(D) isn't there

(　) 4. The Number 3 bus goes there, _____ ?
(A) isn't it　(B) doesn't it　(C) is it　　　(D) does it

(　　) 5. I told you not to buy the car, _____ ?

(A) did I　　(B) did you　　(C) didn't I　　(D) didn't you

(　　) 6. John will come when it stops raining, _____ ?

(A) does it　　(B) won't he　　(C) doesn't he　　(D) will he

(　　) 7. Rose：It's time to go to bed. You have to get up early tomorrow, _____ ?

Nina：Yes, my class is going hiking tomorrow.

(A) can't you　(B) don't you　　(C) aren't you　　(D) haven't you

(　　) 8. He has studied for several hours, _____ ?

(A) has he　　(B) doesn't he　　(C) isn't he　　(D) hasn't he

Unit

02

附
加
問
句

Solution 公佈答案

1. (B)　2. (C)　3. (D)　4. (B)　5. (C)　6. (B)　7. (B)　8. (D)

今日重點回顧筆記

一定要練習寫下來！才能確定自己真的會了喔！

1. 直述句用肯定，附加問句則用_____。
2. 直述句用否定，附加問句則用_____。
3. 附加問句主詞必須用_____詞。

試判斷以下句子是否正確？錯誤的請更正為正確句子。

A. Jenny is from Australia, is Jenny?

....

B. Linda lives in Taipei, isn't she?

....

C. Peter can't play volleyball, can he?

....

Unit
02

附
加
問
句

正確答案：

1. 否定　　2. 肯定　　3. 代名

A. Jenny is from Australia, isn't she?
　　前面是肯定句，後面就要用否定句。而Jenny既然已經出現過
　　了，附加問句中用代名詞she即可。

B. Linda lives in Taipei, doesn't she?
　　live不是be動詞，附加問句不能用isn't。

C. 正確

Chapter 12

Test

問東問西都不能少的進階問句
──綜合測驗篇

🎧 問句觀念選選看 🎧

(　　) 1. You can't go with me, _____ you?

　　(A) don't　　　(B) can't　　　(C) did　　　　(D) can

(　　) 2. David has learned English for many years, _____ he?

　　(A) does　　　(B) has　　　(C) hasn't　　　(D) doesn't

(　　) 3. English is spoken in many countries, _____ it?

　　(A) hasn't　　(B) doesn't　　(C) wasn't　　　(D) isn't

(　　) 4. I am not sure when _____ out.

　　(A) did she go　(B) she go　　(C) does she go　(D) she went

(　　) 5. Can you tell me _____?

　　(A) who are you　(B) who you are　(C) you are who　(D) are you who

(　　) 6. Do you know _____?

　　(A) what did Tom happen　　　(B) what happened to Tom

　　(C) what Tom happened　　　　(D) what Tom did happen

(　　) 7. I don't know _____.

　　(A) what he like　　　　　(B) what does he like

　　(C) what he likes　　　　　(D) he likes what

(　　) 8. She put the trash here, _____ she?

　　(A) did　　　(B) didn't　　(C) was　　　　(D) wasn't

🎧 劃線錯誤處，請改成正確文法 🎧

1. I don't know <u>why was he angry</u>. _____

2. They didn't know <u>what could they do</u>. _____

3. Are you sure <u>when will he come back</u>? _____

4. Do you know <u>where is the post office</u>? _____

5. Tracy likes swimming, doesn't <u>Tracy</u>? _____

6. They have to finish the work by tomorrow, <u>haven't they</u>? _____

7. The game will be watched on TV, <u>isn't it</u>? _____

8. He read the comic book yesterday, <u>doesn't</u> he? _____

❝ 閱讀測驗 ❞

(Robert and Danny are talking in their office.)

Robert：I'm going on a vacation this summer.

Danny：Where do you plan to go?

Robert：Well, Jenny would like to go to Hawawa.

Danny：It's great place for a family trip! And you're taking the dogs on the trip again?

Robert：Sure, **that's much more fun, isn't it?** Doris and David go everywhere with us. We've had great times together.

Danny：How about the hotel? Do you have any idea of where to stay?

Robert：We'll stay at Hawawa Hotel. It opened this spring, and my parents went there once. It has many large rooms, but it's not very expensive. And there are beautiful beaches around it. The best thing is that they allow dogs in the room.

Danny：It sounds wonderful. Don't forget to show me some pictures when you come back.

Robert：No problem!

【基測 95-2】

(   ) 1. Which is true about Hawawa Hotel?

      (A) It is new and expensive.

      (B) It is a hotel with hot springs.

      (C) It is a hotel with nice beaches.

      (D) Its rooms are small but comfortable.

(   ) 2. Who are Doris and David?

      (A) Robert's dogs.

      (B) Robert's parents.

      (C) Robert's children.

      (D) Robert's friends in Hawawa.

66 句子重組測驗 99

1. arrive / don't / when / We / know / will / he

_____

2. Do / know / where / went / he / you / ?

_____

3. me / Tell / I / can / for / what / do / you

_____

4. isn't / is / English / an / Susan / teacher, / she?

_____

5. These / aren't / your / are / students, / they?

_____

6. didn't / Dad / living / put / his / watch / in / the / he? / room,

_____

7. has / Tom / to / the / doesn't / work, / he? / finish

_____

8. John / can / think / can / doesn't / do / Rick / homework, / the / he?

_____

9. America, / He / flies / to / seldom / he? / does

_____

10. favor, / me / a / will / Do / you?

_____

66中翻英測驗 99

1. John 昨天搭火車上學，不是嗎？

   John went to school by train yesterday, _____ he?

2. 我們必須早起，不是嗎？

   We have to get up early, _____ we?

3. Tim 很少去圖書館，不是嗎？

   Tim seldom goes to the library, _____ he?

4. Jimmy 學英文已經很久了，不是嗎？

   Jimmy has learned English for a long time, _____ he?

5. 這窗戶被打開了，不是嗎？

   The window was opened, _____ it?

6. 樹下有一隻狗，不是嗎？

   _____

7. 他從不遲到，不是嗎？

   _____

8. 咱們去看電影，好嗎？

   _____

9. 那是你的筆記本，不是嗎？

   _____

10. Susan 明天將會去市場，不是嗎？

    _____

Chapter 12

Solution

問東問西都不能少的進階問句
──解答篇

💬 問句觀念選選看 💬

1. (D)　　2. (C)　　3. (D)　　4. (D)
5. (B)　　6. (B)　　7. (C)　　8. (B)

💬 劃線錯誤處，請改成正確文法 💬

1. why he was angry.　2. what they could do　3. when he will come back
4. where the post office is　5. she　6. don't　7. won't　8. didn't

💬 閱讀測驗 💬

1. (C)　2. (A)
（羅伯跟丹尼在辦公室裡談話）
羅伯：這個暑假我要去度假。
丹尼：你計畫要去哪？
羅伯：這個嘛，珍妮想要去哈哇哇。
丹尼：那裡對家庭旅遊來說這是個好地方！你這次又會帶著你的狗狗去旅行嗎？
羅伯：當然，那會更有趣，不是嗎？不管我們去哪裡，多莉絲跟大衛都會跟我們一起去。我們一起度過很快樂的時光。
丹尼：那旅館呢？你有想過要住哪一家嗎？
羅伯：我們會待在旅館。這間在今年春天才開的，我父母也去過一次。它有很多大間的房間，但它並不會很貴。它附近也有許多美麗的海灘。最棒的是，他們允許狗狗入住。
丹尼：那聽起來真棒。別忘了拍些照片回來給我看。
羅伯：沒問題！

66 句子重組測驗 99

1. We don't know when he will arrive. （我們不知道他何時將會到達。）

2. Do you know where he went? （你知道他去了哪裡嗎？）

3. Tell me what I can do for you. （告訴我能為你做些什麼。）

4. Susan is an English teacher, isn't she? （蘇珊是英文老師，不是嗎？）

5. These are your students, aren't they? （這些是你的學生，不是嗎？）

6. Dad put his watch in the living room, didn't he?
   （爸爸把他的手錶放在客廳，不是嗎？）

7. Tom has to finish the work, doesn't he? （湯姆必須完成這項工作，不是嗎？）

8. John doesn't think Rick can do the homework, can he?
   （約翰並不認為理克能做這個功課，不是嗎？）

9. He seldom flies to America, does he? （他很少搭飛機去美國，不是嗎？）

10. Do me a favor, will you? （幫我一個忙，好嗎？）

66 中翻英測驗 99

1. didn't

2. don't

3. does

4. hasn't

5. wasn't

6. There is a dog under the tree, isn't there?

7. He is never late, is he?

8. Let's go to a movie, shall we?

9. That is your notebook, isn't it?

10. Susan will go to the market tomorrow, won't she?

原來如此 系列 *E080*

英文文法簡單到不行──暢銷增訂版

沒有學不會的文法，只有不好學的方法！

作　　者	曾韋婕
顧　　問	曾文旭
總 編 輯	王毓芳
編輯統籌	耿文國
主　　編	林侑音
執行編輯	張辰安、汪螢瑩
美術編輯	吳靜宜、王桂芳
特約編輯	盧惠珊
法律顧問	北辰著作權事務所　蕭雄淋律師、嚴裕欽律師

印　　製	世和印製企業有限公司
初　　版	2013年07月
出　　版	捷徑文化出版事業有限公司
電　　話	（02）6636-8398
傳　　真	（02）6636-8397
地　　址	106 台北市大安區忠孝東路四段218-7號7樓

定　　價	新台幣399元／港幣133元
產品內容	1書 + 1光碟（文法口訣MP3 + 教學影片精華）

總 經 銷	采舍國際有限公司
地　　址	235 新北市中和區中山路二段366巷10號3樓
電　　話	（02）8245-8786
傳　　真	（02）8245-8718

港澳地區總經銷	和平圖書有限公司
地　　址	香港柴灣嘉業街12號百樂門大廈17樓
電　　話	（852）2804-6687
傳　　真	（852）2804-6409

捷徑 Book站

現在就上臉書（FACEBOOK）「捷徑BOOK站」並按讚加入粉絲團，
就可享每月不定期新書資訊和粉絲專享小禮物喔！
http://www.facebook.com/royalroadbooks
讀者來函：royalroadbooks@gmail.com

國家圖書館出版品預行編目資料

英文文法簡單到不行─暢銷增訂版 / 曾韋婕著. --
初版. -- 臺北市：捷徑文化, 2013.07
　面；　公分 (原來如此：E080)
ISBN 978-986-6010-75-0 (平裝附光碟片)

1. 英語　2. 語法

805.16　　　　　　　　　　　　102011253